To my precious Rylee Rose,
You are the greatest blessing in my kingdom
I love you forever

THE ALMOST ACCIDENT

"CRAP!" QUINN ROBBINS SHOUTED, slamming on her brakes. As the car skidded to a stop, she whipped her head around; gasping in relief when she discovered there were no other cars behind her.

Now, where was the boy? She hadn't felt an impact, but where had he gone? She craned her neck forward the best she could, trying to make sure there was no teenage boy lying in the street in front of her bumper.

As she looked around, something else caught her attention. Blinking lights a few hundred feet ahead of her, just past the intersection at River Road. Not an emergency vehicle, but not right, either. The windshield wipers made another pass, and in the cleared glass, she could see that the lights were slightly to the side of the road. The hazard lights of a car.

"Is that a naughty word?" Her little sister's small voice piped up from the backseat.

"What?"

"Crap. You said crap. Is that a naughty word?"

"Um, no, it isn't." She could barely concentrate on what Annie was asking. She craned her neck forward over the steering wheel, making

1

sure there was no boy in the road before easing her foot down on the gas pedal.

"Quinn! It's not nice to say naughty words!" Annie's voice rose, as it generally did when she was feeling ignored.

"I know, Annie. Crap isn't a naughty word."

"Oh. What kind of word is it, then?"

"Um," she struggled to focus on her little sister, attempting to calm her shaking hands. "It's a surprised word."

"What are you surprised about?" Annie always had to understand everything.

Deep breath. She's only three, Quinn reminded herself. *Don't freak her out, too.*

"There's something going on up here, Annie. Can you be quiet for a minute?"

"Why?"

She sighed. Asking Annie to be quiet was like asking the river down below them to stop flowing for a minute.

"I want to see what's going on, okay?" Her little sister's insistent questions were starting to pull her out of her reverie, and her racing heart was beginning to slow.

"What's going on?" Annie struggled to look as far around as the car seat straps would allow. "Why did you stop the car?"

"There was a boy who ran in the middle of the road. I was afraid I hit him."

"You *hit* him? With the car?"

"No, I didn't." She was *almost* sure of that now. She pulled slowly through the intersection. On the other side there was a little red hatchback, its hazard lights flashing. Somehow, it had gone into the guardrail. The front of the car was crumpled like an accordion, steam pouring out from under the hood. Glass littered the side of the road from the shattered windshield. The driver's side door was open, and as she pulled past the car, she could see the outline of the driver inside, and someone else kneeling just outside the door.

Heart pounding again, she pulled carefully to the shoulder. "Stay here, Annie," she said as she unbuckled her seat belt.

"I want to come!" Annie's fingers were already fumbling with the chest clip on her car seat.

"I'm not kidding. Stay here. Here," she dug through the glove box and pulled out a small handheld video game, "play with Owen's game."

It wouldn't keep her sister occupied for long, but it was better than nothing. She closed the door and pulled up the hood of her jacket.

As she walked toward the car, she assessed the situation. Out-of-state plates – well, that wasn't unusual during ski season. There was a resort about twenty miles farther up the highway. The rack on top of the car held skis and a snowboard, and another rack on the back carried – oddly – a mountain bike. What the driver planned to do with that in the middle of winter in the Colorado mountains, she wasn't sure.

When she got to the driver's side of the car, her heart nearly stopped. The person kneeling outside the car was him. The boy she'd almost run over. And now she knew who he was. William Rose.

He was a senior at Bristlecone High School, a year older than she was. He must have been really running to get here before her. He was bent over the car's driver, doing something. He'd pushed the seat back, getting the man away from the deployed airbag.

"Did you call 911?" she asked.

William stood up so quickly that he bumped his head on the door frame. When he looked up at her, she got the distinct impression that he wasn't pleased to see her. "No I didn't. I don't have a phone."

He didn't have a phone? What senior in high school didn't have a phone with him at all times?

"Doesn't *he*? Somewhere in the car?"

"I don't know, Quinn. I was too busy trying to keep him from bleeding out to look yet."

As he spoke, he had already knelt back down in front of the driver, and now she could see that he was pressing a large piece of gauze just above the driver's barely open eye. It was already soaked with blood. If the man was conscious, it wasn't by much. A huge gash ran the length of his left arm, too, and blood dripped in little rivulets down past his wrist and to his fingers.

A little queasy, she pulled her own phone out of her pocket and dialed 911. *Quinn. He'd called her Quinn.* She was standing here on the side of the road with an almost-unconscious tourist, and the thing that shocked her most was that William Rose knew her name.

A couple of minutes later, after talking to the dispatcher, she leaned back toward the car. "The police and an ambulance are on their way."

He nodded, reaching into a large backpack that was sitting next to him on the road, and pulling out a thick roll of clean, white gauze. *What in the …*

"What happened here?" she asked.

William didn't look up at her as he wound a long piece of the gauze around the driver's head, securing the pressure bandage in place before he turned his attention to the gash on the man's arm. "I don't know," he said. "I just saw the car here and started running. There's black ice just on the edge of the intersection there. I think that probably had something to do with this."

The driver gave a low moan as William touched his injury, but otherwise didn't respond.

"What are you…" she didn't know how to form the question she wanted to ask – what he'd been doing out here in the first place.

"They're sending an ambulance?" he asked.

"Yes."

"Good." He glanced up at the sky, looking over the mountains where the sun had now almost disappeared. "Here, hold this for me," he said, pointing to the pad he had pressed against the worst part of the driver's cut.

Too far in shock to think about what she was doing, she followed his instructions and replaced his hand with hers, being extremely careful to keep her hand only on the clean gauze, and away from the blood that seemed to be everywhere.

Once she had pressure on the cut, William opened the back door of the car, and dug under the back seat. "Here," he said, setting something down on the road beside her. She glanced down to see an open first-aid kit, the fancy wilderness kind. She carried one similar to it in her saddlebag on the ranch where she led horseback riding groups in the summer.

William pulled open a little pouch that held latex gloves. Wordlessly, he took her free hand and slipped a glove on it. Keeping the gauze in place with the gloved hand now, she held out her other hand for the second glove.

Although she was trained in first aid, and had some idea of what she was doing, she'd never been around this much blood before, and she was beginning to feel nauseous. Keeping her hands firmly pressed against the gauze, she looked down at the ground, taking deep breaths, and studying the shards of glass under her feet.

A moment or so later, she caught sight of red and blue flashing lights out of the corner of her eye. "They're coming," she said, looking up for William, but he wasn't standing next to her anymore.

"William!" she called, but he didn't answer.

The first police cruiser to reach them was marked with the familiar county logo. Even more familiar was the officer who rushed to her side. "Quinn? Is that you?"

"Yeah, it's me, Louis." She was never going to get used to the fact that Louis Chavez – her best friend's older brother – was now a cop. Although it did explain the fascination he'd had with handcuffing her and Abigail together with plastic handcuffs when they were all little.

"What happened?"

"I don't know. I just saw the car when I was driving by."

"You didn't see the accident?" Louis pulled his own pair of latex gloves out of a pouch on his belt, and a few seconds later, he took over applying pressure on the man's arm.

"No," she said. "It had already happened when I got here." She pulled off her own gloves, and took a couple of deep breaths of fresh air, relieved to be away from the smell of the car.

"You were the one who called 911?"

"Yeah, I called." She was suddenly distracted by another movement on the road. "Annie!" she shouted, running over to the little girl. "I told you to stay in the car."

"But I didn't want to be there all alone," her sister said, tears streaming down her face. "I couldn't see you. I don't like it when you leave me." The choking sounds in Annie's voice told Quinn that she'd probably been crying the whole time, and she felt guilty. It probably *had* frightened Annie to be alone over there. She scooped her sister into her arms.

The trickling sleet was turning into a torrent now, and Annie had left her coat in the car. Quinn pulled her own coat around the little girl as best she could. More flashing lights were approaching in the distance.

"You don't have to stay if you didn't see anything," Louis was telling her. "You'd better get Annie in the car and get home before your mom starts worrying. I know where to find you if I need you. There's black ice everywhere. Probably just someone not used to driving up here. Make sure you drive carefully."

Quinn nodded. She didn't need the warning after seeing *that*.

She was buckling Annie back into her car seat when she realized that she hadn't mentioned anything about William. Two state patrol cars were pulling up now though, and an ambulance was just a little way up the road. She didn't want to go back into that mess. Besides, she had no idea where he had gone. *Where had he gone?*

Instead of heading straight home, she turned the car around, heading back to the spot where she'd nearly run William over a little while ago. She believed him that he'd just seen the accident and gone running – but she still had no idea why he'd been out here in the first place. And where had he gone now?

The problem was, there was nowhere for him to have gone. The stretch of highway they were on was pretty isolated. If he had come back this way, she should be able to see him. Really, he would have to be either walking along the narrow shoulder, or down by the riverbank, which was a ridiculous possibility. Nobody would be down by the river in this weather. The freezing rain was beginning to turn to snow.

"Why were there police?" Annie asked.

"Because that guy had a car crash," Quinn answered, giving up and turning the car around, scanning the area once again for William, just in case. The whole thing was starting to freak her out a little bit, and she was starting to crash from the adrenaline rush of nearly hitting William earlier.

"Did he die?"

"No, he didn't die. I think he's going to be okay."

"But why did he crash?"

"I don't know. He just did."

"But why?" The insistence in her little sister's voice told her that there was no way Annie was going to just let it go.

"Hey, Annie, want to sing Jingle Bells?" Quinn asked, turning on the CD player. Annie had been obsessed with the song since Christmas a few weeks before.

By the time she pulled into the two-car garage, both girls were singing loudly and giggling; she was hopeful that Annie had forgotten all about the incident. Her mom wasn't home yet, fortunately.

Inside the house, she turned on Annie's current favorite DVD - this week it was "Fireman Sam" - and retreated into the bathroom.

The whole incident – almost hitting William, and then seeing that accident – had scared her more than she wanted to admit. Her hands still felt shaky as she turned on the faucet, sending a flow of warm water into the sink. She reached into the linen closet and removed a clean washcloth and a small, brown bottle with a purple lid. After thoroughly soaking the washcloth in the steaming water, she carefully placed two drops of the lavender-and-vanilla scented oil in the middle of the cloth. Folding it into a smaller square, she buried her face deep inside, breathing the calming scent in deeply, the way her mother had taught her to do when she was little.

She stayed in the bathroom for a long time, wanting to be completely calm before facing her mother. Her mom didn't need to know about this; she had enough on her plate right now as it was. Besides, nothing had actually happened.

Finally somewhat settled down, she managed to get started on making an enchilada casserole just a few moments before she heard her mother's car in the garage. She put all of her energy into the preparations, trying to keep her mind occupied. Although she knew it was going overboard, she took a long time preparing an extensive salad with lots of vegetables that needed chopping, and she washed all of the dishes by hand.

Megan Robbins was usually exhausted on Friday evenings, which was one reason that Quinn had taken over making dinner most of the time. She hoped her mother would be too tired to notice how antsy she was as she scrubbed the counters and set the table.

Of course, it was stupid to think her mom wasn't going to find out. An hour later, as the girls sat down to dinner with their mother and their brother, seven-year-old Owen, Annie turned to their mother. "Mommy! Guess what?"

"What, sweetie?"

"We saw a car crash! And there were lots of police! And a fire truck. Just like on Fireman Sam!"

Quinn hadn't even noticed the fire truck.

"Quinn! What happened?" Megan turned to her in alarm, concern written all over her face.

She sighed. It wasn't always easy to appreciate how verbal Annie was becoming. "Some tourist ran his car into the guardrail right at the intersection to River Road. I stopped and called 911."

"Are you guys okay, honey? That must have been scary." Megan scooped Annie into her arms, hugging her tight, and reached across the table to grab Quinn's hand. "Was the driver okay?"

She shrugged. "He looked like he was going to be okay, he was pretty out of it though. He had big cuts on his arm and his forehead."

"Maybe I shouldn't be having you pick up Annie when it's getting dark so early..."

"It's fine, Mom, really. We didn't crash. We're safe." She didn't want this conversation going too far in the wrong direction. She knew it made her mother anxious to have both her and Annie in the car alone.

"Quinn always drives safe," Owen's quiet voice interrupted. "It'll be okay mom."

She looked gratefully across the table at her little brother, who had glanced up from his book long enough to join in the conversation. She loved her sweet, quiet little brother. Owen was always so straightforward and literal; it was easy to believe everything he said.

"Yeah, Mommy! Quinn drives safe. And buckles her seat belt!" Annie chimed in.

She anxiously watched her mother's eyes as she looked carefully at each of her children in turn. Finally, she closed her eyes, took a deep breath, and spoke.

"All right, sweetheart. I'll try not to worry. Are you sure you're okay, not too shaken?"

"I'm sure, Mom."

Quinn retreated to her room after dinner, hoping that immersing herself in the English essay would distract her enough to stop the endless playback of the near-accident that was running through her brain. She had just crumpled up the second paper that had doodles on it instead of words when there was a soft knock on the door.

"Hi sweetheart. Can I come in?"

She sat up on the bed and shuffled her books and papers into a pile, making room for her mother to come and sit beside her.

"How are you doing, honey?"

"I'm okay."

Megan eyes were on her intently. Sometimes she felt as if those green eyes could see right through her. Tonight, they were laced with the same concern and anxiety Quinn was feeling. "Really?"

She sighed. "I think so. I was pretty freaked out." And she hadn't even told her mom about the part that had scared her most. The part where she'd almost hit William in the street. Her heart sped abnormally every time that memory crossed her mind.

"And now?"

"I keep seeing it over and over in my head." She didn't know why, but she couldn't bring herself to tell her mom about seeing William Rose there.

Her mom nodded. "That happens sometimes when something really scares me, too." She paused, and her eyes drifted to a framed photograph on the nightstand. "And that would really scare me."

Quinn followed her mother's gaze. It was a picture of her real father, Samuel. He had died in a hit-and-run car accident when she was three. Someone had hit him in the road, the same way she'd almost done to William tonight. In the picture, he was grinning widely, his gray eyes twinkling as he hoisted a tiny Quinn into the air. They both stared at the picture for several minutes.

"Still think I should have gotten my driver's license already?" Her voice was wry.

Her mother looked directly into Quinn's eyes. "Yes, I do. You're almost seventeen, Quinn. You can do this. Things happen. You can't control everything. I know it's scary for you. Trust me, it's terrifying for me. Someday you'll understand when it's your child. But you can't hide from everything that scares you." She pulled Quinn into her arms and hugged her tightly, kissing her on the forehead before she let her go. "It will be okay, honey, it really will."

"I know," she said. But she didn't really.

Halfway to the door, her mother turned back to face her again. "I think you should come to Denver with us tomorrow."

Quinn raised an eyebrow.

"I know you don't love going down there all the time anymore, but Richard and Denise haven't seen you in a while."

"They just saw me at Christmas." It wasn't that she didn't like Jeff's parents. They'd been supportive when he had adopted Quinn, and they were always nice to her and made her feel welcome, but they weren't her grandparents the way they were Owen's and Annie's. She'd never really had her own grandparents. Her mom's mother had died when she was little, and her grandfather had remarried and moved far away. They saw him every other year or so. She didn't know anything at all about her father's parents. Megan had told her they'd died before she was born.

It felt weird to her now, watching her little brother and sister with grandparents who doted on them, who got antsy about seeing them if more than a couple of weeks passed between visits.

"Look, sweetie ... I just don't think I could spend a weekend away from you right now, okay? Please come."

She sighed. It wasn't like she had big plans here in Bristlecone for the weekend anyway. "I thought you said you were okay."

Megan kissed her on the head again. "I'm fine, and so are you. I just ... want you close, okay?"

As she watched her mother walk out of the room, Quinn wondered which of them she had been trying to convince. The last few months, since Jeff's team had taken the contracting job in Afghanistan, she knew her mother's anxieties had been soaring. It was hard on all of them really, to be missing him.

She stared at the picture again, thinking now about the fact that she'd almost hit William. It still scared her. What if she'd hurt him as badly as someone had once hurt her father?

Her phone buzzed, startling her out of her reverie and when she looked at the screen, she realized that she was still more freaked out than she'd thought. It was a text message from Abigail, and just the thought of reading it abruptly exhausted her. She was sure that Abbie had heard about the accident from her brother, and she was going to want all of the details.

What could she even tell her? Now that she thought about it, she hadn't told *anyone* about William being there. Louis had probably just assumed that Quinn had been the one to pull out the first aid kit and patch that guy up.

Right now, she didn't even want to think about it. So she did something she'd never done before. Without reading the message, she turned off the phone and went to bed.

She had dreamed the same dream hundreds of times; the details changed very little. They had started when she was just a small child, although even as they happened, she knew she was only dreaming, she could never fully remember them once she woke up.

The old man was there, as always, standing behind a low table. The expression on his face was serene, giving away nothing, though his eyes seemed kind. On the table stood two vases, their crystal facets refracting rays of sunlight into tiny rainbows all over the room. The bottom third of each container was filled, not with water, but with rich, black soil. Each vase held a single flower.

In the vase on the left bloomed an enormous dandelion. She had never liked dandelions, but this one was surprisingly beautiful in large detail, its golden petals splayed in flawless symmetry. The sweet aroma arising from it brought an immediate image of a fresh, new spring. Its stem and leaves were lush and green, soft and inviting.

The vase on the right held a perfect, white rose, blossoming in full glory; it was the most exquisite flower she had ever seen. Even if it hadn't looked too delicate to touch without spoiling, she wouldn't have; spiky thorns spiraled around the entire stem, all the way to the base of the bud. Even the small branches leading to the rich, green leaves were heavily guarded.

Suddenly, the image shifted. No longer inside, she stood directly in front of the

table, in the middle of a vast field; waving grasses stretched endlessly toward every
horizon.

The old man's voice came from behind her. "The choice is yours."

As she turned to face him, uncomprehending, the vision disappeared.

Quinn woke up feeling unsettled. It didn't feel like it could be morning already. She glanced at the digital clock on her nightstand. The red numbers glared at her. 1:23. Strange, she never woke up in the middle of the night. She could almost remember the dream she'd been having, but not quite. Something about ... flowers? It left her with an odd feeling that she just couldn't shake. As if it was somehow important, as if she needed to be able to remember it, but the memory kept slipping away, just as she thought she might grasp it.

For almost three hours, she tossed and turned in the bed, telling herself she must have just had a crazy dream brought on by the stress of the almost-accident, and that everything was okay, but sleep refused to return.

Finally, faced with the approach of morning, Quinn resorted to something she would never admit to – she crept quietly to the next room. Inside, her mother lay sleeping, Annie curled peacefully next to her on the king-sized bed – the same way Quinn had slept every night until she was six, until a few months before her mother had married Jeff.

Gingerly, so she wouldn't wake either of them, Quinn climbed in next to Annie. The little girl's face was so relaxed, adorable, deep in sleep, that Quinn couldn't resist stroking her soft cheek for a moment. Though she didn't wake at all, Annie's hand reached for Quinn, wrapping her chubby little fingers around Quinn's thumb. Their mother, a light sleeper always, stirred and reached across the sleeping Annie to find Quinn's arm. For a long moment she lay there, soaking up the comforting warmth of her mother's loving hand on her arm, and the sounds of Annie breathing peacefully. A few moments later, she drifted off into a dreamless sleep.

WILLIAM ROSE

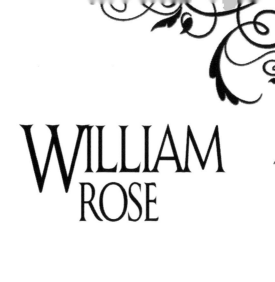

ON MONDAY MORNING AS she drove to school, Quinn had knots in her stomach. In a move that was really uncharacteristic of her, she'd left her phone at home all weekend when she went to Denver. The incident on Friday night was still scaring her, and it wasn't just the tourist. She still wasn't ready to talk about what had almost happened with William.

She couldn't understand why she couldn't just let it go. Nothing had even really happened – had it? It was the kind of thing that she normally would have told Abigail, and she couldn't explain to herself why, right now, she didn't want her best friend to know.

The trip to Denver should have been nice. She had liked being able to go to a big mall, and see a movie that she knew would never come to a small theater like Bristlecone Cinema. Her options in Denver were endless, but she'd spent much of the weekend doing homework and reading, which she would have been doing at home, anyway. She thought it should have been relaxing, to be away from her cell phone and the demands of her life here.

But the last thing her weekend had been was relaxing. She hadn't felt like herself since Friday. For three nights now, she had barely slept; waking each night from bizarre dreams that she could only remember parts of. Small flashes of the dream would assault her throughout the day, but she couldn't get a concrete picture.

Nothing happened. She mentally repeated that phrase like a mantra. She hadn't hit him. Not when she was awake, anyway. In at least some of her dreams she had hit him. And in others she had watched him vanish, over and over in to the night. It felt like something else was going on here, but she couldn't begin to figure out what it was. It was driving her crazy, though.

Now it was Monday, time to get back to her normal life, and she still wasn't ready.

As she expected, Abigail was waiting by her locker to pounce, her short black locks bobbing in agitation. One of the strands that she had recently dyed purple swung into her face. Quinn felt an immediate stab of guilt at the worry she saw in Abigail's expression.

"Quinn! What is going on with you? What happened? Why didn't you text me back? Are you okay?"

Quinn eyed her warily. "One question at a time, Abbie, please."

Abigail wasn't having it; irritation flashed in her blue eyes. "Quinn, what the heck? Where have you been? I was trying to call you and text you all day yesterday."

Quinn knew that. There were probably fifty unread text messages on her phone right now. "I went to Denver with my mom, to see Richard and Denise."

"Why?"

"I haven't seen them for a while?"

"Is that a question, Quinn? Why didn't you tell me you were going?"

Quinn didn't have an answer for her. She had no answers at all.

"I don't know, Abbie, I'm sorry."

Her friend's eyes softened, although the suspicion didn't disappear entirely. "So what happened on Friday night? You saved some tourist? My brother told me you really helped that guy."

Now, now would be the time to tell her the whole story – about William, about what happened with the accident, about him disappearing into nowhere. But she didn't. Instead, she shrugged. "It was just first aid, Abbie."

"Still, wasn't it scary?"

"Yeah. I've been kind of messed up about it all weekend – that's probably why I didn't call you. I'm sorry."

Now her friend's expression melted completely. A flash of guilt almost had Quinn spilling everything, but then she caught sight of something across the hall, and she was distracted again. William Rose was standing there. He watched her for a moment, his eyes wary behind his glasses. When her eyes met his, he looked away, and then disappeared into a classroom. *What in the…*

"Quinn! Quinn!"

"What? Sorry, Abbie."

"Are you sure you're okay? You weren't hurt in that accident or something, were you?"

"No, I'm fine, I promise. It's just …" she didn't know what it was just, so she opted for distraction, instead. "Are you ready for the World History test?"

"I think so." Abigail nodded. "No thanks to you. We were supposed to study together this weekend, before you flaked out on me."

She swallowed. She had completely forgotten that she and Abigail had planned to spend Sunday afternoon studying. Now she really felt guilty as she realized the meaning behind at least some of the text messages. Heat flooded her face. How could she fix this? "Want me to make it up to you by helping you write your English essay?"

She could see Abigail contemplating the offer. She was still looking at Quinn in a concerned way, so maybe it wouldn't take much.

Quinn's writing skills were well known, and writing was a subject her friend struggled with. She was relieved when Abbie's eyes lit up; maybe she would just let it go after this.

Although she was putting all her effort into staying focused on her work, it was harder than it should have been. *What in the heck had just happened in the hallway?* She had always told Abigail everything – mostly, anyway. Why couldn't she tell her about this? And what was that with William? She tried in vain to settle into answering the questions on her World History test, but her thoughts kept drifting to William Rose.

William had always been sort of an enigma in Bristlecone anyway. He'd arrived at the small K-8 school when he was in third grade, an instant object of curiosity in a community where new people were pretty rare. Even Quinn, only in second grade at the time, had been aware of the "new kid" in the classroom next door. By lunchtime on that first day, the third graders had spread everything they knew about him to the entire school, which had turned out to be not much.

He had come here to live with his uncle, Nathaniel Rose, who was a doctor at the small community hospital in Pinespar, about twenty minutes away. Like all kids in Bristlecone, Quinn had known Doctor Rose her whole life. He was friendly, but quiet. He'd never married, despite the fact that there were a number of women in both Bristlecone and Pinespar who would have been more than willing to fix that.

Doctor Rose was kind and personable. In addition to occasionally being on call at the hospital, he ran a small clinic in Bristlecone on random days. He was liked enough that the people in their small community usually called him first before trying one of the other close-by clinics – Quinn's family included. Occasionally, he even made house calls. Nice as he was, though, he was a very private person.

Nobody had ever heard where William's parents were, or why he was here living with his uncle. There had always been rumors, of course, but both William and Doctor Rose were adept at fading into the background and avoiding answering invasive questions. And since most people liked Doctor Rose too much to really pry, the details of their lives had remained quiet.

Now that she thought about it, she realized that she really knew very little about William. Much like her little brother, Owen, every time she'd seen William at school, he'd had his nose buried in a book. She remembered so long ago, when he'd first appeared on the playground, the other students had hounded him with their questions, and with teasing about his constant reading, but William would never react to any of it.

By the end of that first school year, most of the questions had stopped. He'd somehow managed to just fade into the background until nobody really noticed him anymore. *Hardly anyone, anyway,* she thought, as she found herself able to drag up a surprising number of memories of him. He hadn't changed his behaviors since then, though, and now he was just part of the background.

How was that even possible? She'd seen him so many times – buried in books on the playground, in study halls, even most nights that she worked her after-school job at the public library, and yet …

Now that she thought about it, she wasn't sure she even knew what he looked like well enough to describe him. He was quite tall, with dark, nearly black, hair. His eyes were...what color were his eyes? Had she ever seen them? She must have. He did wear glasses; maybe that's why she'd never noticed? The most distinctive thing she could identify about him was the dark purple sweater he was nearly always wearing. It had been replaced over the years with new ones as he'd grown taller.

"I'll be collecting the tests in twenty minutes, finished or not." Mr. Black's voice pulled Quinn out of her abstraction.

Crap! That was twice this week she had had a near miss because of William Rose. She looked back down at her paper. Twenty minutes, and she still had nearly two pages of essay questions to answer. She had been so lost in her thoughts that she had started doodling on the margins of the page. Some design she had never drawn before ... pretty, but not on a test. She quickly rubbed it out with her eraser, and rushed through the rest of the questions on the test, pushing William Rose as far from her thoughts as he would go.

By the time she finished her World History test, she was able to clear her head enough to concentrate on school. She didn't even think about William Rose again until lunchtime. As she set her tray down at a table with Abigail and the rest of their usual group of friends, she saw him.

Surely he ate lunch in here with the rest of the students every day, and yet, she'd never noticed him before. Today, though, the pile of books that surrounded him were like a huge flag, waving in the wind, calling for her to pay attention. He was only two tables away, but nobody else seemed to notice him. A small, black insulated bag sat next to him, and every few minutes he would take a bite of something from a glass bowl, using a real metal spoon. *Who did that?* she wondered, glancing down at the plastic silverware on her cafeteria lunch tray.

Mostly, though, he wasn't eating at all. He was reading from a thick book, jotting notes down in a black binder. Whatever it was he was working on held his attention completely. Forehead propped on his hand, he wrote furiously and flipped through the pages of his book, never once seeming to even realize that he was in a room full of teenagers carrying on social lives.

She wasn't aware that she'd been staring, until someone tapped her on the shoulder, and she nearly fell out of her chair.

"Hey, Quinn, are you all right?"

She steadied herself, trying to remember to breathe, and looked up. Right into the brown eyes of Zander Cunningham. Her whole face, her whole body probably, flushed a deep crimson. She had no idea what Zander was doing, standing here. He hadn't left the football players' table and come over to talk to her the entire time they'd been in high school together.

"Yeah, I'm fine, why?" Had he seen her staring at William like that? Was she making an idiot out of herself?

"My mom told me you saw that accident out on the highway the other night. I heard you gave first aid to that guy or something, and your mom told her it kind of scared you. I just wanted to make sure you were okay."

Why, oh why was his concern making her throat tight? She blinked several times, fighting back the sudden emotion that his words had brought on. Zander's mom and her mom had been best friends since they were in high school. Maggie Cunningham still watched Annie during the day while her mom worked. When she and Zander were younger, they'd been close friends, but ever since he had gone to high school a year before her, all of that had changed, and they very rarely talked anymore. She couldn't remember *ever* talking to him at school.

"It wasn't a big deal, Zander. I just saw the accident after it happened. I called 911, and put pressure on the guy's cut until the ambulance got there. That's all. I'm fine."

He took a step back at her tone, but the concern didn't leave his eyes. "You're sure?"

"I'm sure." She softened her voice. It *was* kind of him to ask.

"You'll let me know if you need anything?"

"Um …" *Really?* "Okay."

"Good." He reached toward her, giving her a sort of awkward pat between her shoulder blades, before returning to his usual table, full of senior football players and a few cheerleaders.

"What was *that?*" Abigail's eyes were wide when Quinn turned back toward the table.

"I don't know."

"Since when does *Zander Cunningham* just come over to talk to you at lunch?"

Aware of the curious eyes at the table around her, Quinn busied herself with her lunch, capturing peas with her fork, despite the fact that she had no interest in eating them. When she finally looked up again, everyone had gone back to their conversations. Nobody at her table was paying any attention to her. But someone was.

Two tables away, William Rose was staring over at her, with an expression that managed to be both surprised and intrigued. His silent communication was brief and definitive. He'd heard her conversation with Zander. He knew she hadn't told anyone he was there. And she didn't know why, but he was grateful.

Suddenly, she decided that she just didn't want to know. It was over now. William had been there, he'd helped that driver, and he didn't want anybody to know. She didn't know why, but did it really matter? He'd helped someone, not committed a crime. Maybe he *really* just didn't want anyone paying attention to him.

If she kept up with this level of distraction, her friends were eventually going to notice. And she was going to have to deal with things like Zander Cunningham coming over during lunch to ask her if she was okay. She would be happier right now if she hadn't seen that accident, either. Quinn had never exactly been an attention-seeking person herself. Yes, it was definitely best to just let this be done.

For the rest of the week, Quinn fought to just let everything go back to normal. And it might have been easy, except for the dreams she kept having. At school, she focused on her classes, on her friends, on helping Abigail with her English essay. She forced herself to look away, even when she noticed William in the hallways and the cafeteria. But she couldn't banish him from her dreams.

By Friday, she was exhausted. As she drove to Maggie's house to pick up Annie after school, she thought the only thing she wanted to do was get home and take a nap, and pray that she'd be able to stay asleep through it.

She was fantasizing about curling up on the couch with Annie and putting on a movie as she climbed the steps to the Cunningham's porch.

The afternoon was cold. The heavy coat she wore was not enough to keep her from shivering as she rang the doorbell.

When the door finally opened, her heart came to a screeching halt. It wasn't Maggie who answered. It was Zander. She didn't know what he was doing here; he was almost never home these days, especially on a Friday. And even when he was, Quinn rarely actually saw him; she was only aware that he was home because of the music pounding from the direction of his bedroom, and the little black truck parked by the curb.

What surprised her even more was the huge grin that lit up his face when he saw her.

"Hey, Quinn." He pushed the screen door open and stood aside, making space for her to step into the familiar living room. Standing next to him, she realized just how long it had been since she'd been this close to him. His height was startling; her head now reached only to his chin.

"Hey, Zander," she answered, finally managing to find her voice.

"Hey, kiddo, your sister's here!" Zander called into the dining room where she could see Annie sitting at the long table and coloring, a smear of purple marker across her right cheek.

Annie didn't respond right away; her head was bent over the white page, her little hand intently making short strokes in the middle of the paper.

Zander raised his eyebrows at Quinn; there was a spark of amusement in his brown eyes. "She's concentrating."

She chuckled, willing herself to relax. "Apparently," she said, appraising him as they stood there in the small confines of the entryway. He made no move to put space between them. He was filling out. From this close, she could see the outlines of burgeoning muscles underneath his green "Bristlecone High School Football Team" hoodie.

His eyes followed hers, and when she finally looked up, he grinned.

"Where's your mom?" she asked, suddenly more than a little self-conscious.

"Ashley had a dentist appointment. I have study hall seventh period, so I came home early to keep an eye on the kids for her. Friday night money." He smiled as he flashed a ten-dollar bill from the pocket of his sweatshirt.

Quinn nodded. Ashley was Zander's seven-year-old sister.

"Did you lose Sophia, then?" she wondered, looking around the room for Zander's other little sister, who was four.

He chuckled. "She's taking a nap, thank God. Those two are insane when they're together." He nodded toward Annie. "Last week, they made me play Trolls and Fairies for a solid hour."

Of course. Even Annie spent more time with Zander these days than Quinn did.

In the dining room, Annie carefully snapped the lid back on to the marker she'd been using, and replaced it in a tub that had once held baby wipes. She ran to Quinn, brandishing the paper she had been working on so carefully.

"I made this for you!" she screeched, jumping into Quinn's outstretched arms.

"Thanks! It's beautiful!" She hugged her sister as she studied the page. She could almost make out the shape of a face with several circles in the middle; some of them were clearly intended to be eyes.

"Hey! I thought you were making that for me!" Zander teased, tousling Annie's brown curls.

"No, silly! It's for Quinn!" Annie made a face at him.

"Me? Silly? You're the silly goofball head!" Zander tickled Annie's tummy and she squealed.

"You're the silly goofball head!" Annie reached for the light brown hair that he had so carefully styled to sweep over his right temple, but he ducked away from her hand in time.

"All right, you little monster, go get your coat and shoes!" He swept her from Quinn's arms, and swung her to the floor, under the coat rack. Annie was still giggling, but she reached obediently for her furry purple snow boots.

Zander turned his attention back to Quinn. "What about you? Big plans for Friday night?"

The question startled her, and she felt the heat of a blush beginning to form at the base of her neck. "No, not really." Not at all, actually. Unless a nap, and, just maybe, microwave popcorn counted as "big plans".

"Jake Price is having a party at his house tonight. His parents just installed a hot tub."

Jake Price was a senior, the quarterback on the football team. Quinn had never once talked to him. She wasn't sure why Zander was telling her this. "That sounds … fun."

"Do you want to go?"

"What? Me?" she was stunned. "Uh, I don't think I was invited."

"I'm inviting you." Zander turned to Annie, who was struggling to pull her coat sleeves the right way out. "We were both wrong, kiddo. Quinn is the silly goofball head." As he said it, he reached over to Quinn and tucked a wayward strand of hair behind her ear, causing a swarm of butterflies to flutter into her stomach.

"Yeah!" Annie declared. "Quinn, you're the silly goofball head!"

"So do you want to go?" Zander's face was earnest.

Her heart was pounding, and the blush reached up to her hairline, even warming her ears, though she wasn't sure why. She'd known Zander her whole life; this should have been easy, but somehow it was completely unexpected. "Um, yeah, maybe," she finally choked out. "I'll have to check with my mom first, see if anything is going on at home." Not that her mother would ever object to her going somewhere with Zander.

"Sure." His smile was easy, casual. "Text me later if you decide you wanna go, I could pick you up around 7:30."

"Uh, ok." Her throat still felt tight.

Wide awake now, she thought about Zander's invitation the whole time she was driving toward her house. What did this mean? Why had he invited her? Did she even want to go to Jake Price's party? Parties weren't really her thing, but somehow Zander's invitation was a little appealing.

She was just wondering what her mom's reaction would be to her asking to go to the party, when she saw something that almost made her crash again.

It was the same stretch of highway where she'd nearly hit him a week earlier, and there he was again. William Rose. He was wearing the purple sweater underneath his long, dark jacket, the familiar large, fancy backpack from last week hanging from his shoulders. This time, his back was to Quinn. He was heading down toward the riverbank. In February. Where was he going?

"Quinn! You have to stop at red lights." Annie's voice behind her pulled her eyes back to the road just in time to stop for the red light.

"Sorry. I guess I got distracted."

"What were you looking at?" Annie asked, as Quinn came to a stop.

"I thought I saw …. I don't know," she trailed off. She wasn't going to try to explain this to a three-year-old.

"What did you see?"

"Nothing…" the light turned green, and she couldn't stop herself. Rather than going straight, toward home, she made a right turn onto

River Road, which crossed the river and headed up into the mountains.

"Where are we going? This isn't how we get home."

"Hold on, Annie. I just want to look at something." She pulled the car over to the shoulder and stopped. Ignoring Annie's questions and protests, she got out and walked around the front of the car, scanning the narrow valley below to find William, to see where he was going. She didn't know why she cared, but the sudden curiosity blazed through every part of her. She had to know.

She stepped over the guardrail and took a few careful steps down the rocky slope, stopping when her head dipped below the road. From where she stood, she could see a solid mile and a half of the river. Far to her front and right, along the adjoining highway, was the small break in the guardrail that opened onto a little, twisting footpath that someone could follow down to the riverbank. At the bottom of the path was a wide, rocky area.

Because it was the middle of winter, the river was quite low, more a stream now than a river. The rocks were dry. Once the snow melted, Quinn knew, the river would flow much higher and faster, leaving a smaller bank. Although several trails led down to this area from the surrounding houses, many of them were blocked now by leftover snow from a big storm they'd had a couple of weeks ago. The only trail that was really clear was the little footpath leading down from the highway. The area where she stood couldn't exactly be called a path, but if she wanted to, she could climb down to the riverbank on the rocks without much difficulty.

In the middle of the flat, rocky riverbank was an odd structure. It was old. It had quite possibly been longer than a century since the bridge had spanned the small section of river. All that remained were the broken stone-and-mortar steps on one side, and the remains of mortar supports hanging from the face of the tall mountain cliff on the other. Even when the bridge had stood, it had obviously never gone anywhere, besides over the river.

Perhaps someone had built it as a fishing spot, a way to stand over the middle of the river in the summer when the water flowed deep enough to house fish, and hang a fishing line. Quinn didn't have to wonder why it hadn't been rebuilt after the center of the bridge had crumbled into the water below.

And there, walking down the little footpath from the highway, nearly to the riverbank now, was William. He was focused as he walked, never looking up, or he probably would have seen her where she stood. The thought should have worried her, but right now, her curiosity overpowered everything else.

"What are you doing, Quinn?" Annie's voice behind her sliced into her reverie and she was almost irritated.

"Nothing." She turned to see Annie's little face, smiling at her from behind the guardrail. "Why did you get out of your car seat? You *know* you're not supposed to do that."

Annie wasn't fazed. "I wanted to come with you. What are you looking for?"

She walked back up the slope and stepped over the rail. "I don't know Annie, just seeing what was down there, I guess." Scooping her sister into her arms, she turned and looked back down at the valley, still inexplicably desperate to see exactly what William was up to down there.

But he was gone.

She frowned, scanning the whole valley for him. There was no chance he could have made it back up to the highway or through one of the snow-packed trails yet.

"I want to see what's down there," Annie said.

So did Quinn. After zipping up Annie's coat, she lifted the little girl carefully over the guardrail, and then climbed back over herself. "Let's go see, okay?"

Annie was eager for the adventure, and she held Quinn's hand tightly as they navigated down the rocks. The whole time, Quinn was scanning the area, looking for any sign of where William was, or where he could have gone, but even once they reached the bottom, there was no sign of him. This was impossible; she was sure he had been here.

He wasn't there. He wasn't anywhere.

She whirled around, searching the entire valley with her eyes, even carefully scrutinizing the shallow water flowing over the rocks in the riverbed. He had to be here.

But he wasn't.

Frustrated, she found herself walking all over the riverbank in the cold evening air, looking behind trees and boulders. The sun had set almost completely. Soon she wouldn't be able to see anything. Except for Annie, who was now busy searching through the rocks, looking for the "shiny" kind that she liked, there was no sign of another human being anywhere on the riverbank. It was impossible. He hadn't had time to go anywhere. What was going on here?

In a last, desperate move, she walked toward the broken bridge. She edged close to the water as far as she could, hoping to peer beneath the base of the bridge. Maybe he was hiding there? She had to get so close to the water that she got her shoes a little wet, but she could finally see behind the dark outcropping. Nothing. He wasn't there, either.

The sun had set now, and only a dim glow lit the horizon. She sighed. None of this made any sense. Annie was still occupied, so she climbed up the crumbling steps and stood for a moment on what was left of the platform at the top. From here, she could see literally everything, even behind some of the smaller boulders she had searched. They were alone.

At that moment, a strange idea popped into her head. What if he had climbed up the bridge and kept on walking? What if it wasn't really broken?

She knew the thought was absurd. She was standing here, and the bridge was broken. William Rose could not have kept on walking. Yet the thought resonated with something deep inside of her, a feeling she didn't understand rising from her chest. She walked forward to the broken edge and looked over. He still wasn't down there. The water swirled below her in freezing ribbons.

Carefully, she put her right foot over the edge, feeling the space.

There was nothing there, of course, only air. Laughing at herself, she pulled her foot back before she lost her balance. The odd feeling passed.

Feeling defeated, she climbed down and made her way back to her car. Underneath the disappointment, though, a new feeling was building. Determination. She was going to find out what was going on with William Rose.

ZANDER

QUINN'S PHONE BUZZED JUST as she pulled her car into the garage. After pressing the button to close the garage door, she flipped open the phone to read the text message. What she saw there sent her thoughts spinning in a completely different direction.

> Hey, Quinn,
> Just wondering if you'd decided
> about the party. Let me know, okay?
> Zander

She stared at the screen for several seconds, trying to sort out her thoughts. Behind her, Annie unbuckled herself, opened the car door, and went inside, but Quinn wasn't ready to move yet.

This was real. Zander really wanted her to go to the party. She didn't know what it meant. Was this supposed to be a date, or was he just asking her to be nice? When they were younger, he'd always been a little protective of her. Were people starting to think she was strange because she never went to parties, and he was just trying to help her out? She didn't know. Of course, she thought, taking a deep breath to calm her nerves, there was only one way to find out.

She pulled the key out of the ignition, grabbed her backpack, and walked inside the house.

At 7:15, she was ready to go. Figuring she had fifteen minutes or so before Zander arrived, she crossed the hallway into her little brother's room. "Hey, buddy. What'cha doing?"

Owen looked up from his book. He was often lost in his own little world, but he would usually come back to reality for a little while for Quinn.

"Where are you going?" he asked, his watchful eyes taking in her soft, white sweater and crisp, dark jeans. She'd even put on a little make-up, though it seemed sort of silly to do so, given that she'd also packed a swimsuit in her purse for going in the hot tub.

"Zander invited me to a party."

Owen raised an eyebrow, which made her giggle. Her brother was mildly autistic, and he didn't always have the right social reactions, but somehow he'd always been tuned in to Quinn.

At that moment, the doorbell rang. All of the color drained from her face. Zander was early. Was she ready for this?

"Have fun, Quinn," Owen said.

She nodded, and leaned over to kiss him on the head.

After taking several more deep breaths, she headed down the stairs. When she was about halfway down, she spotted him, standing there at the bottom, watching her. When she caught his gaze, he smiled. *Oh.*

"Eleven o'clock, please, Zander," her mom was saying.

"I'll have her home on time Megan, I promise." His tone was light, pleasant. He was comfortable with her mom. "Hey, Quinn," he said, as she reached the bottom of the stairs.

"Hey, Zander." She suddenly felt very shy.

She reached for her winter jacket, which she'd hung on the bannister at the bottom of the stairs, but Zander was too quick for her. Pink flooded her cheeks as he held it open, slipping it first over one arm, and then the other. Her mother raised an eyebrow as she opened the door for them, which made her feel entirely different than when Owen had done it.

The walk to the truck was awkward. Zander stayed right behind her, but just as they reached the door on the passenger side, he stepped in front of her to pull it open. As she climbed into the cab, she got the distinct impression that he'd vacuumed the inside very recently.

This was beginning to feel a lot like a date. She didn't know if that thought made her giddy or nervous. Probably both. Zander slid into the seat beside her, and turned on the engine, then adjusted the heater. "I hope it didn't get too cold," he said. *Yes, definitely both.*

Jake Price lived only a few blocks from Quinn – in nicer weather, they could have walked – and so there were only a few minutes of the awkward silence in the car before Zander was walking around to open her door. There were a few other cars parked along the stretches of trees between the houses, but not as many as she would have expected.

"How big is this party?" she asked Zander, as she tried to ignore his hand on her arm, steadying her on the ice.

He shrugged. "Just senior football players – and whoever they bring." They reached the porch, and his hand moved from under her elbow to the empty air in front of her – he was clearly expecting her to take it. "Ready?" he asked, tipping his head toward the door, his whole face lighting up with a grin.

Heart hammering furiously, she reached to take it. As soon as his fingers closed around hers, it got easier. This was *Zander*. He'd been her best friend before even Abigail.

Once they were inside, the evening felt much less like a date. Well, after the round of surprised looks generated both by Quinn's presence there in the first place *and* that Zander was holding her hand. There were quite a few people she didn't know well, but Bristlecone High School wasn't big enough to accommodate strangers. Jake's mom managed a card shop in Pinespar where Quinn liked to shop sometimes, and she smiled kindly at Quinn before she and her husband disappeared upstairs.

About fifteen minutes after she and Zander got there, Abigail showed up, on the arm of Adam Lamos. Now it was Quinn's turn to raise an eyebrow.

As soon as Zander and Adam were engrossed in a battle on the foosball table, she made a beeline for her friend. "You've been holding out on me."

"Me?" Abigail's eyes were wide. "I've been after Adam for weeks – he just finally gave up the fight. But *you?* So, Zander was just coming to check on you at lunch the other day because your moms are friends, then? Since when does Quinn Robbins come to a party at the quarterback's house?"

Quinn opened her mouth, but then closed it again. She didn't have a response, and she wasn't ready to talk about this – it was too new, and she hadn't had a chance to sort out her own feelings yet. And she wasn't sure how Zander really felt, either. Sure, tonight *seemed* like a date, but he hadn't said so. Fortunately, Abigail was easy to divert.

"So when did Adam ask you here?"

Abigail shrugged, although her eyes were bright and excited. "I think it was Wednesday before lunch. I was going to tell you about it, but I swear, you've been so distracted this week. Every time I see you, you're out in space somewhere. Lately, you've been about as social as William Rose."

A jolt of electricity shot through her chest. "Wh … what do you mean?"

"Jeez, Quinn, you look like I said you murdered someone or something. I was just trying to make a joke. I didn't really mean you're as weird as William – just that you've been so … distant or something. Are you sure that accident didn't freak you out worse than you thought?"

She couldn't do this, didn't have answers for her friend. She thought she'd been doing well this week, focusing on Abbie, trying to be normal. Maybe it was just because she was so tired from not sleeping. "The boys are done playing," she said. "Should we go and check out the hot tub?"

"Did you have a good time?" Zander asked, climbing into the truck beside her and turning the key in the ignition.

"Yeah, actually." Quinn reached for the control panel, turning the heat to high. She was rewarded with a blast of cold air in her face, so she adjusted the vents, avoiding looking up at Zander. On the walk back to the truck, she'd suddenly become self-conscious again.

"Does that surprise you?"

"What?"

"That you had fun."

She frowned, finally lifting her eyes to study his expression. He looked genuinely curious; his brown eyes were warm and gentle as he blinked back at her. "I don't know." She shrugged. "Is it supposed to surprise me?"

He was silent for a minute, and then he, too, shrugged. "You play a mean game of air hockey." He grinned, and rubbed his thumb. A little bruise was starting to form there, where she'd hit him, hard, with the puck.

"You have only yourself to blame for that one. I seem to remember you teaching me that move."

"That was a long time ago, Quinn."

"Yeah, it kind of was."

"Where have you been?"

"Me? I've been right here the whole time. You're the one who's always off doing something when we come to your house. When's the last time you were home to eat dinner and play air hockey when your parents invite us over?"

"Why aren't you out doing stuff with us? This is the first time you've ever come to a party – even with Abigail."

"I don't know, I guess I'm usually busy. I'm usually helping my mom with the kids, or doing homework, or working. Does it matter?"

He looked down at his hands, and for a second, she wondered if they were trembling. "I just miss you, Quinn, that's all."

Oh. Now her hands were shaking. "I miss you, too."

"And ..." he stared down at his hands again. They were definitely trembling. "And I was wondering if you wanted to go to the Valentine Dance with me?"

She blinked several times. "You're asking me to the Valentine Dance?"

"I think I just did." He leaned down, catching her gaze.

"Um ... you know I can't dance, right?" She was stalling, trying to regain her composure.

He chuckled. "Neither can I, but I think it could still be fun."

"With me?"

"Yes, Quinn. With you. I want to go to the Valentine Dance with you. Actually dancing is optional."

A strange fluttering feeling filled her stomach. Shoving her hands under her legs to stop them from shaking, she gathered up whatever courage she had. "Okay, sure."

"You'll go with me?"

"Yes, I'll go with you."

Zander's face lit up with a smile that did strange things to her insides. She had to work to catch her breath as she watched him shift the truck into drive.

They were both silent for the short trip, but the grin on Zander's face didn't diminish. By the time he pulled into the driveway in front of her house, she was smiling too, suddenly a little giddy.

"So ... I'll see you at school on Monday?" She was unsure how this whole process worked. Did his asking her to the dance change other things between them?

"Um, no, actually. Next week is the senior football ski trip. We leave early Monday morning, and won't be back until after school on Friday."

"Oh, right." She'd never thought about any of the senior football players at school before; she was surprised to discover that the thought of them being gone on Monday was a little ... *disappointing*.

"I can text you, though," he said as he climbed out of the cab. A second later she was grateful that she was still too much in shock to remember how to open the door and get herself out, because she would have felt awkward when he showed up to do it for her.

He walked her up to the porch, and they stood there for a minute. She could feel her cheeks turning pink, and it wasn't just from the cold.

"Do you want me to text you?" he asked, sounding a little nervous again.

She nodded, slowly coming to understand that she very much *did*.

"All right, then ..." He hesitated, and then quickly brushed his lips against her forehead. Heat flashed all the way to her toes, and she had a hard time catching her breath as she watched him walk back to the truck, grinning the whole way.

By the time she let herself into the house, she couldn't contain her own grin. She took her coat off slowly, arranging it carefully on a hanger as she tried to process what had just happened.

"So, how was it?" Her mother's voice from behind her startled her, and the hanger clattered noisily to the floor.

"It was fun," she said, once her heart had started beating again.

"Did anything *interesting* happen?"

Her heart nearly stopped again at the inflection in her mom's voice. "You knew?"

"I knew that Zander wanted to ask you something."

She let out a heavy sigh. "Oh my gosh, Mom. You and Maggie …"

"Are no different than you and Abigail." Her mother smiled.

Quinn felt a stab of guilt at those words. Lately she hadn't been telling Abigail much of anything.

"Now," her mom started, sitting down on the end of the couch, "I want details."

"Mom!" She rolled her eyes, but sat down next to her, the excited, fluttery feeling returning to her stomach. "Tell me what you know first."

"I want to hear it from your side."

"No deal. You first."

This time it was her mother doing the eye-rolling. "Well, I know that Zander was going to ask you to the dance."

"You and Maggie were *in* on that?" Quinn was mortified.

Her mother laughed. She didn't even have the courtesy to be embarrassed at being caught. "Why wouldn't we be?" she teased. "Maggie and I have been joking about the two of you getting together since you were toddlers and one of you would cry whenever it was finally time to separate you. Zander used to kiss you on the forehead and call you 'my best fwiend Quinn.' How could we resist being in on it when he finally got up the courage to ask you to a Valentine dance?"

Her heart was racing. She didn't think she was ready for this to be quite such a big event. "Mom, it's just a dance. It's no big deal."

"So you said yes?" her mother squealed.

"Mom! Seriously. It's not a big thing. It's just one dance."

"Yes sweetheart, just a first date, and then there might be a second," she grinned. "And if there is a third, well..." Quinn rolled her eyes and groaned, but she couldn't stop her heart beating just a little faster at the idea of subsequent dates.

"If there is a third date then you can do all the gushing you want to do, but until then, can it just be okay that I'm going to the dance with a friend?"

"Of course it can." Megan smiled – a little too widely, but Quinn couldn't deny her own excitement. "Now, it's late. You should get up to bed."

DETERMINED

"QUINN! COME ON! YOU'RE going to miss it."

She looked up from where she was sitting, next to Annie and Owen in the middle of an enormous field of dandelions. She took the chain she'd been making from the soft, yellow flowers, and handed it to her sister.

"I'll be back," she said, as tears started to form in Annie's eyes.

The little girl didn't answer, but Owen took Annie's hand and nodded at Quinn. She stood to go, suddenly in a hurry as the sun started to sink below the horizon.

The boy paused at the top of the stairs, waiting for her to join him, his gray eyes twinkling. "Hurry!"

"I am!"

He stretched his hand to assist her up the support of the broken bridge, urgency in his action as he almost pulled her to the top. "That was close," he said, as she stepped in to the empty air over the water, and then to the other side.

"Very," she agreed. "Give me more warning next time."

The sun was hot overhead now, baking down on an endless field of red roses, their aroma almost intoxicating as it filled the air around her. She closed her eyes, lifting her face toward the sky, breathing in the scent. Somewhere in the distance, there were faint squawks from birds circling in the air.

Opening her eyes, she surveyed the scene in front of her. The boy stood off to the side, staring down at something. She walked over to see what had so captured his interest.

It was a rose, just like the thousands that surrounded them, only this one was white. Pure white, so pristine that it shimmered in the afternoon sunshine. It was so perfect that she couldn't help reaching down for it, down into the quivering mass of flowers.

"Ouch!" She drew her hand back immediately, bringing it up where she could see the damage. A bright red drop of blood glistened on her finger.

"Quinn!"

"Quinn! Quinn!"

She opened her eyes, trying to figure out where she was, who was calling her name. The first thing she saw was Annie's blinking eyes, an inch away from her nose.

"Quinn! Wake up. We're going out for breakfast!"

"What?" She was disoriented; she couldn't understand for a minute what was going on.

"Mommy said to tell you it's almost nine and it's time to get up. We're going out for breakfast."

Almost nine? Slowly she remembered waking up several hours ago, tossing and turning in the bed. She must have eventually fallen back asleep – had that all just been a dream, then?"

"Okay, Annie, I'll get up. Go on out of here, and let me get dressed."

Once her little sister had closed the door behind her, Quinn closed her eyes and took several breaths, trying to clear her head.

A lot of the time, she didn't remember her dreams, but this one had felt so real, so vivid – she still felt like she was inside it. She held up her finger, looking for the drop of blood that had been there a minute ago, but now there was nothing wrong with her finger – at least not visibly. It ached, though, as if it had been injured, and she rubbed it for a minute until the pain subsided.

She didn't know why, exactly, but she was convinced that the dream had something to do with William Rose. The boy in her dream hadn't been William — at least, not exactly, but he reminded her of him somehow. And the broken bridge in her dream — that had to be a direct result of her excursion on Friday.

Checking her finger one more time, making absolutely sure there was no real blood there, she climbed down from her bed and went to get dressed. Perhaps it was time to start ordering coffee with breakfast.

Quinn picked up her phone and then set it back down again for probably the hundredth time that afternoon, telling herself that calling there was not a good choice. She had no idea what she would say if she did call. What if William did answer the phone? What would she do? Hang up? Ask him where he had disappeared to by the river on Friday afternoon? Definitely not.

She wondered if she was starting to lose her mind. Or maybe more than just starting. After two more nights of the dreams that were getting more and more specific — last night William had actually been present, she had been obsessing about his disappearance at the bridge all weekend. When she wasn't obsessing about Zander, anyway.

Zander had texted her several times yesterday, and a couple more today, always with quick, short messages — hi, what are u up to? and smiles. Quinn, still shy about the whole thing, kept replying with equally short answers. She wondered if it was always this hard. In a way, it was a relief that Zander wasn't going to be at school this week, and she would have time to get used to this whole idea.

Her cell phone buzzed then, and she picked it up to read the message.

Where are u? We need to talk! What is going on with u and Zander?

She sighed. Abigail again. She knew she was going to have to deal with her eventually, and that she would be paying for her lack of response later, but she was just not ready to explain herself to her best friend yet.

She picked up the phone again. Might as well just do it, and then maybe she could stop thinking about it. Feeling like some kind of criminal, she blocked her own number before dialing.

The phone rang three times and then clicked to life.

"Hello?" It was a man's voice, surely Dr. Nathaniel Rose.

Her heartbeat sped to a manic pace; she actually had to grip her wrist to stop herself from just hanging up on him. "Hi … is William there?"

There was a long pause. "No, I'm sorry. He won't be home until this evening. May I ask who's calling?"

"Um, I'll just try him later."

"Okay."

Quinn snapped the phone shut and slid it halfway across her bed, as if it might bite her. She sat there for several minutes, until her breathing was under control, and finally went downstairs.

Her mother was in the kitchen with Annie and Owen, who were helping her knead bread dough. Owen's dough was in a neat ball. He was methodically kneading it in exactly the same pattern as the pictures of the hands in the cookbook, which he had propped open in front of him.

Annie was covered from head to toe in flour, with sticky dough clinging to her forearms. Quinn stifled a giggle.

"We're helping Mommy make bread!" Annie announced proudly.

"I can see that," Quinn told her. "You look like you're being a big helper."

Annie grinned.

"Do you need any more … uh, *help*, Mom?"

"Hey sweetie," her mom planted a kiss on her forehead, holding her own flour-covered arms to the side. She glanced over at Annie and sighed, then shrugged and smiled. "I think we're okay here for now. Have you been up there working on homework all afternoon?"

"Um, yeah," She was glad she hadn't had much homework over the weekend, but there actually were a couple of assignments she hadn't been able to get into the right frame of mind to complete yet.

"So, what is all this bread for?" she asked, eyeing the mess. Her mom always baked bread for the week on Sundays, but this was a lot more than usual.

"I just thought I'd get ahead a little, since I'll be gone next weekend. Put a couple of loaves in the freezer for next week."

"Oh, right." Quinn had forgotten the upcoming conference in Denver. Her mom went every year. She would leave on Thursday afternoon with Annie and Owen, and wouldn't be back until Sunday.

"Are you still sure you don't want to come with us? We could go shopping. Maybe hit up that little boutique in Cherry Creek and look for a dress for the dance?"

"That sounds fun, Mom. But…"

"I know, I know. It would mess up your perfect attendance."

"Right." Quinn wasn't about to tell her mom the other reason she wasn't interested in leaving Bristlecone for an entire weekend right now.

"Hey Mom, do you mind if I run over to Abigail's for a little while?"

"I guess that would be all right. Come back for dinner please, though, okay?"

"Sure. Thanks, Mom."

All the way to the highway, Quinn genuinely entertained the notion of going to Abigail's house. She knew it was where she should go. Her life would be so much easier if she just drove over there, and spilled out all the details about Zander – and maybe all the details about William, too. Knowing Abigail, she would just walk right up to

William at school tomorrow and ask him what was going on. She wouldn't run around trying to puzzle out the mystery for weeks on end. One question and she would have her answer.

Quinn wondered what would happen if she just walked up to William and asked, or called him on the phone tonight, when his uncle said he would be home. Right. Quinn knew she would never have the guts to do something like that.

Anyway, she wasn't so sure that anyone would be able to get an answer that easily. Whatever William was hiding, he was hiding it well. Even if she could bring herself to just walk up to him and ask, would he tell her? Somehow she knew that if she was going to find out anything about him, she was going to have to figure it out for herself.

Another thought was plaguing her. If William wasn't going to be home until later tonight, where was he now? Suddenly, she wished she had called his house yesterday. Had he been home at all this weekend? Without really meaning to, she found herself driving down Bray Street.

She knew she was crossing a line. Anyone might recognize her as she parked a little way up the street from Doctor Rose's house, on the opposite side so that she could see their sidewalk and driveway clearly. She just hoped that the cold temperatures and the approaching evening would keep everyone in their houses and away from her car as she watched for William to return to his house.

She didn't know what kind of car he drove, or even if he had a car at all. Of course, it was kind of the hope, wasn't it, that he wouldn't be driving home from somewhere in Bristlecone? She wasn't sure what she was hoping to see as she sat here, but if he simply pulled into his driveway and went inside, this was going to be a wasted trip. She pulled a blanket out of the back seat, and her copy of the book she was supposed to be reading for English out of her bag, figuring she might as well get something done while she sat here.

After about twenty minutes, she was starting to get cold, even with the blanket, and light was quickly fading from the sky. This was stupid. Her key was halfway to the ignition when she glanced up a final time, and her keys fell out of her hand.

There he was, walking up the street on the opposite side of her, wearing the same long coat and heavy-duty backpack. He hadn't come from the end of the street – he had to have been on the little hiking trail. He was coming back from the river; he had to be.

Again with the river. She watched in silence as he walked up to his house and disappeared into the front door.

In that instant, she knew that she was not going crazy or imagining things. Something seriously – not normal – was going on with him.

After dinner, when she finally checked her text messages again, there were several from Abigail. She groaned at the most recent one, left nearly an hour ago.

What is going on? R U mad at me?

Guilt wrenched her insides over letting this thing with William get in the way of their friendship. Abigail annoyed her sometimes, it was true, especially in the last year or so since she'd really gotten into boys and the social scene, but she was still the friend Quinn could trust the most.

She knew that Abigail would keep her secret if she shared it. She would think Quinn was crazy, but Abigail would help her. Despite that, she also knew that she wasn't going to tell Abigail anything about William Rose; she didn't know why, but she just – couldn't. Not now, anyway.

What she could do was spill the details about Zander. Abigail would like that, and she really was dying to, anyway. For the next few days, she promised herself, she would focus on patching things up with her friend and looking forward to the Valentine dance, which was not quite two weeks away.

She would worry about William Rose later; she had a feeling he would be back at the bridge again on Friday, and with her mom and her siblings going out of town, maybe she would have the chance to find out why.

CURIOUS

FOR TWO WHOLE DAYS at school, Quinn was able to keep her promise to herself. She paid attention to her classes and her friendship with Abigail, taking advantage of the fact that both Zander and Adam were away on the field trip, and Abigail wasn't worrying about impressing a boy during lunch.

But on Tuesday evening, as she was shelving a cart full of books at Bristlecone Public Library, William Rose once again caught her attention. It shouldn't have surprised her, seeing him there. She had worked part-time at the library since she was fourteen, and William had always been a regular. So regular that she'd stopped noticing him long ago.

As soon as she saw him though, she realized that he hadn't come in last week during either of her shifts. *Why did she know that?* It made her uncomfortable, realizing how closely she'd been paying attention to him – even before the second time she'd seen him by the river. She'd never been like that before – had she? Well, whether she'd ever been like that before was kind of beside the point now.

Tonight, he was on her radar as soon as he entered the library, heading straight for a small table in the back of the reference section.

He carried a backpack, but only a small inexpensive one, the kind nearly everyone at school wore, not the expensive hiking-type she had seen him wearing on Friday.

It was frustrating, the way she could not seem to get him out of her head. His appearances in her dreams at night were becoming more and more vivid; nearly being run over by her car, disappearing into the river, ducking into classrooms at school.

Last night, she had dreamed that she was outside somewhere with him, walking under a blue sky, surrounded by trees and open fields, and laughing about something. The dream had ended, and she had awakened feeling disconcerted, but now the feeling that she had to know what was going on with this strange boy was becoming urgent.

She finished re-shelving half the books on the cart, and surreptitiously wheeled it over toward the reference section, parking three-quarters of the way down the back row, in a spot where she could see him, but he wouldn't be able to see her. He sat at the table, surrounded by three piles of thick books. He was leafing through some kind of reference journal, but she could not read the title from where she was. It looked like an odd collection of reading material for a seventeen-year-old boy, but he was engrossed in his task, making notes about whatever he was reading in a thick, black binder.

Unable to contain the impulse, she walked over to him. "Anything I can help you find?"

He didn't even look up as he answered. "No, thank you."

Was he hoping to win some kind of award for making it to graduation without ever interacting with another human being? She stole a glance at the titles in his neat stacks of books before retreating to her hiding spot, politely muttering, "Well, let me know," as she walked away.

Safely back by her cart, she peeked at him again. The *New England Journal of Medicine*? He couldn't possibly need that for a high-school Biology class. All of the books in his stacks had been from the medical reference shelves. Unable to see him clearly, she crept silently to the corner, where she could steal a closer view.

Suddenly, William looked up from his task, straight to the spot where she was standing and staring at him. Before she could duck back around the corner, his eyes met hers. The intensity of the irritation she saw there momentarily vanquished her burning curiosity. Heat rushed from the base of her neck to the top of her forehead as she turned and fled to the other end of the library.

The rest of the night, she stayed far enough away from him to avoid direct contact, but she silently kept tabs on him until he left, only a few minutes before the library closed. He was gone, of course, by the time she made her way back to her car to head home.

Not wanting a repeat of what had happened at the library, Quinn's observations of William at school became stealthier, but at the same time her interest grew more intense. She just couldn't help herself.

On Thursday morning, as she was digging through her locker, looking for the books she needed for her first class, she was also scanning the hallway for William out of the corner of her eye.

Abigail was standing at her locker, next to Quinn's, wondering whether Adam was going to ask her to the Valentine Dance. Quinn had sort of felt guilty when she'd told Abigail about Zander asking her. Now, she listened only enough to insert a vague "uh-huh," and "I think so," in the appropriate pauses.

He wasn't difficult to spot, wearing his usual deep purple sweater and the backpack she'd scrutinized at the library the night before. He seemed as oblivious to the rest of the students as he always was, keeping his eyes straight ahead as he walked into an English classroom.

"Quinn! Quinn! Over here!" Abigail's voice demanded her attention.

She gulped. She had gotten carried away watching William, and lost track of her conversation with Abigail. "Sorry, Ab, I'm listening."

Her friend frowned. "What is up with you lately?"

She swallowed hard; she must have missed something that Abigail thought was important. "I don't know. I just keep getting … distracted."

"Yeah, no kidding. Every time I try to talk to you, you're out in space somewhere. Are you okay?"

Was she? She had been trying to keep her behavior under control. "I'm fine. I think I'm just a little tired, maybe stressed out a bit."

"Stressed over what?"

She shrugged, trying to come up with an excuse. "Things are hard on my mom right now, with Jeff gone and everything. I keep having these weird dreams and then I can't get back to sleep." At least part of her explanation was true, though she felt a wave of guilt over the sympathy that appeared in Abigail's eyes.

A bell rang just then, reminding them that they had one minute to get to class before they would be marked tardy. "Anyway, Abby, I'm sorry. I'll try to snap out of it." Quinn ended the conversation by slamming her locker shut and hurrying to Trigonometry.

It should have felt creepy, this following William around, stalking his every move … she couldn't understand what made her do it. Over and over she'd told herself that it wasn't like there was any reason for her to care what this boy was doing, why he avoided talking to people, why he spent so much time in the library looking through medical books.

There was just something about the whole situation that set off a strange, compelling signal somewhere inside of her.

Something about it all was so – familiar? That wasn't the right word for it, but it was the closest she could come to describing the feeling that washed over her every time she encountered William doing something that just didn't seem right. It was all so out of the ordinary, mysterious... and it was something that she just needed to understand.

On Thursday night, when she worked again at the library, Quinn found herself watching for him. This time, she was determined to keep her distance, but she had to find out exactly what he was researching. Tuesday night, after she had watched him leave carrying nothing but his nearly empty backpack, she had gone over to his table to re-shelve the materials he had been reading, but the table was empty.

The area looked as if nobody had been there. She had checked all of the nearby bins where patrons could deposit books they were finished using, but found no medical books in any of them. Not one item was out of place on the shelves he had pulled them from, either. So tonight, she would look more closely. She waited for him as she worked, staying in the front area of the library, looking up every time she heard the whoosh of the door, but he never came.

By Friday, She felt as if her curiosity was going to eat her alive. All day at school, she kept a tighter eye on William than she ever had before. She didn't see anything different about him. As always, he walked quietly between his classes, keeping to himself, engaging in few conversations with other students. Occasionally he might offer an "excuse me" if he were trying to squeeze by someone, but Quinn never overheard a string of more than five words at a time.

It was lunchtime when she noticed something amiss. She was sitting at her usual table. With the senior football players gone, the cafeteria was a little quieter than usual. Abigail was busy gossiping with a couple of their other friends about the Valentine Dance. They'd given up on Quinn joining in with them, though she knew she probably should.

She glanced around the cafeteria looking for William, certain she would see him occupying one of his usual spots, one of the smaller tables that dotted the middle of the room, busily reading or completing a homework assignment. That was William's true talent, she had realized, hiding in the middle of everything, while attracting no notice whatsoever. But he wasn't there. Puzzled, she let her eyes slowly scan all of the tables in the room, mostly occupied by familiar clumps of students. He wasn't anywhere.

Vaguely mentioning something about the restroom, she left her lunch and wandered into the hallway to find him.

He wasn't difficult to locate. After walking past his locker and nonchalantly standing near the restroom doors for several minutes, she realized that she should have checked the library first. There he was, huddled over the keyboard of one of the ancient computers, his backpack hanging neatly over the back of the wooden chair. Before she even realized what she was doing, she was in the middle of the library. Careful as she'd been to avoid him noticing her all week, now she wasn't even thinking about what he might do if he saw her as she strode toward the side wall.

"Quinn! Can I help you find something, honey?" The voice startled her, nearly making her jump out of her skin. She hadn't even seen Mrs. Johnson in here. Bristlecone's tiny school district could only afford one librarian; the high school shared the kind, older woman with the K-8 school. "Sorry, sweetheart. I didn't mean to scare you. What can I do for you?"

A sickening sensation rolled through her stomach as William turned around in his seat to watch her conversation with Mrs. Johnson.

"Um..." she scrambled for something to say. "Do you have the Norton Anthology of Poetry? I need to look up something for my essay that's due on Monday." This was an outright lie; the essay for her English class was already finished.

Mrs. Johnson frowned, her wire-rimmed glasses slipping just slightly down her nose. "I'm sorry sweetheart. All of my copies are checked out right now. They don't have it at the public library?"

"Theirs is checked out, too." She'd never lied to a teacher before; could Mrs. Johnson see it on her face?

"I see. Is there something else we can look for that might help?"

"No. Thank you anyway, though." All she wanted right then was to end the conversation. Every part of her wanted to turn and run out of the library as fast as she could.

"Are you sure? We have several other anthologies."

"Yeah." Her cheeks glowed warmer and warmer. "I have the one I really need – I just wanted to look up something else if it was here."

"Sure, honey. It's nice to see you in here. You don't come in much anymore, now that you're working at the big library." She swallowed hard at these words. She'd loved Mrs. Johnson since the first week of kindergarten, the kind woman with the room full of books. She glanced over at the corner; William was still staring at her, his eyebrows raised.

"It's nice to see you too, Mrs. Johnson. I suppose I should go, though, before I miss my entire lunch."

"All right, honey, go on. But don't be such a stranger."

She forced herself to smile, then hurried out of the library, feeling William's eyes on her back the whole way.

THE BRIDGE

THIS WAS IT. Quinn took a deep breath as she searched for a rock to tuck her car keys and cell phone under. Finding a smooth, flat piece of granite, she lifted it and propped a small stick underneath, both to keep the weight of the rock off her items and to make the place easier to find again.

After the incident in the library today, she had decided that she was absolutely done waiting. She was going to follow him this afternoon, and if he went to the bridge again, she was going to follow.

And that's exactly what had happened. She had watched William climb up the broken steps of the old bridge from a hiding spot behind a boulder on the riverbank, and again he had somehow just disappeared. She had seen him climb the first two steps, and then a pine tree had blocked her view. Now, he wasn't anywhere. Her eyes scanned the entire length of the riverbank and the shallow running water. She was alone.

Fully feeling the weight of her stupidity, she climbed the four crumbling stone steps, toward the end of the broken-off bridge. This time, she did not hold back or hesitate. She closed her eyes and stepped forward. Expecting only a loss of balance and the resulting short drop into the cold water below, she was surprised when it didn't come. There was solid stone underneath her right foot. Maybe she had missed. When a second attempt with her left foot also failed to produce an icy-cold plunge into the stream, she opened her eyes.

William had never been so freaked out – or irritated – in his entire life. He had known the girl was paying attention to him after that stupid accident – had known that she had been following him at school and watching him in the library. That was obvious. However, he had never dreamed that she would follow him closely enough to see him going through the gate.

He was used to the curiosity, of course. That had plagued him off and on ever since he had first started staying with Nathaniel in Bristlecone, and had enrolled in the third grade at Bristlecone K-8. This was not the first time someone had tried to learn more about him.

There had even been a time, in eighth grade, when Allison Rivera had imagined she had a crush on the strange boy she barely knew. He had seen her watching him whenever they were in the same room together. He had noticed her attempts to sit by him in classes or choose him for partner work. She'd come up with silly excuses to start conversations with him, and twice, William had returned from his time in Eirentheos to find several missed calls on the caller ID from her number.

His intentional ignoring and paying zero attention to her had taken care of the issue quickly. She had moved on to Victor Marks, who had been happy to have her notice. The deliberate ignoring strategy had always worked, even on the inquisitive third graders, back in the days when William was a new phenomenon, a novelty in the small town, although it had taken awhile at first.

It had never been that difficult for William, to keep his distance from everyone. It wasn't that he wouldn't have been allowed to make an acquaintance or spend time with kids his own age while he was in Bristlecone – sure, it would have been difficult to maintain both a good friendship and his enormous secret, especially when he disappeared every weekend, and would never have been around to attend birthday parties or snowboarding trips. It would have been difficult, but probably not impossible.

The thing was – he had never wanted to. He could never wrap his mind around the kids in Bristlecone. They weren't like him, or maybe he wasn't like them. Most of them were only interested in such ridiculous things — television shows and video games.

William didn't understand any of it, couldn't join in with the conversations. He always spent most of his time in Bristlecone studying, reading, and missing his home — always missing home.

How had he not noticed how much the girl had seen? Maybe he had just never perceived that kind of persistence being possible coming from her. Quinn Robbins had always been a quiet girl herself. She was a year younger than William was, so he had never been in class with her, but he knew from things he had overheard that other kids and teachers considered her smart.

Her mother was the town's second grade teacher, so he had heard a lot about the family, though he'd started living in Bristlecone a year too late to have experienced being in Megan Robbins' class himself.

Quinn had always had friends among the classmates she had grown up with, and everyone seemed to like her, though William had often seen her group of friends congregate in places around town without her.

She was close to her family; he had noticed, a few times when she was out with her younger brother and sister, how she smiled and laughed when she was with them.

Honestly, Quinn Robbins was the last person he would have ever expected to find him at the bridge, let alone to follow him closely enough to see him going through.

It had been stupid of him not to be more careful, more secretive around the gate. It had been the first thing drilled into him, when he had started living with Nathaniel in Bristlecone, to always be careful, never act suspicious, never even to approach the gate if there were signs that anyone was around. He guessed he had grown complacent. He had never even come close to being caught. He hadn't been watching. Stupid. Now, the girl had seen him.

Just as he had climbed up the second step of the bridge, he had seen her, caught a glimpse of her watching him, almost hidden by a boulder, about halfway up the riverbank. There he had been, exposed, one foot already invisible. It hadn't been a decision, really. There wasn't time, and he was too stunned to be rational about anything. He had just done it: stepped through the gate and disappeared.

Once through the gate, William, heart racing, sat down by the wide riverbank, trying to catch his breath. What had he just done? How much had she seen? What would she do? How could he have let this happen?

She was bound to freak out. She might even start searching for him. What if she called the police? Even if she didn't, what was he going to say when he went back to school and she started asking him questions? He sat there for a long moment. When he was finally calm enough to manage it, he let out a low whistle.

Immediately, there was a rustling sound from the leaves of a nearby tree. A moment later, a large bird swooped toward him, folding in her massive black-tipped wings as she glided to a stop a few feet from him. He rummaged in the front pocket of his backpack, pulling out the treat he'd saved: beef jerky from Art's Pump n' Stuff. He broke off a small piece, pinching it between his fingers. The bird strutted straight toward him as he held out his offering, allowing William a quick pat on her snowy head before she snatched up the snack.

"Hello, Aelwyn. I've missed you."

The bird responded by poking her beak into his hand, looking for more beef jerky.

He chuckled, and broke off another small piece for her. Suddenly, a small movement in the corner of his eye made him freeze in place. Of all the possible consequences of the girl seeing him disappear through the gate that had been running through his mind, this was beyond his worst imaginings.

There, above him on the bridge, the girl had just materialized. She had followed him. She was here. Fear flooded through him. What was he going to do now? He scrambled through his backpack for a scrap of paper and a pencil, quickly scribbling a short note.

He whispered a quick command to the bird, and offered her the remainder of the beef jerky. There was a quick flutter of wings, and in the next heartbeat, she was soaring above the trees.

Quinn gasped. The broken end of the half-missing structure was no longer broken, and it no longer ended. Instead of the disintegrating, broken concrete-and-stone edge, a wide stone walkway arced across the entire river. Cautiously, she put her other foot forward. The stone and mortar that should not have been there held firm. She spun around, ready to run back down the stone steps, but the sight stopped her cold.

The sun that should have been directly in front of her had moved, and now dipped below the tree line far to her left, casting strangely long shadows that cut obtrusively across the landscape. Even in the fading light of the irregular dusk, she could see that everything was different. Where the rocky riverbank should have sloped up to the highway, there was now a vast expanse of trees and open fields. Lights from unfamiliar buildings glimmered and sparked to life in the distance.

Slowly, she let her eyes scan the area around her. The river was no longer a rocky, mountain creek underneath the bridge. Now, a wide expanse of water flowed lazily between the bush-covered banks on either side. Downstream, the river continued uninterrupted to the southwest but seemed to widen significantly just past a break in the tree line. The view upstream was the most shocking. Instead of sloping up into the familiar peaks of the mountains she had seen all her life, a long valley spread out before her, sparsely populated by stands of trees and varieties of grass and wildflowers. In the distance where the horizon began to merge with the night sky, she could just make out the outline of a thick forest.

"Now you've done it." The sound of the voice below her jolted her like an electric shock. In the same instant that she registered the frowning face of William Rose, she stumbled and fell down the steps at the end of the bridge, right into the bushes.

"Fabulous," William muttered, bending down toward her to assess the damage.

Her mind reeled as she tried to reason with herself. The rational part of her that had decided that she was dreaming was at war with the side that could see the strange landscape, hear the unfamiliar calls of strange birds and feel the blood seeping into her jeans from the gash on the inside of her right leg. She let William help her out of the shrubbery. He sat her down at the end of the bridge, and she leaned back against the steps as he pulled up the leg of her jeans to examine the source of the bleeding.

"It doesn't look too bad; a little deep, but I'm going try to patch it up without stitches, at least out here," William told her, removing a small pouch from his bag. He worked quickly and methodically, cleaning the wound with a bit of clear fluid from a glass vial, and spreading on some kind of thick, yellow goo.

Quinn stared; nothing he was saying made any sense. She watched his steady, practiced movements and tried to clear her head. Suddenly, a stinging sensation brought everything sharply into focus.

"Ow!" She jerked her leg out of his grasp.

"Sorry. That's gauna root; it stings at first but it will help it heal faster. Don't rub it."

She scowled, pulling her hand back. *Gauna root?* "Where are we?" she demanded.

William's expression was calm as his eyes met hers for the first time. Gray eyes, deep gray, nearly the same color as her own. He studied her face, looking as if he were trying to decide something as he wrapped her leg in a long bandage, and then began re-packing his supplies into the compartments of his leather pouch. A look of determination crossed his face, and he finally spoke. "Can you stand? It will be dark soon and we still have a fair distance to walk."

Quinn coughed. The shock and strangeness of the situation combined were becoming too much for her. Her mind screamed for something – anything familiar. Part of her began to sincerely hope that this was a dream and she would awaken in a few moments in the safety of her own bed.

My mom! She thought suddenly. She needed to be home before her mother called in the morning.

"I'm not walking anywhere, except back to my car and home."

He sighed, studying her face again. When he answered her this time, his tone was resigned, but sincere. "There's no way back to your home tonight." He finished storing the pouch back in his bag and stood, hoisting the heavy backpack onto his shoulders, glancing up at the now-dark sky. "The gate is closed. You're just going to have to come with me and we'll get this sorted out later. Do you think you're okay to walk?" He offered her a hand.

Gate? "What? Wait." An edge of panic was rising in her voice. "Go with you where? Where *are* we?" She quickly pulled herself to her feet, refusing his hand. The pain she felt when she first put weight on her leg only served to heighten her anxiety. He had wrapped it very tightly. Wincing, she turned slightly, pretending to look at the river, hiding the sudden moisture at the corners of her eyes.

"Try taking some deep breaths," he suggested.

His calm, almost disinterested demeanor finally got to her. "Oh that helps, William. Like saying 'don't panic' ever helped anyone stay calm." Ignoring her still-stinging leg, she stormed at the foot of the bridge, looking in every direction as if somewhere amidst the trees she would see the path back to reality. When that yielded no answers, she turned back to William. "You didn't answer me. Where are we?"

"My home." He turned and gestured toward the forest in the distance.

"Excuse me? Your *home*? You live with your uncle on Bray Street."

"You were following me there as well?"

She blushed slightly at the accusation, but she was still angry, and she didn't relent. "Well, if anything about you made sense – first you run in front of my car, and I almost hit you, then with the accident, and then you just *disappearing* all the time. What was I supposed to think, William?" Suddenly, she could see very clearly just what a bad idea it had been to try to satisfy her curiosity.

"You weren't supposed to *think* anything. You followed me. Where did you suppose I was going?"

Quinn paused. William's questions were too direct. "I don't know," she finally admitted.

"Why have you been following me?"

She shrugged and stammered for a moment, her mind searching for what she hoped would be the least embarrassing response, finally opting for offense as the best defense. "What kind of person walks off into the woods in the middle of nowhere every Friday at sunset?"

"What kind of person wonders *that* and then just steps off a broken bridge in the middle of a river?" His unimpressed and unsympathetic retort came quickly and left her unable to respond.

"You got yourself into this," he said shortly. He turned and started walking. "This way." Without checking to see if she was following, he began heading down the narrow slope to a point where the dirt path widened out and curved in the direction of the twinkling lights. Not until he reached the bottom did he stop and turn, raising a questioning eyebrow at her.

She wondered what if this was what it felt like to go crazy. Briefly, she contemplated just going back up on the bridge, to see if it would take her back home, but dismissed the thought as soon as it came. As much trouble as her curiosity had already gotten her in, the same instinctive need to know that had caused her to walk off the end of the bridge soon had her following him.

William appraised her limping stride as she made her way down the slope. For a split second, it looked as though he was extending his hand toward her again, but she might have imagined it.

"Would you like some ibuprofen?" he asked.

"Guana root and ibuprofen?" She snorted. Her irritation still had the best of her. "I'm fine, thanks."

She heard him sigh beside her, but he didn't say anything, just started walking. He led her along the dirt footpath winding downhill from the bridge, in and out of patches of enormous trees. They walked for a while, the stands of trees giving way to farmlands and soon to roads and houses scattered through the valley until a small town appeared in the distance.

"We're going to my home..." He paused in a way that indicated there was more to his words than he was prepared to say. "This is my real home, the kingdom of Eirentheos," he added, as she started to respond. "My Uncle Nathaniel is here already, and the rest of my family as well. I've sent a message on ahead to let them know you're with me."

"A message? You have a cell phone that only works here?"

The expression on his face as he regarded that question told her she would get no more answers from him now. Thoughts and questions bounced around in her mind like Ping-Pong balls. Though she hid it from him, as they walked, she tried his advice – taking deep breaths, trying to calm herself and regain control of her thoughts. The pain radiating through her leg made this more difficult, but she was determined not to mention it to William. Wherever they were headed, she would walk on her own.

After about fifteen minutes of walking, the exercise and fresh air had worked to calm her down. Wherever they were, it was beautiful here.

The night was warm, and although the sun had now completely disappeared, a bright full moon hung in the sky, allowing them to see their way easily. Something was strange about the moon, but she couldn't place it. She had never seen so many stars. She scanned the sky for a long time, looking for constellations she recognized, but she could find no familiar patterns in the sparkling night.

As they grew closer to what was obviously a more populated area she could see brick walls surrounding the town proper. Cottages and shops nestled together along the narrow, stone streets. The glittering lights came from windows and low streetlamps that lined the streets. A tall, long building dominated the western landscape, forming a shape she'd only seen before in books and movies.

"Is that a castle?"

"Yes, it is," he replied simply. He seemed lost in thoughts of his own.

The pain in her leg was growing steadily, and gradually she became aware of a warm, wet sensation in the lower part of her jeans and her sock. A wave of nausea washed over her as she realized what was causing it. Suddenly dizzy, she felt an overpowering need to sit down.

"Uh, William?"

"Yes?" he turned to her quickly, looking alarmed by the sound of her voice. His eyes immediately darted to her leg. Somehow, in the next instant, she found herself lying on the ground in a patch of soft grass.

Propping her head on her rolled-up jacket, he pulled out his pouch of medical supplies. Before she had time to protest, he produced a pair of scissors and began cutting away the bloodied bottom half of the leg of her jeans. She'd liked those jeans, too.

"I'm sorry," he said, looking up at her after he'd appraised the cut. "I should have stitched it to begin with. I just wasn't sure how I was going to get you all the way home from the bridge if you couldn't walk."

After digging around in his leather pouch again, he pulled out a small glass vial and an odd-looking syringe; it was made of glass and metal, and was very old-fashioned looking. It was also the scariest thing she'd ever seen as she suddenly registered the word "stitched" with what he was about to do.

A larger wave of nausea hit and beads of sweat broke out along her forehead.

He must have seen the color draining from her face, because he quickly hid the needle again inside the pouch, but it was too late; she'd seen it. "Are you okay?" he asked.

"Yeah, it's just..." the nausea won, and she rolled to her side and vomited in the grass. Mortified, she didn't know how to respond when he gently reached over and pulled her hair out of the way. When she was finished, he helped her sit back up, handing her a small cloth he produced from the leather pouch so she could wipe her mouth. He watched her expression – she wondered if he was mentally placing bets over which color was going to take over first – the nauseous green, or beet red.

"Looks like she handles needles about as well as you do." A new voice startled both of them.

"Thomas! What are you doing out here?" William rose to greet the boy who had walked up behind them. The two of them hugged tightly for a long moment, which utterly surprised her. So maybe William wasn't *completely* anti-social.

The first thing she noticed about the boy was his incredible resemblance to William. They both had the same dark hair, deep gray eyes, high cheekbones, and pale skin. Comparing their heights, she could tell that the boy was younger than William was, but his shoulders were already much broader and he was more muscular.

Red was definitely winning now – it had been bad enough having one person see her like this.

Studying him caused a niggling feeling inside her, too. He was so – familiar, even though she was sure she'd never met him before. She'd seen him though … *but where?*

"After Aelwyn brought your note that the girl had followed you, I thought I'd come see what was going on for myself." The new boy grinned. "It looks like you might need some help."

She didn't have much time to decipher what they were talking about. William went back to messing around in the pouch, and for the first time in weeks, she wasn't the least bit curious about what he was doing.

The other boy knelt down in front of her. "He sure knows how to make friends, doesn't he?" He grinned. "I'm Thomas, by the way. I'm Will's brother. I'm guessing you must be Quinn?" She nodded, unable to wrap her mind around the situation. William had a brother? How did Thomas already know her name? And Will? She had never imagined the stoic William with a nickname.

Thomas withdrew a metal canteen from William's backpack, and although she was still feeling like she'd rather crawl under a rock, she let him help take a sip of it. "Good girl," he said.

"Sorry," she said, still embarrassed as she lay back down against her jacket, her queasy stomach finally starting to settle a little.

Thomas' eyebrows knitted together. "For what? Hurting yourself? I can't imagine you did it on purpose. Don't be sorry, don't be worried, just let Will finish patching you up, and then we'll take you home with us." The way he smiled at her told her that he meant it, which was surprisingly comforting given that she had no idea what he meant by them taking her home with them.

He poured some of the cold water onto a cloth and held it against her forehead, which helped even more, but the pleasant feeling was quickly interrupted by a freezing, wet sensation on her leg that made her jump. A second later, she caught the scent of rubbing alcohol, and her stomach flipped over again. Her first instinct was to pull her leg away, but Thomas, who had been studying her face rather intently, placed his hand gently, but firmly, against the top of her calf, securing her leg to the ground.

"I know, sweetheart, but that's not going to help. I need you to hold still for a minute. Take a deep breath and focus on something else." Normally, she would have been irritated at being held down, and at being called sweetheart by some boy she'd just barely met, a boy who was younger than she was, but somehow Thomas put her at ease immediately.

Thinking about anything except how humiliating this was, she inhaled deeply and tried to concentrate on the alternating pattern of light and dark green stripes on the sleeve of her shirt. It almost worked, but she lost her focus and winced at the sharp pinch of the needle. Thomas used his free hand to squeeze her fingers gently until the sting of the anesthetic subsided a little, and she managed to exhale.

"Sorry, honey," Thomas said, "this wasn't what you signed up for, was it?"

She shook her head, grateful that at least she hadn't cried on top of everything else. "I don't remember signing up for any of this. Is he finished?" The nausea was starting to come back; she could *feel* the green seeping back in at the edges of her temples.

Thomas chuckled, though he looked concerned. "Not yet." He turned to William. "Will, stop for a second. Do you have any valoris seed in your bag?"

William nodded, putting down the syringe and tossing the leather pouch to Thomas. He kept applying pressure to the wound, but looked up at Quinn. "You doing okay?" he asked, surprising her with the gentleness in his voice.

The lightheadedness was back in full force, but she managed a weak, "Yeah, I'm fine."

"Uh-huh; I believe you." Thomas' smile was wide, and his gray eyes sparkled with friendliness. "I do something to myself that requires stitches about every other moon." He grinned kindly at her, rooting through the leather pouch. "I don't like this part, either. The numbing medicine is the worst bit, I promise. Do you want me to give you something that will help? It's magic stuff."

Although she had no idea what he meant, she nodded, grateful for the kind and soothing presence of this boy. A moment later, she felt something powdery and slightly sweet on her tongue. Almost instantly, she started to feel calmer and her thoughts grew a little fuzzy.

"Better?" Thomas asked, after a minute. She nodded again; the nausea was dissipating, too – although the lightheadedness might have been getting a bit worse. "Good. You should see Will when he's the one on the other end of something sharp and pointy," he added, grinning.

The look that William shot Thomas then made her smile in spite of herself. Then, William shocked her again by directing a look at her that was purely sympathetic, his eyes briefly even kinder than Thomas'. Maybe she only imagined it though; suddenly she couldn't really focus on anything.

"Is it starting to get numb?" William asked. She nodded, although the motion didn't feel quite like it was supposed to. She almost reached up to see if her head really was floating away from her shoulders. "I'm almost done with this part, and then it won't hurt anymore." William said as he went back to work, his voice softer than she'd imagined it could be.

There was another pinch on the other side of her wound, but she couldn't concentrate on it. She didn't know if it was the powder that Thomas had given to her, but she didn't feel right at all.

"Quinn?" Thomas' voice was alarmed. "Quinn?"

THE CASTLE

QUINN WOKE UP FEELING disoriented, unsure of where she was. For a moment, she thought she was in her own bed, in her own room on Saturday morning, waking slowly after another bizarre dream. As she became more lucid, however, she realized that was not the case. Or that maybe she wasn't really waking up.

She opened her eyes. It was a bedroom; she was lying in a large, four-poster bed, underneath a thick white comforter. The pillow under her head was incredibly soft. She was too comfortable to move right away.

A small old-fashioned lamp burned on the table next to her, giving the room a dim glow. She was facing a large window, covered with heavy, brocaded curtains. No light seeped around any edge of them. She turned her head to get a view of the rest of the room.

"Quinn! You're awake." The voice startled her, making her jump. Her heart racing once again, she looked up into the familiar, kind face of Doctor Nathaniel Rose. All at once, the night's events came rushing back to her, and she struggled to sit up.

"Quinn, please be careful," Dr. Rose put his hand on her shoulder, gently preventing her from rising.

"What... Why... Where am I?" she demanded.

Dr. Rose looked uncomfortable. "I'm afraid that's rather ... complicated. How are you feeling? Are you in any pain?"

She paused, trying to feel herself out. "N...no, I don't think so. My head feels a little fuzzy, but it doesn't hurt. My throat is pretty dry."

"Here," he helped her to a sitting position, propped up against several more of the soft pillows before handing her a glass of water from the small wooden table next to her.

"Thanks." She sipped at the water for a long moment before adding, "My leg does feel kind of strange."

"Yes, well your leg will probably be a bit numb for another hour or two. William had to put in a few stitches."

She set the heavy glass back down on the table before pulling back the thick white-and-gold duvet that covered her. At some point, her ruined jeans and green-striped pullover had been replaced by a long white nightgown.

Her cheeks grew pink as she wondered who had done that – hopefully not William. She lifted up the ruffled hem and found it, a neat little white cotton square secured with medical tape, on the inside of her right leg, just a couple of inches above her ankle.

"Doesn't look scary enough to have caused all this trouble, does it?" She blinked up at Dr. Rose's gentle smile. "William said it was pretty deep, though. You must have fallen just wrong on one of the bushes by the bridge. He found a small chunk of wood in there when he went to stitch it up."

She started to feel a little lightheaded again – maybe she didn't need so many details. "What did Thomas give me – that made me sleep?" she asked, changing the subject.

"Valoris seed powder. It comes from a plant that grows here. Generally it just helps someone relax, and dulls pain a bit. The reaction you had to it was very rare. I think it may have affected you more because of the shock you'd just experienced." There was a catch in his voice when he said that, like there was something he wasn't telling her, but it wasn't her biggest concern right then.

"How long was I asleep?" She was suddenly worried about what else she might have missed.

"Only a little over an hour."

A soft knock at the door just then distracted them both.

"How is she doing, Master Rose?" A soft voice drifted over from the doorway.

"Come on in, Mia. Our little patient is awake." His voice was as warm and friendly as ever.

A short, slender young woman entered the room. Quinn guessed she was probably around her own age, sixteen or so. Her long, thick, midnight-black hair was pulled back into a neat French braid. A starched white apron covered the simple navy blue dress she wore. Her bright green eyes were cheerful and friendly underneath her dark eyelashes, and sprinkling of freckles dotted her rosy cheeks. She carried a brown wicker basket full of freshly folded laundry.

"Mia, this is Quinn, our guest. And Quinn, I would like you to meet Mia. Mia is one of the most esteemed members of our housekeeping staff." The maid's bright cheeks flushed even pinker at the doctor's compliment.

Interesting that wherever they were had a housekeeping staff. She didn't think Doctor Rose had anything like that in Bristlecone.

"It's nice to meet you, Miss Quinn," Mia said cheerfully, setting the basket down on a fluffy white ottoman. "I washed your shirt for you, and it's drying now. I am afraid the pants had seen their last day. I've brought some more clothes so you will have things you need in your cupboard, and some fresh underthings you might like to have as well. Is the sleeping gown all right? I know it's not really the style where you're from. We could have some sleeping tops and bottoms made for you instead, if you would rather. That's what Master William's sisters have taken to wearing these days."

Quinn's eyes were wide by the end of Mia's rapid speech. Mia now stared at her expectantly, and she wasn't sure how to respond.

"I, uh ... the nightgown's fine," she finally stammered. "Thank you." She wasn't going to put someone to the trouble of making new pajamas for her for one night. She was so relieved to realize that she was still wearing her own underwear that she wasn't bothered at all by the frilly nightgown. For all of its ruffles, it was incredibly soft. It would be okay for tonight.

Master William was a new one for her, though.

"It's been a long evening for you Quinn," Dr. Rose said pointedly, concern on his face. "You're probably hungry, aren't you?"

Now that he mentioned it, she was starving. "Yes, I suppose I am."

"I'll bring up a tray right away Miss!" Mia disappeared through the door almost instantly.

Dr. Rose turned his warm smile back to Quinn. "I'm guessing you might also like a few moments to yourself?"

She nodded; she was starting to feel a bit overwhelmed. More than a bit, even.

"Let me help you up, you can move around a bit, and take care of any needs you might have," Dr. Rose said, placing his hand underneath her elbow.

Putting weight on her leg wasn't nearly as bad as it had been earlier when she was walking with William. After a couple of stiff steps, she was feeling much more like herself.

"There's a bathroom just in there." Dr. Rose pointed to a heavy wooden door at the far corner of the room. "Mia's been busy making sure it's stocked with just about anything you could need. I'll give you a little while and then I'll bring some ibuprofen after you've had your dinner. Your leg will probably be pretty sore once the numbness wears off."

She nodded, unsure of what else to say, and Dr. Rose disappeared through the door, leaving her alone in the room.

She took a deep breath, relieved to have a few minutes to think without having to talk to someone and answer questions. She had too many questions of her own to concentrate on theirs. Taking a deep breath, she looked at her surroundings.

The room she was in was large and beautiful. Dark wood paneling extended halfway up the walls, and the top half was covered in some kind of rich gold-and-white fabric that matched the duvet on the enormous four-poster bed. Near the window were a table and two soft armchairs. In the middle of the room stood an overstuffed white couch with a low coffee table in front of it.

Someone had recently placed a vase of fresh flowers in the middle of that table. She could not identify the dark violet blooms. The pale gray carpeting was thick and soft underneath her feet. Although she wanted to explore all of it, pressing need drove her quickly to the door in the corner that Dr. Rose had pointed out a moment ago.

The bathroom was every bit as lavish as the bedroom to which it was connected. Piles of fluffy white towels lay on the marble counter tops surrounding both the large sink and the deep bathtub.

After taking care of her immediate needs, she investigated the rest of the preparations that Mia had made for her. She found a long, thick bathrobe hanging from a hook on the back of the door, and a pair of fuzzy white slippers on a low shelf along the back wall. In the long, shallow woven baskets that sat on the shelves under the sink, she found a new hairbrush, comb, and ponytail holders.

There was also a toothbrush, and an odd little covered tin filled with what looked and smelled like toothpaste. Every item she encountered left her with more questions. Much care had been taken in the preparations for her night in this room. Most surprising, next to the basket of washcloths, Quinn discovered a small, brown glass bottle, exactly like the one in her bathroom at home.

It couldn't be the same, could it? Nobody else she knew used essential oils like that. Picking up the bottle, she pulled out the stopper and gasped as the familiar scent of lavender and vanilla filled the room.

Now she really wasn't sure whether she was awake or dreaming. Her hands shook as she replaced the little bottle on the shelf.

After the night's adventures, she felt grubby, and the deep marble bathtub looked very inviting. Her hand was almost on the strange metal tap when she realized that she hadn't asked Dr. Rose if it would be okay to get her stitches wet or not. She shuddered thinking about it; the last thing she wanted was to have to have them replaced. She was grateful for the small size of her injury and its discreet location. How would she have ever explained stitches to her mother? She sighed and headed instead for the sink.

Twenty minutes later, when she emerged from the bathroom as clean as she could get herself, she noticed small changes in the room. The laundry basket had disappeared, and the bed looked as though she'd never been in it. She looked all around the room, but didn't see anyone in there with her. On the small table by the window, she discovered a covered silver tray and a matching pitcher, dripping with condensation – for the first time, she noticed that it was kind of warm in here. She was about to pull the cover off the tray when she was interrupted by the sound of a knock and then the door opening.

"Quinn? Okay if I come in?" Thomas didn't wait for her to respond before coming the rest of the way into the room. He carried a smaller covered tray in his hand, and wore the same sparkling smile she had seen earlier.

"Um, sure..." He was already in; did she have a choice?

"I brought you something." His grin grew even wider. "One of our cooks, Cassie, makes the most amazing chocolate cake you've ever tasted." He set his tray on the small table, and turned back to her. Though he was still smiling, his eyes looked concerned again. "You doing okay?"

A housekeeping staff and cooks, plural? "Much better now, thanks."

"You had us worried there for a minute; that's a pretty rare reaction to have from valoris seed. I wouldn't have given it to you if..."

She shrugged. "Maybe it's better for me that it did. I'm okay now."

"How's the leg?"

"It's better, I think. I still can't really feel it."

"Will's good at stitching. You'll be good as new in no time."

Although she'd been calm since she'd woken up, her curiosity over the new environment overriding her fear and uncertainty, Thomas' laid-back attitude about the whole thing sent her reeling again. Irritation roared inside her like a tidal wave. "Explain to me please, how, exactly, a seventeen-year-old kid is 'good at stitching'?"

Her outburst didn't appear to faze Thomas. "I suppose that's not really normal where you're from, is it?"

"Where I'm from? No. And that's another thing, where am I?" The stress of the situation and the strangeness of the night's events were really starting to get to her now.

"William didn't tell you anything, did he?"

"He said 'this is my real home' like I should have already known that. And then he started poking needles into me."

Thomas looked like he was restraining himself from laughing aloud. "Sounds like Will," he said.

"So, WHERE. AM. I?"

Thomas cleared his throat. "You," he began, "are in Rosewood Castle."

She stared at him.

"Not helpful?" Thomas wondered.

"No, not exactly. Rosewood *Castle?* Do you mean the castle I saw out there while we were walking?"

Thomas nodded.

Well, that explained the opulent surroundings and the servants. "How did I get to Rosewood Castle?"

"On my horse?"

She narrowed her eyes. "I think you know that's not what I mean."

"You followed Will through the gate from your world into ours."

"What does that even mean? How..." she trailed off, not even sure what question she meant to ask.

"That's the question of the day, isn't it? There's a big uproar downstairs. You, my lady, are quite the mystery to everyone. They're all trying to understand how you got here. Nobody from your world has ever just followed someone through the gate before." His grin still hadn't faded. Despite the obvious confusion surrounding him, he clearly found this entertaining.

"And," he continued, "you haven't even touched your dinner. The food that's prepared in honor of William's homecomings is not something you want to miss." He sat down in one of the two chairs at the little table and lifted the silver lid from the platter. "Join me, will you?"

She eyed him skeptically. "Will you explain to me what's going on here if I do?"

He seemed amused. "Suit yourself; it's getting cold." Smiling, he dipped a silver fork into a steaming pile of mashed potatoes, waving it near her face. The food smelled amazing, and she was starving.

She sighed, and sat down in the chair opposite Thomas, grabbing the fork from his hand.

He smiled. "Much better." It was odd how comfortable she already was with him. He felt like an old friend rather than someone she'd met only hours ago - in a strange world. A strange world?

"So let me get this straight, I somehow followed your brother into a different world?"

"Yes," his response was matter-of-fact.

She blinked. "I don't understand."

He studied her face carefully, "It is awfully strange, I suppose."

"You suppose? Is this something that's normal in your ... world? People just walk over bridges and find themselves on a different planet?"

"We've never figured out if your world and ours are simply different planets, or something else altogether. William has this theory about dimensions..."

She just stared at him.

"I suppose that's not really the point you were going for, is it?" Thomas' bright smile hadn't faded at all. She was finding it difficult to be irritated with him. Besides, she had to admit that this was all a little fascinating.

"No," he continued, "it's not normal in our world, either. We do have stories, hundreds of cycles old, legends, really, of our people traveling back and forth between your world and ours, but it's in fairly recent history that our family discovered a genuine passage we could travel through. It's a secret we guard pretty closely."

"Why would William, who apparently has all this," she gestured around her, "leave and live in a place like Bristlecone?"

The look on Thomas' face became thoughtful. "There are many similarities between our worlds, but many differences as well. We don't have many of the resources, or the knowledge that your world has access to. Particularly knowledge of technology and medicine. William - and Nathaniel, for that matter, spend time living in your world to study your medicine, and to bring those skills back to our people."

At that moment, Nathaniel appeared in the open doorway. "Not talking her ear off too much are you, Thomas? She needs to eat."

"She's eating," Thomas answered, looking pointedly at Quinn, who obediently tossed a forkful of salad into her mouth.

"How are you feeling, Quinn? Is your leg sore now?"

She shook her head, still chewing some strange, crunchy vegetable.

"Well, I brought you something anyway," he told her, setting a small glass bottle on the table. Inside she could see several tiny white pills; the shape was familiar. "Some ibuprofen, from home. Take two of them after you've finished your dinner and two more when you wake up in the morning. It works best if you take them before you start hurting," he added, silencing her unspoken objection. "And your leg is going to be sore tomorrow."

She nodded; her leg didn't hurt yet, but she could tell that, just at the edges, the numbness was beginning to fade a bit.

"Finish eating, and then you should probably get some rest. Would you like me to stay with you for a while?"

"I'll take care of her, Nathaniel. See that she finishes her dinner and gets to sleep. If that's all right with you, Quinn?"

She nodded; she was enjoying Thomas' company - and his willingness to answer questions.

Nathaniel looked back and forth between the two of them and smiled.

"Okay then, but no wearing her out too much. Some things can wait until the morning. Is there anything else you need for tonight, Quinn?"

"I don't think so, thank you."

"All right then. Have a good night."

"Goodnight, Dr. Rose."

He looked like he was about to say something else, but then he just smiled. "Good-night, Quinn."

She turned back to Thomas, who shook his head. "Eat," he commanded.

By the time she had finished her dinner, and eaten the chocolate cake, which, as promised, was the best chocolate cake she had ever tasted, she was feeling the stress of the day. She yawned widely. Curious as she was, it was beginning to be a struggle to keep her eyes open.

"Time for bed," Thomas said.

"You were going to answer my questions."

"You're tired. More answers in the morning, I promise." He stood and started collecting the dishes.

"How about just one more?"

He stopped and looked at her, an amused expression on his face. "I suppose that depends on what it is. Too much talk about alternate universes is going to interfere with your sleep."

"Because I'm going to be able to sleep in a strange universe?"

Thomas chuckled. "Is that your one question?"

"Okay, how about this question. Why do you live in a castle?"

"That one's easy. Because my father is the king."

"Your father's the king? Meaning you're what? A prince or something?"

"Yes, but that's two questions. Goodnight." Thomas disappeared through the door with the dishes before she could think of a response.

STUCK

QUINN HAD AWAKENED too early in the morning, and now she had no idea what to do with herself. For probably the tenth time that morning, she walked over to the tall windows. When she had first woken up and pulled on the cord that operated the heavy draperies, it had still been nearly pitch black outside, only the barest glow beginning to form on the horizon.

Realizing that there was no chance she would be going back to sleep, she had busied herself with the few small tasks she could create for herself in the immaculate room. First, she had made the bed, pulling the sheets tight and smoothing the soft duvet. She'd thought she was pretty decent at making a bed, but she was completely unable to recreate Mia's work.

She had cleaned herself up again in the enormous bathroom, washing her hair in the deep sink, and taking the time to pull her long, auburn hair into a neat French braid. After brushing her teeth for far longer than was strictly necessary, she had investigated the large armoire in the corner of the room. She had been comforted to find her favorite shirt on top of a pile of freshly laundered tops. On the bottom shelf, she was surprised to discover two pairs of blue jeans, quite similar in style to the pair she had ruined the night before. Though they bore no brand-name tags, and were fastened only with buttons – no snaps or zippers – she thought she would probably get them past her mother without scrutiny.

Her mother – that was the source of her anxiety as she stood again at the window, watching the sun slowly begin to rise, spreading waves of pink, purple, and orange over the few clouds in the increasingly blue sky. What if she tried to call last night? What if she freaked out when Quinn didn't answer her phone calls today? Was the whole town going to be out looking for her?

She was getting desperate to get back to her cell phone to text her mom. She knew that if her mother grew worried at all, she would cut her Denver trip short and come rushing back to Bristlecone to make sure everything was all right. Aside from the possibility of her mother getting angry with her, she got a sick feeling in her stomach thinking she might make her mom worry.

She was halfway tempted to just find her own way out of the castle, and search for the trail that would take her back to the bridge. Halfway to her door though, she realized that she didn't even have the faintest idea how she had gotten into the castle the night before, and had little idea where the trail might begin even if she did find her way out without being stopped by one of the many people who surely were here in the castle with her. What if there were guards? Also, she wasn't sure where her shoes were, so she resumed her search of the bedroom.

It really only took her a few minutes to find her shoes where someone, most likely Mia, had neatly stored them in the small cupboard at the bottom right of the armoire. She could find no evidence of the blood she was sure would have stained the side of her right shoe the night before.

Growing antsier by the second, she headed back toward the bedroom door. She had no idea what was expected of her this morning. She didn't want to put anyone to any more trouble, or to cause a scene. She just wanted to get back to the bridge so she could get home. Holding her ear near the edge of the door, she heard no noises at all in the corridor outside.

She pulled on the heavy lever as quietly as she could, and opened the door just wide enough to peek out. The long hallway was dark, lit only every few yards by small lights glowing a few inches from the floor. They reminded her of nightlights – which was probably what they were. The few doors that she could see were closed. There were no people anywhere. Feeling nervous, she closed the door softly, and resumed her pacing back and forth to the window.

Outside, the sunrise was amazing. She had lived surrounded by the Rocky Mountains her entire life, so watching the sun rise over flat land was an unusual experience for her. Although the horizon was thickly forested, seeing the sun itself appear over the tops of the trees so quickly after its rays colored the sky was incredibly different from home.

The height of the window led her to guess that she was probably about three floors above the ground in the castle. Directly below her, she could see wide, manicured lawns stretching several hundred yards to where she could just make out the shape of a tall stone wall. As she watched, a pair of small brownish-red bunnies hopped across one of the stone walkways and into one of the well-tended flowerbeds.

Bored now, as well as anxious, she headed back to the doorway. This time she wasn't quite as careful to be silent in opening it. Her head was all the way into the corridor before she noticed the small difference. One of the doors was halfway open. Startled, she ducked back into the room.

Before she could get her door completely closed, she heard the shrieking giggles and slamming door that let her know that one room, at least, was occupied by children. Quickly, she retreated to the soft couch in the middle of the room and curled up on it, watching the sky become more and more blue through the window.

Sitting there, anxious and desperate as she was to get back home, to return to normal, to not scare her mother half to death, another emotion was starting to filter in. The curiosity that had plagued her for the last several weeks was back with a vengeance.

All of these weeks of following William, of trying to figure out where he so often disappeared to, had yielded her an answer she had never expected, and the answer had left her with a million more questions. She still had no idea exactly where she was or how she had gotten here. This couldn't be real, could it? Suddenly, she realized that she wanted to find out more about what had happened here than she really wanted to go home. And then, she wasn't completely certain that she wasn't dreaming.

She stood again, and began wandering the room, inspecting everything again, staring out the window once more. Something else about this place was nagging at the back of her mind, but she couldn't put her finger on what it was.

A knock at the door interrupted Quinn's reverie. Just as he had the night before, Thomas entered the room without waiting for her response.

"You are up! My little sisters told me you were poking your head out. You sure have a talent for causing excitement around here." He flashed his happy grin at her.

She grimaced; she wasn't sure how happy she was to be attracting all of this attention.

"Are you hungry? It'll be breakfast time soon." Thomas' twinkling gray eyes appeared a bit sleepy this morning, but he had clearly been awake for at least a little while. The curls of his dark hair were a bit wet. He looked nice; wearing freshly pressed black pants and a short-sleeved steel-gray sweater over a white shirt; the starched collar was folded down crisply by his neck. Quinn suddenly felt a bit under-dressed.

"I am a little hungry, I guess," she told him. "But, mostly I just want to get home."

A look of concern mingled with confusion swept over Thomas' usually-carefree face. He was silent for a moment before his smile returned, a little more subdued and kinder. "I'm sorry. I'm sure it must be hard for you, coming here unexpectedly and being stuck. Breakfast will help with the hungry part, though!"

He had lost her on a single word: stuck. "What do you mean, stuck? William comes back all the time." In that instant, she realized how much she had assumed. She mentally played back the scene at the bridge with William from the night before. What had he said? *There's no way back to your home tonight.*

She had locked on to the 'tonight,' part, maybe thinking that the 'gate' closed at dark. Assuming she would be able to get back through in the morning.

Thomas watched her for a long moment, seeming to notice her internal struggle. He finally spoke. "In your world, it must seem that way – that William goes back and forth 'all the time'." He paused, scrutinizing Quinn's face carefully. "It doesn't work exactly that way on this end."

This completely bewildered her, and her breathing started to speed up. "What do you mean?"

At that moment, there was a knock at the bedroom door, and Thomas rose to open it, disrupting Quinn's oncoming panic attack.

"Master Thomas, you're in here!" Mia's voice was surprised. "I've brought breakfast for Miss Quinn." She carried a covered silver tray; identical to the one from which Quinn had eaten dinner the night before. She set it down on the small table by the window. "Would you like me to bring you up a tray, or will you be eating downstairs this morning?"

Thomas frowned at her, a strange expression on his face. "Mia, isn't it your day off today?"

Quinn watched dark pink color Mia's round cheeks.

"Yes, well, it would be, Master Thomas, but I thought I would stay this morning and help make sure Miss Quinn is settling in."

Something in Mia's voice made Quinn think there was more to it than that.

"That was very kind of you, Mia," Thomas' smile was genuine and warm. "I'm sure we have enough help. I will sort out breakfast for myself, thank you. I don't want you missing your day with your family."

"Thank you, Master Thomas." Mia kept her eyes on the floor near Thomas' feet. Her blush hadn't faded.

"Of course. Have a wonderful time. We'll see you tomorrow afternoon?"

"Yes, Master Thomas. Thank you again."

As Mia exited, Quinn heard giggling in the hallway.

Thomas turned to look at her. "I think some of my little sisters are anxious to see who all the fuss is about," he smiled. "Do you mind?"

"No, I don't mind." And she didn't. Children had never intimidated her the way other people sometimes did. The sudden realization that William and Thomas had other siblings momentarily overshadowed her distress.

Thomas strode into the hallway, and then returned a moment later, three little girls in tow. One skipped eagerly ahead of him into the room. Quinn guessed her to be about six. She had the same dark, curly locks as Thomas, although hers reached down to the middle of her back. Her gray eyes held the same sparkle of friendliness and spunk as Thomas'.

Another little girl clung right to Thomas, hiding behind his back. A bit younger, maybe four or so, she reminded Quinn much more of her other big brother, William. Quieter, more serious. Her dark hair was long and straight. These gray eyes also studied Quinn from behind glasses.

The third child was only a toddler. She nestled in her big brother's arms, poking her fingers into his mouth, while he playfully pretended to be biting them off.

The oldest girl walked right up to Quinn. "Hi! I'm Emma. Who are you?"

Quinn smiled back at her. "Hi Emma. I'm Quinn."

"Emma here is our little instigator of all things giggle-related," he said, tickling her ribs until she squealed, then smiled winningly up at Quinn.

He ran his fingers through the second little girl's hair. "This is Alice. She's a little quiet until she gets to know you. And this," he tickled the littlest one under her chin, causing her to reveal deep dimples in her rosy cheeks, "is Miss Sarah."

Quinn smiled.

"Are you really William's friend from another kingdom?" Emma looked at Quinn expectantly.

"Um," Quinn looked to Thomas for help, but he was ready.

"Of course she is! It's nice to have a guest, isn't it, girls?" Thomas set Sarah down on the floor. They all watched as she toddled around the room, looking at everything.

Quinn was reminded of Annie's toddlerhood as Sarah pulled one of the flowers from the vase on the low table and immediately proceeded to put it into her mouth. Thomas quickly retrieved the flower and replaced it, but Sarah's curiosity was undeterred, and she toddled toward the other table, reaching up for the shiny cover on the tray Mia had brought.

Thomas sighed, and then grinned sheepishly at Quinn. "You girls must be hungry. Let's go get you to breakfast." Thomas scooped Sarah back up and ushered the girls to the door, over Emma's objections. "We need to let Quinn eat her breakfast, too."

She watched Thomas disappear through the door with the girls, wondering why he had only allowed them into the room so briefly. She wondered exactly where the little girls believed she was from. Another kingdom? How much did they know? Why was Thomas so vague with them?

Of course, as little as the girls seemed to know, Quinn realized that she knew even less. She had no idea where she was or how she had gotten here. What did Thomas mean about her being stuck here? A thrill of panic ran through Quinn ... what *did* he mean about her being stuck here? She was going to be able to go home, wasn't she? For the first time, the situation started to feel extremely real, and anxiety overtook her.

Thomas was only gone for a couple of moments, but it was long enough for Quinn to have been alone for too long. When he re-entered the room, Thomas found her in a ball on the couch, tears running down her face.

"Hey, what's going on?" Thomas rushed across the room to her.

"What's going on? That's what I would like to know! What *is* going on? Where am I? How did I get here? How am I going to get home? *When* am I going to get home? I *am* going to be able to go home, aren't I? *Am I?*"

Thomas looked a bit taken aback by Quinn's outburst, but he recovered quickly, "It's okay, Quinn. Calm down. Yes, you *are* going to be able to go home."

Her breathing slowed a bit at Thomas' calm reassurance, but the room still felt like it was spinning.

He studied her for a second, and then laid his hand gently in the middle of her back. "It's going to be okay. Why don't you come take a walk with me?" He helped her up, and guided her gently to the door.

"A walk? I want to know what's going on here, not go for a walk!"

Thomas' voice was calm and patient. "I will explain it to you. I promise. You can ask me any question you like. I just think that fresh air and privacy would both be helpful, okay?"

Quinn took a deep breath, thinking it over, and then nodded.

When they got into the hallway, Thomas turned to her. "Let's sneak you out quietly and give you a chance to think without the rest of my family bombarding you with their curiosity."

She nodded, and started to wipe her tears on her sleeve, but Thomas was too fast for her, pulling a soft, white handkerchief out of his pocket and handing it to her. He led her down the hallway, all the way to a wooden door at the end. He opened it, and they stepped inside.

It was a stairwell, she realized. They were on a landing in a stairwell. A curving staircase rose above them, and dipped down below. Morning sunlight slanted in through arched windows near each floor. Thomas led her quickly down two flights of stairs, and then pressed his ear against the door on the landing. Quinn heard him mutter something, but she couldn't make it out; it almost sounded like an expletive.

"What?"

He looked abashed, "Sorry. It's just that I hear some of my brothers and cousins in there, and I don't think we want to run into them right now. Fortunately for you, I have a few more tricks up my sleeve than that." He grinned and pulled her down the last flight of stairs, and through the door at the bottom.

Now they were standing in a long, curving hallway. The plain, stone floor here stood in sharp contrast to the polished marble of the upper floor, though it was swept and neat.

"Where are we?" she whispered to Thomas.

"Near the kitchens; these rooms are storage areas." Thomas wasn't whispering here. They walked along the corridor, and then through another wooden door into a room that must have been an enormous pantry. Cupboards and shelves lined the walls, filled with vegetables and sacks of flour and other grains. Thomas led her quickly through here, and paused by the large, swinging double doors at the end. He peeked through the crack in the doors, and Quinn saw him smile.

"Let's go," he took her hand and pulled her through.

She had assumed from his grin that they were entering an empty room, so her heart fell into her stomach when her eyes took in the woman standing at the counter, rolling out dough, staring at Thomas and Quinn with a raised eyebrow.

"'Morning, Delores," Thomas said with a wink, and his most charming grin, casually laying his arm across Quinn's shoulders and quickly ushering her to the door at the other end of the kitchen.

Quinn thought she saw a bit of color light up the older woman's cheeks as she and Thomas disappeared through the door.

THOMAS

QUINN BLINKED IN THE bright sunlight outside the kitchen. They were standing on a gravel path that seemed to wind in several directions. Large hedges lined the walkways, obstructing her view. Thomas led her down the path to the right. After they had walked about twenty feet, they came to a break in the hedgerow, and she could see water bubbling from an enormous stone fountain, in the middle of a stone-paved courtyard.

Thomas led her through this courtyard, and past several large flowerbeds filled with every color of roses that she had ever seen, as well as some that she hadn't. Other flowers were mixed in with the roses; she recognized chrysanthemums and tulips, but many of the other flowers were a mystery to her.

He kept going, far past the fountain, back into more gardens, until they reached a beautiful white gazebo. He climbed the steps, motioning for her to keep following. Once inside, he sat down on one of the cushioned benches that lined the perimeter. He patted the seat beside him.

"Now," he said, "we're somewhere we can talk."

Thomas' friendly company and the walk had calmed Quinn. She was no longer panicking, and she could feel the intense pull of her curiosity beginning to burn again.

"Do you do this often?" she asked.

He looked at her, surprise in his gray eyes, "Do what?"

"Sneak girls through the kitchen and out to the gazebo."

He grinned. "Occasionally."

She rolled her eyes.

"Your mood has improved. Not freaking out anymore? Decided you like it here and want to stay?" He winked.

She ignored him. "Okay, we're outside. Can you please tell me what exactly is going on here? What did you mean when you said that I'm stuck? Stuck for how long?"

"Well..." Thomas stood up and walked to the entrance of the gazebo. He gazed out at the roses for a moment before turning around, leaning his broad shoulders against the post, and looking at her. "I don't know the details exactly. I know that you followed William through the gate last night from your world into ours, just as the sun was setting, so the gate would have closed pretty much right behind you."

"So the gate will be open again at sunset?" That sounded hopeful.

"No. Not today, anyway."

"When?"

"In about ten days. The opening of the gate follows a rough cycle, usually around two weeks. It has something to do with our lunar cycles aligning. This time of year, it opens about every ten days."

Quinn blinked, uncomprehending. Thomas stopped speaking, and sat down next to her on the bench.

After what was possibly the longest moment in her life, she brought her eyes back to meet his.

"Are you telling me that the gate won't open for me to go home for ten days?"

He nodded, and she felt like the floor was falling out from under her.

They sat together on the bench for a long moment in complete silence, while she processed what Thomas had told her. She wouldn't be able to get back to her home for ten days. She wasn't going home today. She was stuck here. Questions flooded her brain. She waited for the panic attack.

That was probably what Thomas was waiting for, too. The show.

It didn't come. She waited and waited, but all she could feel was an unnatural calm settling over her, maybe because there was a huge, glaring piece of missing information. Finally, she decided it was safe to speak.

"If the gate doesn't open," she tried to hold her voice steady, "for *ten days*, then how is William going to get back?"

Thomas' brow furrowed. "Through the gate," he spoke slowly, "when it opens again." It was obvious that he didn't understand Quinn's question.

"How is it that he never misses school? Has he not come back here in years?" It didn't fit with the scenario she'd been constructing in her mind. If he wasn't coming here, where did William keep disappearing to?

The dizziness was coming back; the slow, terrifying feeling was beginning to form in the bottom of her stomach. Her mom.

She could tell when he'd registered the change in her eyes, because his words came out in a jumble. "No, it isn't like that. When the gate opens again in our world, it will only be the next sunset in yours."

She was stunned. "How does that work?"

"I don't know how it works," Thomas shrugged, "I only know that it does. William has been going back and forth through the gate for … years. Nathaniel for longer than him. Others before them. We don't know why or how. We just use it."

"So how is it that Nathaniel isn't gone when William is, then?"

Thomas blinked. "He is gone from your world when he comes here, the same as William. He isn't able to come back every single time William does, though. He has a job there he has to keep up with.

Sometimes he comes back on days when William has school, too, now that Will's almost an adult. They're not always together in either place."

Quinn considered that. It answered some questions, but created so many more. She wasn't sure she could think clearly enough even to begin asking what she wanted to know. Maybe this was all a dream. She was quiet for so long this time that she started to wonder if she was being rude, but Thomas continued to watch her with calm interest.

She still wasn't freaking out the way she thought she should be. Maybe because she was finally getting an answer to the mystery that had puzzled her for weeks and the answer was amazing. William was from an entirely different world?

The news that she would probably be back before her mother reported her to the police was comforting. But what was she supposed to do here for ten days? Finally, she decided it was safe to speak.

"So now what?"

Thomas' brow furrowed. "What do you mean?"

"What do I do here?"

Thomas shrugged and smiled at her, "Well, for now, you are our guest."

"And that's just okay with everyone? A strange girl shows up suddenly from another world and just gets to stay at the castle? Am I in some kind of trouble or something? Where is William, anyway?"

This time, Thomas did laugh out loud.

"No, you are not in trouble. We've shown up uninvited in your world quite often; it wouldn't be quite fair to begrudge you for the same curiosity. Mind you, most people here have no idea about our secret passage. The servants all think William has brought you back from one of the nearby kingdoms he visits sometimes. As do the younger children who are not quite old enough to be discreet. Just keep your secret to yourself, though, please."

As she processed Thomas' words she guessed it made sense. "So where is William?"

Thomas sighed, "He took off on his horse somewhere this morning; I think he's pretty upset with himself for letting you in on the secret."

She blanched. "Is he really mad?"

Thomas was thoughtful, "He's upset, but not at you, I don't think. William can be very hard on himself. I'm sure he's not thrilled with you right now, but he'll come around when he settles down. He'll probably be worried about your leg – he was upset last night that he didn't put the stitches in when you first did it, even though Nathaniel told him you were fine."

"You never did tell me how a seventeen-year-old, a senior in high school, could know so much about medicine, and be putting stitches in people."

A crease appeared between Thomas' eyebrows. He hesitated, watching Quinn's expression closely before he began speaking, "Time doesn't work exactly the same way in our worlds. Here in our world, people have longer life spans than in yours. Well, not really longer life spans, in a way, but growing a whole cycle older takes many more days. William is seventeen years old in your world, yes, but because of the time differences, that 'seventeen years' – or cycles, here, is a much longer period of time here. He has really lived much longer than people his age in your world."

Quinn's eyes felt like they might pop out of their sockets. "What?"

"William attends school in your world to take advantage of your medical knowledge, and system of education. He reads all about the medicines and research there and tries to find equivalents here.

"However, when he leaves to come back here, for what is only a weekend in your world, he has twenty or more days here. Time to study, to take the knowledge he has gained and put it into practice. He is not a full-fledged doctor yet, of course, but he has already been assisting Nathaniel as an apprentice for several cycles. Even in your world, he has worked past most of the courses that would be typical for a student his age. Nathaniel has assisted him in completing college classes, as well."

"Why? I mean, why does a prince want to do all of that?"

"Medicine is my brother's gift, Quinn. Along with an incredible passion for caring for people, for helping them. I honestly couldn't imagine William without medicine. He breathes the stuff. Herbs, remedies, cures, anti-biomo-something, – he won't shut up about the properties of mold. That and healing people are practically his whole life."

Quinn was floored. Logically, what Thomas was telling her made no sense, and yet, it fit. Suddenly, all of the little clues she had been gathering about William were coming together to form a picture.

Abruptly, Thomas looked up and stood, seeing something behind her. She followed his gaze. On the path, walking toward the gazebo's entrance was a beautiful woman. Dark hair flowed in curls down to the middle of her back, and her gray eyes stared at Quinn in wonder. Though she looked far too young to have two nearly-grown sons, Quinn immediately had no doubt about whom she must be. A moment later, her suspicion was confirmed.

"Good morning, Mother." Thomas walked down the steps to greet her. He kissed her on the cheek, and then held out his hands to take the tiny bundle of white blankets cradled in her arms.

"Good morning, Thomas." The woman leaned over and kissed the top of the baby's head, hidden by the blankets and a white hat, before handing it to him.

Thomas pulled the baby close to his chest, holding it comfortably in one arm, and, with his other arm, led his mother up the gazebo steps toward Quinn. The woman looked so elegant she nearly took Quinn's breath away. She was dressed simply, in a long, flowing white skirt and a lavender top with white lace along the collar and the ends of the short sleeves. Her hair was held back from her face with a delicate silver headband. Studying her more closely, Quinn realized that the elegance wasn't in the woman's appearance at all, but in the way she carried herself and the bright, knowing look on her face.

Quinn watched as they glided up the steps, and she suddenly felt self-conscious. If Thomas' father was the king, that must make his mother the queen. She had never met a queen in person before and she had no idea what the proper etiquette might be. Did she shake hands with her? Curtsy? Unable to decide, Quinn just stood there, her face turning crimson.

A quick glance passed between mother and son, but the expression on the queen's face only grew more tender.

"Quinn, I would like to introduce you to my mother, Charlotte, Queen of Eirentheos. Mother, this is Quinn."

"Hello dear. Welcome." Queen Charlotte's smile was every bit as warm and friendly as her son's.

"Thank you, um, Your Majesty?" Quinn had no idea how to address a queen in a strange world.

Thomas looked like he was going to laugh again, but Queen Charlotte's gaze contained only warmth and concern. "Please just call me Charlotte, sweetheart. I am sure all of this is strange and overwhelming."

Just call her Charlotte? What kind of world was this? "Yeah, it is a little overwhelming, for sure."

Queen Charlotte smiled. "How are you feeling? I heard you injured your leg last night." Her tone was motherly.

"I'm doing better, thank you. My leg isn't hurting much at all this morning." Quinn felt immediately comfortable with Charlotte, much the same way she had with Thomas the night before. She thought it was a bit odd though, how easily they were accepting her presence here.

Charlotte nodded. "Well, please let us know if it bothers you at all. Have you had breakfast?"

"Um..." Quinn realized now that she hadn't even touched the tray Mia had brought for her, and she was growing hungry.

"No, she hasn't," Thomas answered for her. "Mia brought her up a tray, but she wasn't quite ready to eat at the time."

"Mia? I thought she was off today?" Queen Charlotte's facial expressions were startlingly similar to her son's.

"So did I." Quinn didn't understand the look on Thomas' face now, but it clearly held meaning for Charlotte, who nodded and turned back to Quinn.

"Surely you must be hungry by now, Quinn?" Charlotte didn't wait for her hesitant nod before asking Thomas to fetch another breakfast tray for her. He handed the bundle of blankets back to his mother before quickly disappearing back in the direction of the kitchens, leaving Quinn alone with Charlotte and the tiny infant.

"Let's go have a seat, dear. Thomas will be back in a moment." The queen led her down the steps and back into a section of the garden where a few small tables dotted the stone walkway. Quinn settled into the soft cushion of a white wicker chair, and Charlotte sat down next to her, holding the baby so that Quinn could see its face.

"This is our newest arrival," Charlotte said, pressing her cheek to the baby's. "Thomas and William's youngest sister."

The baby girl's eyes were open, showing deep gray ringed with long, dark eyelashes. She was beautiful.

"What's her name?"

"She will officially be named in a few days, at her Naming Ceremony." Queen Charlotte replied. As if in response, the tiny girl let out a squeak and waved her fist in the air, trying to get it near her mouth.

"I think she's hungry, too," Charlotte laughed, and unraveled some of the blankets from the baby. A moment later, when the baby was contentedly nursing, Charlotte studied Quinn's face. She opened her mouth, looking as if she was going to say something, and then closed it again. Quinn wasn't sure what to say, either.

Charlotte began again suddenly, "So, Quinn, how is William getting along in your world?"

Quinn's head snapped up, surprised, "I beg your pardon, Your Majesty?"

"Oh, Quinn, really. You don't have to be so formal with me, darling." The queen's expression was almost sad – Quinn couldn't quite shake the feeling that something else was going on here.

"I just thought ... William is always away from me, from home, for so long, with only Nathaniel to keep him company and to let us know how he's doing. It would be nice to hear it from someone who is in school with him, who perhaps knows him in a different way."

Quinn swallowed hard, reminded just then of her own mom. "I ... don't know if I know William all that well..."

Charlotte's face registered surprise, mingled with something else ... *concern?* "Really? He seems to know you. He's talked about you before."

Quinn's eyes opened wide. William had talked about her? To his family? She hadn't been positive he knew her name, and he had been talking about her? What had he said? Had he told them something about her that would explain the strange way some of them were acting?

"Well, I have seen him around a lot, ever since we were little. He kind of keeps to himself a lot, though. I've never really talked to him at home."

Charlotte raised her eyebrows. "Keeps to himself? Does he have friends?"

"I don't know," Quinn answered honestly. "I've never seen him with anybody."

A deep line appeared in Charlotte's forehead, Quinn guessed that hearing this made her sad, and she suddenly saw William Rose in an entirely new light. Where before she'd seen him as reclusive, wondering if he was plotting something, she could now see a lonely kid often separated from his loving family. His strange behaviors told a very different story now that she had a better idea of the truth. She wondered why he did it at all, but wasn't sure that this was the right time to ask his mother that question.

"Does he do well in his classes?" Charlotte asked, changing the subject.

"Yes. Everyone knows that. William is smart and ahead in everything. He's a year ahead of me, but I still know that."

Charlotte smiled. "That's good to hear. Thank you for sharing with me, sweetheart. I don't mean to put you on the spot."

"Of course she does! Isn't that what mothers are for?" Thomas had returned, carrying a loaded tray. He set plates full of food in front of Quinn, and in a spot for himself. There were tall glasses of red juice for all three of them, and a glass bowl of freshly-cut fruit for Charlotte. "I know you've already eaten breakfast, Mother, but I thought you'd like a treat to help you keep up your strength for my little sister."

Charlotte smiled widely as Thomas kissed the top of her head before he sat down to eat.

Just as dinner had been the night before, the breakfast was similar to what she ate at home, but not exactly the same. There was a bowl of some kind of thick, grain cereal. At first, Quinn was hesitant to try it, but once she did she found that she liked it, especially the dark berries that were mixed in. The juice was like nothing she'd ever tasted before – sweet, but she wasn't sure she liked the flavor. There was toast, too, that she enjoyed a lot, soft and warm on the inside, crusty on the outside.

Thomas watched intently as she tried everything, while Charlotte appeared to be trying not to make her feel self-conscious. Once it was clear that Quinn was okay with eating most of it, though, the three of them ate in companionable silence for several minutes, Charlotte swaddling the baby again after she fell asleep.

Suddenly, Quinn heard footsteps on the stone path, directly behind her. Thomas and Charlotte both looked up.

"Hello, Linnea." Charlotte smiled as the girl leaned in to kiss her cheek.

"Hello, Mother, Thomas. Beautiful day, isn't it?"

Thomas grinned and stood up. "I wondered how long you'd be able to back off before you had to satisfy your curiosity."

"Never long. This must be Quinn?" The girl sat down in Thomas' chair, taking a sip of his juice, and appraising Quinn.

"Yes, Linnea, this is Quinn. Quinn, this is my busybody sister, Linnea."

Linnea smiled widely. "It's very nice to meet you, Quinn. Welcome."

Quinn smiled back shyly. "It's nice to meet you, too. Thank you." She studied the newcomer. Linnea looked strikingly similar to Thomas. She had the same friendly, gray eyes framed by thick lashes, and dark curls, too, although hers flowed down past her shoulders. She was shorter and slighter than Thomas, but there couldn't be much difference in their ages. She was both surprised and relieved to see that Linnea was dressed nicely, but simply, in a tailored maroon blouse, and tan pants that ended a few inches past her knees, woven out of something like cotton. Apparently, Quinn wasn't too out of place not wearing a dress.

Linnea looked back at Thomas. "I told you this morning, you wouldn't get to keep her all to yourself for long."

Thomas rolled his eyes in response, smiling in Quinn's direction. "Just trying to keep her from being overwhelmed by all of this."

"Well, time's up. It's my turn now. Quinn, I promise I don't bite. Anyway, Thomas, Nathaniel sent me to find you. A messenger arrived from Mistle Village this morning. Essie's asking for help, and Nathaniel can't find William anywhere. You're the only one who ever knows where he is."

Quinn didn't understand the look in Linnea's eyes, darker than her lighthearted tone implied, but Thomas seemed to take some meaning from it, looking apologetically at Quinn.

Linnea rolled her eyes. "Really, Thomas, she'll be fine here. Won't you, Quinn?"

Quinn nodded. She wasn't sure what was going on, but she liked the spunky Linnea already. Now that she wasn't preoccupied by getting out of here and home, she found herself becoming fascinated by this place, curious to learn more. It felt like walking into one of the fantasy novels she loved to read.

Linnea grinned, her expression matching the one that Quinn was quickly growing accustomed to seeing on Thomas.

"Yes, Thomas, we will see to Quinn's needs here. I'm sure William needs you right now much more than she does." Queen Charlotte rose from her chair, handing the baby to Linnea so that she could embrace Thomas. "Be careful. Send for help if you need to."

"Nathaniel was going to have Jared saddle Storm and ready him for you. Delores was packing up some food." Linnea told her brother. "We'll see you this evening. Quinn will have had a wonderful day."

"All right then, Quinn. I suppose I'd better go track down my brother. How you ever managed to keep a close enough eye on him to follow him here, I'll never know. Don't let my little sister get you into too much trouble."

Linnea shot Thomas a dark look. "Fifteen extra minutes does not make you my big brother."

"Older is older, fifteen minutes or fifteen cycles," Thomas teased, ruffling Linnea's hair.

"All right, you two," Charlotte scolded. "Thomas you should get going. Linnea, why don't you show Quinn around, make sure she knows the way back to her room?"

NEVER ENOUGH

WILLIAM LED HIS HORSE, Skittles, down a narrow path between trees and bushes that led to the river. They emerged from the foliage at a spot where the river widened out into a large, deep pool. He dismounted and sat down in the soft, bright green grass at the edge of the river, and watched the gentle flow of the water over the smooth stones. Skittles walked right into the water up to her knees a few feet away from him and dropped her tawny head down for a long drink.

This was his favorite spot to come when he needed to be alone and to think, and today there was a lot on his mind.

When the girl had followed him through the gate last night, he had assumed he would be in trouble; he had betrayed the secret and possibly put everyone in danger. As deeply annoyed as he was with her, he knew it was his fault. That his own carelessness had allowed this to happen.

So yes, he had expected to be in trouble. But the reaction he'd gotten instead ... he couldn't understand it at all.

On his last few visits, he had told his mother about the girl who had been following him around at school. He always told her any story he could about the kids at school, to make it seem like he had more of a social life than he did. He knew his mother worried that he wouldn't have friends or that he would feel lonely.

She was always interested in his stories, but this time she'd asked even more questions than usual, William had thought maybe because it was about a girl, though he'd never cared one way or another for any girl in Bristlecone. While other girls in Bristlecone had imagined a romantic interest in him, that wasn't the impression he'd gotten from Quinn. No, Quinn Robbins' interest in him had not felt romantic in the slightest. It was something ... else.

Of course, now he knew what that something else had been. What had she been thinking actually following him over that broken bridge? Was she crazy?

And then she'd had the nerve to be mad at him? Well, sorry. It wasn't his fault she'd been reckless enough to land herself here. It almost served her right to be stuck here for ten days.

For a brief moment, he felt a flash of sympathy for her. How scary it must be to have something like that happen. He pushed the thought away almost as quickly as it came, though. She shouldn't have been following him, then.

Regardless of what Quinn's intentions had been in following him, though, he just could not understand what had happened when he had led the horse carrying Thomas and the unconscious girl into the courtyard.

Both of his parents had been there waiting, standing together behind Nathaniel, who had quickly rushed to help William lift Quinn down from the horse.

Nathaniel himself had carried the girl carefully upstairs in the castle.

His mother had been visibly upset, but only with worry over the girl's condition. She seemed unconcerned with the fact that she shouldn't have been there at all. She had questioned William over every detail of Quinn's injury, and then quickly followed Thomas and

Nathaniel upstairs, where Mia had apparently already been preparing a room for the unexpected guest – in his family's own private wing!

This had left William standing there in the courtyard, facing his father, who held the tiny new baby in his arms. His face held slight disquiet, but no outward signs of anger.

He had looked up at his father in shame, afraid of the disappointment he had caused.

But no disappointment came. King Stephen's voice was only concerned. "Will the girl be all right?"

"Yes, Father. The injury was really very minor. I think she might have reacted to the valoris seed I gave her, but her breathing and pulse are fine. Nathaniel should have her sorted out in no time."

"Good. Welcome home, Son. It's wonderful to see your face again." His father had wrapped his free arm around William, embracing him tightly. Then, "Meet your new little sister," he had said, placing the blanket-wrapped child gently into William's outstretched arms. The new baby was adorable; her long, dark eyelashes fluttered softly against her rosy cheeks. She had sighed softly in her sleep as William had rested his face near the top of her head and breathed deeply of the warm new-baby smell.

"Come, Son, everyone is anxiously awaiting your arrival to begin dinner."

That had been all; no words were ever spoken about William's mistake in allowing Quinn to follow him. His mother had fretted over her comfort and well-being. The cover story that she was a guest from one of the surrounding villages was passed around and easily accepted - other guests were slowly drifting in from places around Eirentheos in preparation for the baby's Naming Ceremony. The explanation would work. There was nothing else.

It felt odd to William, like Quinn's arrival had been expected somehow, even anticipated, which made no sense at all. It made him feel like everyone knew something he didn't, as if he was out of some loop. Returning home was always disorienting as it was, having been gone only five days in his mind, but missing several weeks' worth of life here. He was sad that he had missed the baby's birth; he had entertained thoughts that he might be able to assist Nola, the midwife, with the delivery. Though he knew that they would never hold it without him, it still pleased him that his family had held off planning the Naming Ceremony for a time when he would certainly be here.

William stared at the flowing water for a long time, trying to clear his head. It felt good to be here, to be home, and to soak up the warm summer sun after days in the bitter winds of a mountain winter in Bristlecone. Aelwyn, his seeker bird, had clearly missed him. She soared above the trees now, enjoying the sunshine and the small prey she was catching, but every so often, she would swoop down near William, pushing her head under his hand for a pat. It felt as though she were checking to see if he were still here.

All of a sudden, he heard the sound of hooves cutting through the underbrush. He sighed. Of course Thomas would be able to find him here. William rose to greet him, brushing the dirt and leaves off his pants.

"William, there you are," Thomas said, dismounting Storm.

"Like you didn't know where you would find me?"

"You don't usually run off so soon when you first get back." Thomas worked for several moments to remove an extra pair of saddlebags from his mount, gave Storm a long rub on his silvery neck, and then watched as the horse waded into the shallow water to join Skittles.

William watched him, still too absorbed in his own thoughts to process the amount of supplies his brother had been carrying. "I just needed some time to think, without everyone around."

"What's bothering you? What's going on with this girl?"

His chest tightened in renewed irritation. "Nothing is going on with her. She followed me."

"You knew she was following you around school before the last time you were home."

"I had no idea she'd get close enough to see me at the bridge."

"You don't notice much about people, especially in Bristlecone, do you?" Thomas asked, watching the rapid changes in his brother's facial expressions with interest.

He narrowed his eyes at his brother. "What do you mean?"

"I mean, I've known that girl for half a day, and I could have told you she was never going to give up until she figured out what you were hiding."

"It's an important secret. I'm supposed to be hiding it." William crossed his arms defiantly.

"That's not the point. The point is that you were completely oblivious to how this girl was reacting to you."

"She wasn't reacting to me; she just wanted to know where I was going."

Thomas sighed. "Maybe that's not the only thing you're oblivious to."

"What is that supposed to mean?"

Thomas studied his older brother's face carefully; he looked as if he were deciding something. "Nothing, I don't mean anything by it. I'm just glad you're home."

William's fury wasn't so easily abated. "And another thing, why is everyone acting like this is so normal? Like they're not as shocked as I am that she followed me through that gate? What? We're just preparing rooms now for people who follow us here? Welcome to the family?"

Thomas did his best not to smile and anger his brother further. "That one I cannot answer for you, although I'm not sure it would be normal for our family to be unwelcoming either. Have you ever seen anyone turned away who needed help?"

"No, I suppose not." William's fit deflated slightly.

"And that girl clearly needs help. What do you expect her to do, live in the woods for the next ten days and starve, just because you didn't stop her from seeing you?"

William didn't bother answering that one.

"Anyway, speaking purely for myself, you'll never find me raising objections to you bringing home a sweet, pretty girl, no matter where she's from." Thomas beamed, and then ducked away from the well-timed punch William directed at his shoulder.

"Don't tell me you didn't notice," Thomas said, once he was safely out of reach.

William only rolled his eyes.

"Sometimes, Will, you are the most obtuse older brother in the world," he muttered. "Anyway, I hate to interrupt your pleasant day of wallowing here, but Nathaniel actually sent me looking for you. He needs us to go down to Mistle Village today to check on things. He went on ahead, and wants us to follow him."

"Has there been any more news?" William asked, suddenly concerned as he headed to retrieve Skittles.

"There have been some new cases of whatever this thing is. Essie sent a messenger to Nathaniel this morning, asking for help." Storm was already answering Thomas' whistle. "I loaded up all the saddlebags with supplies already, so we can just get going. You can thank me later."

"Don't push it Thomas." Now William was less irritated than determined. He and Thomas worked together quickly to load the second, heavy pair of saddlebags onto Skittles' back.

The brothers mounted their saddles in unison, and led the animals back up the narrow path, winding through the trees for several minutes until they came to a larger road.

"Still no more ideas about where this is coming from?"

"No. Jacob and Essie have just been tending to things as best they can, waiting for you and Nathaniel to come back. It's still so strange. Only affecting children and it doesn't seem to be spreading from person to person. It's striking random families."

The worry in Thomas' words was clear, and William heard something more in his voice, past the worrying – pain?

William rode in silence, letting several minutes pass before he spoke. "What are you not telling me?"

Thomas slowly came to a halt, and paused, waiting for William to bring Skittles to a stop and turn around to face him. Cold trickles of dread ran down his spine. "What, Thomas?"

"We lost one. Sabrina and Galen Howe's little girl, Alanna. She was six."

William felt his heart sink into his stomach. "When?"

"Five days ago."

The two brothers stared at each other in silence, and then simultaneously turned their horses back to the road, taking it at a gallop.

When they reached Mistle Village, they found Nathaniel's horse hitched outside of Jacob and Essie White's medical clinic. Nathaniel heard them approaching, and met them outside on the wide, covered porch.

"What's the news, Nathaniel?"

His uncle's face was grave. "It's not good. Two more children sick in the last week. Several are recovering, but we still don't know exactly what this is or what is causing it. One little boy was brought in last night with a high fever. We haven't been able to get it down at all, even this morning. Seven years old. The family's farm is nearly twenty minutes' ride outside the village. None of the rest of the family or neighbors are sick."

"I packed everything you brought Will." Thomas held a bag of medical supplies out to William, who took the bag and walked into the clinic. Inside, he scanned the room where several children and their families had been staying. Two children were sleeping, and another lay lethargically on her cot while Essie tried convincing her to accept small sips of water. A large blister near the girl's mouth was making the effort visibly painful. Her father sat near her in a chair with worry in his eyes.

A young woman in a handmade farm dress sat cradling the little boy. She sang to him and tears appeared in the corners of her eyes as a ragged cough tore through his tiny, fever-ridden body. William's stomach turned when he saw the terrible red rash that covered the boy's face and arms.

"The other villages?" William asked, finally finding his voice, but fearing the answer.

"The same."

"There won't be enough." William looked at the sick children, opened his bag and started with the boy.

"There is never enough."

DINNER

IT HAD BEEN THE strangest day of Quinn's life. The strangest and the most fascinating. She still couldn't believe that this was real, that she'd followed William into an entirely different world.

Freed from worrying about her mom, and confident in Thomas' reassurances that she would be able to go home, she had spent the day basking in the excitement and satisfaction of having solved an enormous mystery. All of the questions that had been driving her crazy about William Rose for weeks had been answered, in a way she had never expected.

Of course, it had opened up an entirely new mystery, and she was still in shock that something like this could happen. There was a not-small part of her that kept expecting that any minute she would wake up from one of her vivid dreams.

As promised, immediately after breakfast, Linnea had taken Quinn's arm and begun leading her through the "interesting" places in the castle. Quinn had felt immediately comfortable with her, the same way she had felt with Thomas. Linnea seemed naturally thoughtful; she kept to places that were less populated with guests, and after each stop, showed Quinn the quickest way back up to her room, so that she would always know her way back to her little retreat.

"So what do you think of all this so far?" Linnea asked, again leading Quinn back down the hall to her room, this time after a tour of the flower gardens, and the small playground where the youngest Rose siblings had been playing.

There, she had drawn the notice of Emma again, who wanted Quinn to push her on the swing, but Quinn didn't mind. She'd pushed Emma "higher" for several minutes before turning her attention to a little boy, about Emma's size, who'd been watching quietly.

He turned out to be Emma's twin, Alex, who was grateful for his own turn, though Quinn was almost certain he'd never have asked.

"Um... I.. uh..." Quinn stammered for a moment trying to run the day through her head. It had been incredible, overwhelming and amazing all at the same time. How was she supposed to describe all that? Searching for a response, she finally settled on one word that contained how she was feeling. "It's astonishing."

Linnea nodded in understanding. "I can only assume it has been a lot to take in; it's not every day you end up in a different world."

"Yeah, I'm still having trouble believing that it's real – that something like this could actually happen." It did feel slightly more real now, though, and maybe it was the time with the younger children in the gardens that had done it. They were so normal – so happy and sweet – maybe this place wasn't so unlike her own world after all.

"Well, it did, and you're here. And I, for one, am quite pleased about it. The next few days will be much more fun with you around. Now, let's get you dressed for dinner. I have the perfect dress."

"What?"

"You'll need a dress for dinner. It's a big, formal affair tonight; we have lots of out-of-town guests who are starting to arrive."

"I, uh … dinner?" Although she'd enjoyed the children, Quinn had been grateful so far that she'd been secluded from massive amounts of attention. Even lunch had been a picnic basket carried by Linnea to a quiet field where they could watch several of the family's horses grazing nearby. Linnea had peppered her with questions, fascinated by the details of Quinn's life in Bristlecone. Unlike Thomas, Linnea had never been allowed even a short visit in Quinn's world, and it was obvious that she knew much less about it than her twin brother.

If Linnea was this curious, there were bound to be others who were, too, and Quinn wasn't sure at all that she would have any idea how to handle them – and keep the secret of who she was at the same time.

"Yes, dinner. It will be fun, and you will enjoy it. Go have a nice bubble bath, and I'll be back in half an hour with the dress." Linnea had gone out of the room, certain that Quinn would do as she said.

As she climbed in the bath – Nathaniel had told her that it was fine to get her stitches wet – she was able to calm herself a little bit. She'd just keep quiet. Nobody was going to ask about Bristlecone who didn't already know who she was. Maybe she could just listen at dinner, try to learn more about this world. Dinner in a castle should be interesting at least.

Two hours later, she found herself being led down to the dining room by Linnea, who had spent the entire last hour dressing her like a doll, braiding her hair in intricate loops, and helping her into a soft, green gown that flowed in gauzy layers down to her ankles.

She had never worn such a long, heavy dress before; it took several steps down the long hall before she felt balanced. The long, curving staircase in the main hall was another matter altogether. Linnea had to hold her by the elbow the entire time; she couldn't figure out how to keep the hem of the dress from getting under her feet. The borrowed heels she was wearing didn't help, either.

"I am going to fall flat on my face in front of your entire family - what will they think of me then?" she complained to Linnea when they reached the wide landing halfway down.

"Oh, we already know that balance is a problem for you; it'll just become a nightly habit for Will, stitching you back together again." The familiar voice came from behind them on the stairs, and the girls turned to see Thomas running down the steps toward them.

Quinn narrowed her eyes at him. "Not funny."

Thomas smiled back. "Yes, it is funny. Although, it would be a tragedy to mess up that dress. You, my lady, are dazzling."

"It is charming on her, isn't it?" Linnea reached up to Thomas' shoulder, brushing away a nearly-invisible piece of lint from his shoulder. Quinn was startled by his outfit.

Dressed as he was, Thomas looked truly like a prince from another world. Over his white, button-down shirt, he wore a purple velvet cape, fastened at the base of his neck by a silver bar with circular designs at each end. Something about the designs felt familiar to Quinn, but she couldn't place what. Atop his head was a purple velvet beret with a silver medallion of the same design in the center.

"Indeed. I take it this was your work, darling sister? You are quite lovely this evening yourself."

Quinn agreed. Linnea's dress was a soft cream color, overlaid with thin crisscrossing stripes in a purple that nearly matched Thomas' cape. The light color set off Linnea's dark curls and gray eyes.

"Always with the compliments, Sir Thomas, the Charming." Linnea's smile was teasing.

"It's in my nature, little sister. Would it be too much for me to ask for the pleasure of escorting two exquisite ladies downstairs?" Without waiting for an answer, Thomas took Linnea's place at Quinn's elbow, deftly assisting her the rest of the way down the stairs. She never even felt like she was going to fall.

"Where is William? He came back with you, didn't he?" Linnea asked.

"He's back, already in the dining room probably. Doesn't know a thing about taking time to dress for the ladies, you know." Thomas chuckled.

"How are things in Mistle Village?" Linnea wondered.

"Calm, for now. We've left them with enough supplies to get them through until after the ceremony." Quinn had no idea what they were talking about, but she noticed a concerned look in Thomas' eyes that belied his cheerful grin.

Walking into the dining room was exactly like stepping into a scene from a movie, Quinn thought. The longest table she had ever seen stretched through the center of the large room. The table was draped in a purple cloth and set with beautiful silver dishes. Arrangements of fresh flowers in a variety of colors created centerpieces every few feet, lit softly by candles placed in the middle.

There were people all over the room standing in friendly groups. The women were all dressed in beautiful, flowing gowns, and the men in elegant suits.

Young children ran about freely, often testing the sliding power of their dressy shoes against the polished marble floor. Off to one side, Quinn could see a cluster of small children all shrieking and jumping to catch the iridescent bubbles that a young man was blowing.

As Thomas led her further into the room, she was shocked to discover that the bubble-blower was William. She'd never seen him like this, smiling and laughing as the youngest children hopped around him. Tiny Sarah toddled near his feet, and when she was close enough, William directed a stream of bubbles right over her head. The little girl grinned with obvious pride as she grasped the shiny bubbles in her chubby fingers, giggling when they popped.

Although Thomas had teased about William not taking time over his appearance, Quinn couldn't agree at all. In fact, *her* reaction to seeing William in his formalwear startled her. He wore the same style of cape and hat as Thomas, which made him look royal, rather than silly as she might have expected. He was - dashing, she decided. She laughed inwardly at the old-fashioned word, but couldn't think of a better description.

Even his glasses made him seem somehow older, and more sophisticated than she'd ever considered him to be.

"Quinn! I'm so glad you've joined us for dinner." She turned around to see Queen Charlotte approaching, wearing a billowing, violet gown with intricate patterns flowing down the skirt. Her hair was beautiful, dark curls flowing down her shoulders, crowned with a delicate silver tiara adorned with purple jewels. Even with the tiny baby swaddled in a lacy white blanket cradled in her arm, Charlotte truly looked the part of a queen; Quinn was in awe.

"You look lovely, my dear. That color is perfect on you."

Quinn blushed. "Thank you."

"Did Linnea take good care of you today?"

"Yes, Ma'am, she was wonderful."

"Just as I promised, Mother," Linnea said. "I know how to treat a guest."

"I know you do, Linnea. Thank you. You look quite charming yourself tonight, sweetheart." Charlotte planted a kiss on the top of her daughter's head. "And you are quite handsome as well, Thomas. What a lucky mother I am, to have such beautiful children."

"I think we are the luckiest parents around." A tall man stepped up behind Charlotte, placing an arm around her waist and leaning down to kiss her cheek. Then he turned his head "This must be the delightful Quinn. I'm Stephen, my dear, welcome to our home."

Quinn wasn't sure what she'd expected in meeting a king, but this man wasn't quite it. He looked like exactly like one. He was very tall - she could see immediately where William and Thomas had gotten their height. The edges of his deep purple cape were lined with some kind of white fur, fastened at his throat by the same silver bar. The thin, silver crown on his head bore the same design, underneath a triad of gleaming purple jewels.

Everything about him spoke of a powerful king. But she wasn't intimidated by him the way she thought she should be. His gray eyes were intelligent and kind, and the way they looked at her was welcoming and somehow soft.

"Thank you … Your Majesty. I'm sorry for just … barging in."

The king's warm smile reached all the way to his eyes; his sincerity was genuine. "You are truly most welcome here, Quinn. Your presence has caused quite the enchanting stir around here."

"Thank you, then. It's very nice meeting you." She wasn't sure where her sudden confidence was coming from. "It's beautiful here."

Stephen and Charlotte both smiled.

"Thomas, why don't you go with Quinn to find your places? Maybe you and Linnea could introduce Quinn to some of the rest of our family?" Charlotte suggested.

"Of course." Thomas extended his elbow toward Quinn. Reminded again of a movie, she took hold of it and allowed him to lead her to the long table.

At dinner, she found herself sitting between Thomas and Linnea, across from William and some of the younger children. William surprised her by smiling politely as servants moved among them, passing out plates of roast and vegetables.

"Hello Quinn, how's your leg today?"

Quinn smiled back. "Much better, thank you. They tell me you did a great job fixing it."

William looked slightly embarrassed. "It was no problem. I am sorry about the whole valoris seed incident. I had no idea that would happen."

"Well, I'm fine now. Don't worry about it. I'm just glad you were there, and knew what to do. Surprised, but glad."

William just shrugged and smiled. "It's not something I could have just told you about one day at school."

"Even if you had ever talked to me," Quinn agreed.

Thomas snorted. "So the truth comes out – it's Will the recluse."

Chagrin twisted William's expression.

Linnea cast a disparaging look at her twin brother. "Now, Thomas, not everyone has the gift of charm. Be nice." Thomas only grinned in response.

Quinn smiled at the easy camaraderie between the siblings. They were obviously close, even with William who was so often absent. She found herself missing her own siblings, glad, that if what Thomas had told her was true, they were not missing her. She realized, with a sudden ache in her throat, what it must be like for William all the time in Bristlecone, missing his family, and knowing he was missing large chunks of their lives.

Across the table, Emma, who had so eagerly skipped into Quinn's room that morning, was studying her intently. "Quinn, you're pretty!" She blurted out suddenly.

Heat filled her cheeks. "Thank you, Emma."

"She is, isn't she?" Thomas said, looking down at her. "Quite lovely in that dress, don't you think, William?"

William glanced across the table at Thomas, looking more irritated than anything. "Very much so," he answered before returning his attention to his plate.

Emma looked back and forth between Thomas and Quinn. "I'm going to marry Thomas when I grow up," she announced.

Quinn smiled. "Sounds like a good plan."

"But you can marry him for now, if you want."

The table erupted in laughter as Quinn flushed bright scarlet.

"I'll keep that in mind, Miss Emma." Thomas chortled.

After the plates had been cleared, Thomas stood and extended his hand to Quinn. "Shall we?" he asked.

Quinn looked at him questioningly. "Where are we going?"

"It's time for the dancing!" Linnea told her, pulling her up and handing her over to Thomas.

Quinn's heart rate accelerated. "Dancing? I don't dance."

"Everybody dances," Linnea exclaimed, following along as Thomas pulled Quinn from the room.

The idea of dancing, here in a castle, with Thomas and William watching was a thousand times more nerve-wracking than the thought of dancing with Zander at the Valentine dance in Bristlecone.

She'd known Zander her whole life; she knew he was telling the truth when he said he couldn't dance either and that dancing with him would involve little more than swaying in time to the music and chatting with friends.

She was quite certain that ballroom dancing with princes and princesses would entail a bit more than that. The thought of Zander and the Valentine dance sent an unfamiliar throb of emotion through her chest, and she was suddenly glad that she would be home before she was missed by anyone.

Quinn followed Thomas and Linnea into an enormous ballroom. It was beautiful, lit by soft light coming from a crystal chandelier in the center of the high ceiling and hundreds of tiny, twinkling candles everywhere. Small tables dotted the edges of the room, subdued light emanating from even more candles in their centers. Several sets of large, glass double doors were open to the evening air at one end of the room. In a far corner, a group of musicians had begun to play a lively tune. Quinn couldn't identify all of the instruments.

"I suppose this is just a typical evening for you?" she questioned Linnea. She wondered if she were going to spend the next ten days having to dress up every night like this, and another little thrill of fear ran through her as she thought again about being stuck here for that long.

"No, actually, this is quite formal for us." Linnea smiled. "The baby's Naming Ceremony is the day after tomorrow, which is kind of a big deal for us. Our extended family members and many other guests have been traveling in from all over the place. We do like to entertain when we have guests."

The conversation was interrupted then, by the approach of another girl. She was older than Quinn was by a couple of years. Quinn was so instantly reminded of William that she immediately had no doubt that this must be another of the Rose siblings. Linnea had told her earlier today that there were thirteen altogether, counting the newest baby. The girl's long, dark hair fell in a straight curtain down her back; the sides were pinned up by delicate silver combs. The violet accents on her long, lavender gown matched Linnea's.

"Rebecca!" Linnea called out. "Come and meet Quinn!"

Rebecca smiled, her gray eyes twinkling with the same kind of friendliness Thomas and Linnea had extended toward her. "Hello, Quinn … you're William's friend, aren't you?"

"Uh… yes." Quinn wasn't sure how to elaborate.

"Well, it's nice meeting you. I'm Rebecca. Where is William anyway?"

Quinn looked around, searching the unfamiliar faces in the room; she had no idea when William had disappeared again. "It's nice to meet you too, Rebecca," she replied politely.

"Has my little brother been behaving around you?" Rebecca asked, raising her eyebrows toward Thomas.

"Of course I have! Have you no faith in me, dear sister?" Thomas interrupted.

Rebecca directed a teasing grin at Thomas before she turned to Linnea, a darker expression on her face. "Did you see that Tolliver's just arrived?"

Quinn saw Linnea's eyes widen. "No, where is he?"

"Over there," Rebecca gestured, "talking to Gavin, already."

Quinn followed Linnea's gaze to the side of the room, where two men stood talking. One of them was dressed only in a formal-looking suit, but the other, the shorter one, wore a flowing green cape in the same style as the princes were wearing, though the shimmer at his neck was gold, not silver. A thin gold circle sat atop his head.

"Which one is Tolliver?" Quinn wondered. The name had sounded significant when Rebecca had spoken.

"The one in the crown," Linnea answered, an odd expression in her eyes. "Awfully confident he'll be next on that throne, isn't he? Already wearing that around."

"Have you ever known Tolliver to be anything but confident?" William had suddenly returned from wherever he'd gone, coming from behind Quinn.

"I suppose not," Linnea sighed.

"Sometimes a sense of humor gets you further than confidence, though, doesn't it darling?" Another man had walked up behind Rebecca, putting his arms around her waist. Rebecca smiled and turned, planting a kiss on his cheek.

"Quinn, this is Howard, Rebecca's husband. Howard, this is Quinn, a friend of William's."

"Pleased to meet you, Miss Quinn." Howard's green eyes twinkled in the candlelight.

"Nice to meet you, too … Howard," Quinn replied, still a bit awkward in this formal setting.

"Will the rest of you excuse me while I take my lovely bride for a turn on the dance floor?" Howard asked.

"Of course." Linnea returned his grin, and they watched as Rebecca and Howard walked hand-in-hand to the dance floor. He held her close, one arm around her waist, and the other hand holding hers. In the few, short moments that Quinn watched them, she saw

Howard lean in to kiss Rebecca three different times; Rebecca's pink, flushed cheeks were visible from where Quinn was standing.

"Dance with me, William?" Linnea then asked, taking her brother by the hand and leading him over toward the band. Quinn watched in awe as the usually-reserved William twirled his sister effortlessly across the floor, both of them smiling and laughing.

"Shall we?" Thomas asked from beside her, holding out his hand.

"What, and fall flat on my face in these heels?"

"You won't fall. Not with me leading." As he spoke, he took her arm and led her toward the dancing, giving her no choice but to follow.

Quinn was still nervous, but Thomas was right; she wasn't going to fall with him leading her. His arms were strong and sure; she only had to allow herself to follow him, and suddenly she was dancing! It wasn't the elaborate sweeping and twirling that she saw the other couples around the floor doing, but it was certainly more than she'd thought possible. She actually found herself smiling. Thomas grinned in return.

When the song ended, Linnea found her. "Having fun yet, Quinn?"

"Surprisingly, yes."

A new song started, this one with a much faster tempo. Linnea grinned excitedly, "Come on, Quinn; time to learn how to dance Eirentheos-style!"

William and Thomas followed as Linnea led Quinn to a spot near the center of the dance floor, and she soon found herself trying to follow them along in some kind of complicated group dance. It reminded Quinn of learning to square-dance in elementary school gym class as the four of them weaved around each other, and Quinn was passed back and forth between William and Thomas. She struggled to keep up with the siblings, but none of them seemed to mind; even William reached to steady her a couple of times, and to show her where to stand. By the end of the dance, all of them were flushed and laughing. Quinn was almost disappointed when the music changed to a mellower tune.

Linnea was just reaching to take Thomas' arm for the next dance when a man's voice interrupted them.

"Lady Linnea, how delightful it is to watch to you dancing out there. You put the rest of these poor girls to shame." Quinn spun around to see that the words came from the man in the green cape - Tolliver, she thought they had said. "Would you grant me the honor of a dance with a lovely princess?"

Quinn watched as Linnea shot an undecipherable look at Thomas before answering, "Of course, my lord," and allowing Tolliver to lead her away.

She was left standing there, in the middle of the dance floor, with Thomas and William. Noting Quinn's sudden discomfort, Thomas ushered them quickly off to the side of the crowd.

"Who was that?" she wondered.

"Tolliver Bowden." Thomas answered. "His father, Hector, is the prince regent of Philotheum."

"Is that supposed to mean something?"

This time, it was William who smiled. "His father is the current ruler of a kingdom about two days' travel from here."

"But he's not the king?" Quinn was puzzled.

"No. King Jonathan died many years ago, and the queen remarried. Tolliver is the firstborn son from Queen Sophia's second marriage."

"So Tolliver will be the next king?"

"He thinks he will." Thomas jumped back in to the conversation, his eyebrows furrowed, and his expression dark. "It's a little bit trickier than that, but he's so certain it will happen that he's wearing that heir's crown."

"Huh?"

"See, on his head? The small crown that's just a ring?"

Quinn nodded.

"Those are worn by the next direct heir to the throne of a kingdom."

"Okay."

"Look over there," Thomas said, pointing across the room.

Quinn followed his gesture. On the other side of the room was a tall, young-looking man. It was hard to tell exactly what he looked like from this distance, but he was dressed in the same cape as Thomas and William, but instead of a beret, she could see a thin, silver circle atop his head.

"That's our oldest brother, Simon. He is the heir to our father's throne, so he wears the heir's crown of our kingdom."

"Oh," Quinn was interested in what she was learning, and she could tell by William and Thomas' carefully-worded answers that there was more going on here than they were telling her. Further talk was clearly going to have to wait until later, though, because the dance had ended, and Linnea was walking toward them, with Tolliver.

"Evening, William, Thomas," Tolliver greeted them. "Nice party."

"Good evening, Tolliver, thank you." William's response was formal.

"No. Thank you, for allowing me the privilege of borrowing your enchanting sister."

"Certainly, Tolliver. Our family appreciates your traveling so far to celebrate with us."

"Of course. And who is your pretty, young ... companion?" Tolliver asked, his eyes on Quinn. He was smiling, but there was something in his expression that made Quinn uneasy. She felt Thomas bristle beside her.

"This is Quinn, a dear family friend," Thomas answered him.

"Is she, indeed? Well, she's looking charming on your arm tonight, Thomas. Dance with me again, Linnea?"

Quinn watched as Tolliver escorted Linnea back to the dance floor, a renewed sense of exactly how far outside of her own world she was running through her.

"Would you like a turn, William?" Thomas asked.

"At?" William's look was quizzical.

"Dancing with Quinn, of course."

"Oh, ah ... certainly. Quinn?"

"Um, sure." Quinn was flabbergasted by the difference in William's behavior tonight. He had always been so distant, uninvolved in anything in Bristlecone. Last night, when she had first crossed the bridge and entered his world, he had been so... annoyed with her. This was something entirely new.

Dancing with William was different than dancing with Thomas. He was just as good at leading; his arms directed her body in all the right ways, sure and strong. Unlike Thomas, though, he would stop, showing Quinn how to do a particular step, or where to put her hands. By the time the song ended, Quinn was beginning to understand some of the moves.

The next song began, and Quinn's eyes widened in familiarity. She looked up at William, and was surprised to see him grinning sheepishly at her.

"This is a song Will brought back from your world when he was younger," Thomas said, coming up behind them and taking Quinn's hand as the crowd thinned into a circle.

"Yeah, well, I liked the Hokey Pokey when I learned it at school." William shrugged.

Quinn laughed. "Me too," she said, "...when I was younger. Now my little brother and sister love it."

A moment later, they were joined by Linnea, with Emma and Alice in tow. Quinn noticed that Tolliver was not on the dance floor; she caught a glimpse of him far to the side of the room, accepting a glass of wine from one of the servants. For a moment, she was curious about this, but then she got lost in the music and laughter of dancing.

HORSEBACK RIDE

QUINN'S SECOND DAY IN Eirentheos had dawned hot and bright. It clearly wasn't winter here the way it was in Bristlecone. Emma and Alice had awakened her this morning, standing by her bed and shushing each other while they giggled. It reminded her of Annie on weekend mornings at home.

After Quinn had bathed and dressed, Linnea had come to drag her downstairs to join the family for breakfast. Linnea had been speaking the truth last night; not all meals in the castle were formal occasions. Breakfast was in a much smaller room, the table able to accommodate only about twenty people - on the small side for a family whose immediate members alone numbered fifteen, Quinn thought.

Many of the faces here were starting to become familiar now, even the ones she hadn't been formally introduced to. William's oldest brother, Simon, and his sister Rebecca, who she had met last night, were not there at breakfast, but Linnea introduced Quinn to Maxwell, the second-born son. He was just as friendly as the rest of the family, though he seemed preoccupied about something.

125

After Thomas and Linnea came two boys, Joshua and Daniel, both pre-teens. Quinn had trouble remembering which one was which, though she *thought* Joshua was the older one.

Then there was Emma and her twin brother, Alex, the two tiny girls, Alice and Sarah, and finally, the new baby. Number thirteen. It was disconcerting to Quinn that the baby didn't have a name yet — such a different tradition than in her own world.

Breakfast was a chaotic affair, with people coming in and out of the room, and children who spent much more time running around, playing, and asking Quinn questions than they did eating. Quinn had enjoyed it thoroughly.

After breakfast, she'd found herself spending time again with William, Linnea, and Thomas. It seemed that William and Thomas were an inseparable pair whenever William was at home. Linnea was enjoying having another girl around to "even things up," she said.

They took Quinn on a tour of parts of the castle and grounds that she hadn't gotten to see yesterday. Quinn was excited when Thomas led her into the stables and introduced her to his horse, Storm, William's mare, Skittles, and to Linnea's white mare, Snow.

Quinn had loved horses for as long as she could remember, and had started taking horseback riding lessons when she was six, though looking back she wasn't quite sure how her mother could have afforded something like that before she'd married Jeff.

For the past two summers, she had worked weekends at a local mountain resort, helping to lead tourists on horseback trail rides through the nearby national forest.

Linnea watched with interest as Quinn approached Snow, stroking her flank and looking her in the eye. "Do you ride?"

"Yes; I love horses," she answered, chuckling as Snow pushed her nose against her hand, obviously looking for a treat. "Spoiled, are you?"

The horse whuffled a response that sounded almost like a "yes."

"Want to go for a ride?" Thomas asked, tossing her an apple he'd grabbed from somewhere so she could give it to Snow.

"What? Really? ... I would love to." Quinn smiled.

The next thing she knew, Quinn was riding on a beautiful brown horse, appropriately named Chestnut. The three siblings led her first along a wide riding trail near the castle, but when they realized that she was, indeed, a skilled rider, they ventured further – taking her into the nearby forest and down toward the river.

Quinn relished the sunshine and the warm air of the summer day, grateful for this strange reprieve from the bitter mountain winter at home. It was beautiful here in Eirentheos. When they reached the river, they all dismounted, letting the horses get a drink, and sitting down by the water to soak in the fresh air.

"I've never heard a bird call like that before," Quinn commented, listening to the unfamiliar sound that drifted through the trees.

"We have many different kinds of birds here than you have in your world," William told her, a strange smile on his face.

"Really?"

"Indeed." William let out a long, low whistle and then paused, seemingly waiting for something.

Suddenly, a large bird flew into their little group from somewhere across the river, so close to Quinn's head that she could feel her hair move. The bird flew straight to William's side, landing and tucking in its wings. Quinn was stunned.

"Quinn, this is Aelwyn, my seeker," William said, rubbing the bird's head lightly with one finger.

The bird was beautiful; the feathers on her head were a pure alabaster in color. The rest of her body was a shimmery gray, almost silver, all the way to the tips of her wings, where the feathers turned a smoky black. Obviously a raptor of some sort, Aelwyn's talons were sharp and dangerous-looking. Quinn had never been this close to an animal like her before.

"She's amazing," she breathed softly, afraid of startling the bird. "She's a ... pet?"

"Sort of," Thomas answered for his brother. "Seekers have long been bred as companion birds, though they live in the wild and fend for themselves as adults. Once they are trained, they are fully loyal only to one master, and they will never stray out of hearing range of their master's call."

Quinn thought her eyes might pop out of her head.

"More a friend than a pet," William said.

Thomas and Linnea both let out whistles of their own, and a moment later, they were joined at the river by two more seekers, Thomas' bird Sirian, and Zylia, who was Linnea's. Quinn watched; she was fascinated at the way the birds responded, to both their owners and each other.

"What does Aelwyn do when you're in Bristlecone?" she asked. "If she's never out of range of hearing you?"

A sad look passed over William's face – it was almost enough to make her sorry she'd asked.

"It was difficult for her at first," he said. "She still doesn't much like it, and she's always waiting for me at the gate when I return, but she's gotten used to it – and she has Sirian."

"We suspect Sirian and Aelwyn may have become a mating pair," Thomas told her, as they watched the birds strut near each other, touching the crowns of their heads together. "We haven't found any nesting sites yet, though."

"But you miss her when you're there, don't you?" Quinn asked William.

He nodded.

After a few moments, the birds seemed to realize they weren't needed for any specific purpose, and almost simultaneously disappeared into the trees again.

"I suppose we should be heading back before too long. It seems unfair to leave Simon and Max to baby-sit Tolliver the whole day," Thomas said, standing and brushing dirt and leaves from his pants.

"I'm sure you're right," William replied, as he stood. "I have no idea what to do with him though; we can only take him on so many tours of the garden and stables."

"How about a game? We haven't played crumple in a while, and with Uriah and Cabel arriving this morning we have enough for a proper four-on-four game."

"Well that would certainly be better than trying to make small talk with him."

"Yeah, I'd prefer tackling him into the dirt any day." The retort came from Linnea and the group turned to look at her in mock horror before breaking out into laughter.

"What exactly is 'crumple'?" Quinn asked.

William grinned. "It's the great Eirenthean sport. Nothing like it in Bristlecone."

"Sweaty boys in shorts pounding each other into the ground." Linnea smiled. "Plenty of fun to watch -- when you're not related to all of them."

Quinn couldn't quite suppress her giggle.

CRUMPLE

AFTER LUNCH, LINNEA LED Quinn through the grounds until they reached some kind of sports field. Lines of white paint marked the playing area. Stands of white, wooden bleachers lined either side of the field.

"So... crumple is a pretty big deal here?" she asked Linnea, noting the formal setup.

"Sometimes." Linnea smiled. "We do play more than just crumple here."

"You're going to have to explain this whole crumple thing to me."

"It's pretty simple. I'll explain as they play, but you'll pick it up really fast."

Quinn studied the field. Set up at each end were what looked like two goals. One was about the size of a hockey goal; the other was smaller. The two sides were set up opposite each other, a small goal directly across from a large one.

Thomas and William arrived then, climbing the bleachers to greet the girls. They were wearing white t-shirts and long, white athletic-type shorts. Quinn sucked in her breath at the sight of them;

suddenly sure that watching the game was going to be as fun as Linnea had promised.

"Let's see some action," Linnea teased.

"As you wish, my lady." Thomas grinned back.

More players were starting to arrive on the field. Quinn recognized the two oldest Rose brothers, Simon and Maxwell, and Tolliver. Another was familiar; she had seen him talking to Tolliver last night, but couldn't remember his name, although she was sure someone had said it. "Who are the two walking onto the field now?" she asked.

Thomas turned and looked. "Cabel and Uriah. They're cousins of ours, brothers. Looks like everyone's here, actually." As he spoke, Quinn could see Rebecca and her husband, Howard arriving. "Guess we should get started."

Quinn watched with interest as they spent a few minutes deciding teams, distributing red and blue arm bands. Thomas teamed with Simon, Cabel, and the one whose name she couldn't remember on the red team. William was on the blue team with Maxwell, Tolliver, and Uriah. Howard volunteered to referee.

"They try to keep it friendly," Linnea explained, "and make the teams as even as possible."

After a few minutes of discussion on the field, Maxwell went to stand in front of the larger goal on one end of the field. Cabel did the same on the other end. "They'll be the goal-keepers," Linnea told her.

"What're the smaller goals for?" Quinn wondered.

"Putting the ball in the smaller goal is worth two points, because they are unguarded. Getting it in the larger goal scores ten."

The rest of the players lined up at the center line, facing each other. Howard stood off to one side, holding the ball. The ball was made of brown leather, and probably a little smaller than a soccer ball, Quinn thought. Howard blew a whistle and threw the ball into the middle of the players. There was a mad scramble, and then Quinn saw the ball in Thomas' hands. He quickly threw it to Simon, who had run down the field.

"Who's the other one on Thomas' team?" she asked.

"Gavin. He's another cousin of ours." Linnea wrinkled her nose.

"You don't like him?" Quinn guessed.

"We've had our issues."

Quinn watched as Simon attempted to throw the ball to Gavin, but William jumped in front of him and caught it, throwing it the other way down the field to Uriah.

"So what are the rules?"

"There aren't many. You basically have to throw or kick the ball; you can't run with it, except for the goal-keepers who can run five steps and throw it if they catch it. And you have to keep the ball inside the boundaries. If it goes out, it has to be thrown back in, and it's fair game for either team."

At that moment, Tolliver threw the ball toward the smaller goal, but missed getting it in. "Thomas was in my way," he complained, as he walked to retrieve it and throw it back in.

Linnea rolled her eyes. "Being in the way is kind of the point," she muttered.

It was fun to watch, if tricky to keep up. The ball moved constantly between the two teams. Simon scored the first goal, an impressive toss right over Maxwell's shoulder, scoring ten points for the red team. That was quickly followed by William and Uriah managing to keep the ball in their zone long enough to make three 2-point goals for the blue. They passed the ball to Tolliver next; he threw the ball with enormous force right at Cabel's head, but Cabel still managed to make the save.

"Is that legal – aiming for someone's face?" Quinn asked Linnea.

"Um, there aren't any rules against it – there aren't many rules in crumple at all – but most guys try to keep it clean when they play, especially when they're playing a friendly game with family."

The score was nearly tied, 16-14 blue when Howard blew the whistle for a break. The boys came over to sit in the bleachers and chat. Quinn was surprised when Tolliver climbed up and sat down right next to Linnea. "A kiss for your favorite crumple player, princess?" he asked.

Quinn's eyes widened. She'd been getting the distinct impression that Linnea wasn't overly fond of Tolliver.

"In your dreams, perhaps, my lord."

The casual conversation that had been taking place around them stopped. Every eye was trained on Tolliver, to see his response to that.

Tolliver was undeterred. "And what lovely dreams they are. I do so anxiously await the day they become reality."

Quinn heard a sharp intake of breath from somewhere behind her. Suddenly, Quinn, Linnea, and Rebecca found themselves surrounded by Thomas and his brothers.

"I think the lady is giving you a chance to bow out gracefully, my lord." There was no mistaking the subtle undertone in Thomas' voice.

"Why don't you let the lady speak for herself? Or does she still need help from her big brother to talk?"

"I thought I had made my feelings explicitly clear to you last night, Lord Tolliver. I am not interested." Linnea stood then and walked down the bleachers.

Howard and Thomas helped Rebecca and Quinn stand, motioning that they should follow.

Linnea walked quickly, back toward the castle. Quinn and Rebecca nearly had to run to keep up.

"That ... UGH!" was all Linnea had to say as they reached the entrance near the kitchens.

"He's quite the piece of work, isn't he?" Rebecca asked her. "As grateful as I am to be out of his reach, I'm so sorry he's moved on to vying for you."

"That makes two of us," Linnea almost growled.

At that moment, Queen Charlotte appeared in the hall. She smiled when she saw the girls standing there. "Rebecca! Linnea! I was hoping I would find you. And Quinn, how are you dear?"

"I'm fine, thank you, Your ... um ... Charlotte."

Charlotte's smile was warm as ever. "I'm glad to hear it. Have my children been keeping you entertained?

"Quinn just saw her first game of crumple," Linnea said. "And she came with us on a horseback ride this morning. She's quite the accomplished rider. She was a natural with Chestnut."

"Are you, my dear? That's wonderful. Perhaps we should have you select one to use as your own while you are here with us. What do you think?"

Quinn blushed, her eyes growing wide. She was grateful when Linnea jumped in to answer for her. "She would love that of course, wouldn't you, Quinn?"

"It's...really not necessary."

"Nonsense. If you're a rider, you need a ride." Charlotte was adamant. "Linnea can take you down to the stables in the morning. Now, girls, I was hoping for your help with choosing some of the centerpieces for the ceremony tomorrow. Could I borrow you for a while?"

Rebecca turned to Quinn. "Run away while you can," she whispered. "I know it must have already been quite a long day for you, and this is not as exciting as my mother is making it sound."

Quinn smiled. She was about to open her mouth to object, but yawned instead. It had been a long day.

"Want me to walk you up to your room?" Linnea asked her.

"No, I can manage. I know my way now."

"Are you sure?"

"I'm positive."

"All right. I'll be up soon and we can get ready for dinner together."

"On your way to your room?" Quinn looked up, surprised by the voice. What Tolliver was doing back in the castle so soon, she wasn't sure. She hadn't seen him in the hallway. She quickly turned toward him, uncertain how she was supposed to greet a foreign dignitary without the company of one of the royal family. Though it was clear that Linnea and Rebecca both had no fond feelings toward him, he was still a potential king, and it was probably best to be polite.

"Yes...Lord Tolliver, I am."

She'd apparently done something right, because the pasty grin on the man's face deepened.

"Allow me to escort you upstairs."

Uh... "Thank you, but I'm sure I can manage."

"Oh but I insist." He took her arm. Whether she liked it or not, it seemed she would have to put up with him.

"Quinn, is it?" She nodded as they walked, he was grasping her arm firmly, almost to the point of pain but she told herself not to pull away, they would be at her room in a few minutes and he would go on his way.

"And it seems you have made quite the impression on young Thomas. He appears to be very fond of you."

"Thomas is very nice."

"And all this... living in the castle, gowns, fine food and wine. Thomas certainly doesn't skimp on his ladies."

Cold fear gripped her insides as she understood what he was getting at, but she chose to ignore it. "No, Thomas has been very kind; the whole family has been generous."

"Oh, I see." Somehow, the look on Tolliver's face changed without moving a muscle; in an instant, it went from inquisitive to predatory.

Suddenly, Quinn realized just how close Tolliver was standing to her. They had reached the hallway that would lead to the royal family's quarters.

"He's actually keeping you in his own quarters? How delightful. I had no idea Thomas had it in him." Tolliver pressed closer to her; she could feel his breath, hot on her cheek.

In a flash, she caught his intentions, and the fear exploded inside her, reaching every part of her body. What was she going to do?

Instinctively, she pulled back. Tolliver's grip tightened on her arm, and she gasped in pain.

"Going somewhere, my dear? I'm sure Thomas would be happy to see you keeping his guests entertained. What say you to taking a tour of my accommodations in the castle?" Without waiting for a response, Tolliver began to pull her toward a different hallway. She tried to resist, but Tolliver twisted her arm, gripping it so tightly that it brought tears to her eyes.

Suddenly, a door opened just across the hallway. Tolliver dropped her arm as Joshua and Daniel, William's two younger brothers, entered the hallway. They sized up Tolliver in his athletic wear.

"Did we miss the whole game already?" Daniel asked.

"No, no... They're still playing," Tolliver's response was too quick. "Why don't you two go and join them? If you hurry, I think they might still need another player."

Daniel looked ready to turn and bolt down the stairs, but Joshua had a puzzled look on his face. "Then what are you doing in here?"

"Quinn was just about to show me a bit of the castle I haven't seen before. Weren't you?"

Heart still racing, Quinn took her chance, "I'm just not feeling up to it anymore, Tolliver. I think I'll go and rest now. Alone."

The look on his face was one she was sure she would see in her nightmares for a long time to come. "Well another time then, I'm sure we'll have plenty of opportunities before I leave." The threat was implicit.

Quinn turned and walked back down the hallway as fast as she could without running, closing the door of her bedroom and locking it before she fell on the bed and burst into tears.

FURIOUS

AFTER RETURNING FROM HER day-off visit with her family in the village, Mia was anxious to check on the visitor's room and make sure she had anything she needed. She was surprised when she reached the door and found it locked. Tentatively, she knocked. There was no answer.

She tried again, calling through the door, "Miss Quinn?" Still nothing. She decided that perhaps Quinn was bathing to prepare for dinner in an hour, and that she could duck in and tidy up without bothering her. She unlocked the door and slipped quietly into the room.

Mia gasped when she saw Quinn lying on the bed, perfectly still. Her eyes were open. Sticky, wet streaks ran down both of her cheeks though she wasn't still crying. Her face was lying in a large, wet spot on the white duvet. Clearly, she had had quite a crying spell. "Miss Quinn! What is it? What's wrong?"

Quinn turned her head at the sound of Mia's voice, but she didn't answer. Mia saw moisture building again in the corners of her eyes. "I'll be right back, Miss!" Mia ran to find Linnea.

When Linnea entered the room, she climbed right up on the bed next to Quinn. "Quinn? What's wrong? What's happened?" Quinn just looked at her and shook her head, tears spilling onto her cheeks again. "Are you homesick?" Quinn only closed her eyes and silently shook her head. Linnea decided not to press her any further until she'd had a chance to calm down. "Let's get you into a nice warm bath; see if that helps."

At Linnea's words, Mia strode quickly into the bathroom. Linnea could hear the water running into the bathtub, and could hear the soft clinking of small bottles – Mia was probably adding calming essential oils to the water.

When the maid emerged from the bathroom again, she was carrying Quinn's robe.

Mia and Linnea worked together to help Quinn out of the sweaty and tear-stained shirt she had worn to the crumple game. As she pulled the sleeve over Quinn's arm, Linnea gasped. Just above Quinn's elbow, a large reddish-purple bruise was beginning to bloom. The distinctive outlines of someone's fingers curled around the back of Quinn's arm.

"Quinn! Who did this to you?" she demanded.

Quinn opened her mouth, as if to speak, but then closed it again. Tears were flowing freely down her face again.

Linnea felt as if the floor were dropping out from underneath her. "Was it Tolliver?"

Quinn's expression was fearful; she dropped her eyes to the floor and gave one short nod, the silent tears hot and flowing heavily. A wave of searing heat washed over Linnea's entire body.

"Mia, stay here." She held her voice deliberately calm. "Quinn, I'll be right back." She didn't wait for a response before she flew from the room.

She found William and Thomas together, in what was technically Thomas' room, but they both slept here while William was at home.

Their casual banter and laughter stopped the instant they both registered the expression on Linnea's face.

"What is it, Nay?" Thomas crossed the large room in four quick steps.

"William, it's Quinn. Tolliver..."

"Tolliver what?"

"I... I don't know what he did. But she has this horrible bruise on her arm..." Thomas and William both took off at a run.

"Hey, Quinn." Despite the anger that threatened to choke him, William made his voice as quiet and gentle as he could as he eased himself slowly on to the bed next to her.

The girl was calm now, sort of, though dried stains from tears ran down both of her cheeks. Mia had wrapped a thick robe around the top of her; she still wore her jeans underneath. "Is it okay if I take a look at your arm?"

It took her a second to respond; he could tell she was trying desperately to keep herself calm, and he waited patiently. He didn't want to upset her further. Finally, she took a deep breath and nodded. William used an extremely light touch to lift up the long, loose sleeve of Quinn's robe. It wouldn't go all the way up, but he got it far enough to see the mark that nearly made him lose his lunch. He swallowed hard, trying to hold onto his composure. "This is Tolliver's hand print?"

She nodded again and his stomach rolled, as his bubbling anger was joined with a thrill of panic. What had Tolliver done? And himself? Had he actually let this girl follow him to his world, and then not managed to keep her safe?

William sent up a quick prayer before he asked the next question. Across the bed, he could see his emotions reflected in Thomas' and Linnea's eyes.

"Did he hurt you anywhere else?" *Please say no, please say no ...*

"No." Quinn's voice was small, but the relief in the room was tangible, as everyone was able to breathe again.

"Did he do ... anything else to you?"

"No." Quinn swallowed as fresh tears began pouring down. "He tried to pull me toward his room, but I ... got away."

William flashed a look at Thomas and gave one quick nod.

"Stay here, Linnea." He commanded as Thomas disappeared through the door. He needed Linnea here; he couldn't do this on his own.

"Mia, can you please bring me some ice from the kitchen?"

"Certainly, Master William."

"Linnea, the salve in the bathroom, please?" Quickly, he added mentally. The injury he knew what to do about – Quinn's tears were another matter altogether. He felt a pang of envy for Thomas and his older brothers, who were going to have the opportunity to confront that ... He didn't have the right word.

Linnea seemed to understand the urgency – or else she didn't want to leave the girl alone, either. She reappeared only a few seconds later with the small tin.

"I'm sorry," Quinn whispered, as he carefully began to rub the soothing balm onto her bruise.

A sudden flash of fire blazed in his chest. She was *sorry*? He was going to need something to hit when he was done here. "You have nothing to be sorry for. Don't you *ever* apologize for this. We are the ones who should be sorry for failing to protect you from that ... poor excuse for a human being." It still wasn't a strong enough sentiment, but it was going to have to do in front of Quinn.

Thomas didn't have the patience to wait for a response to his banging on the door of the guest suite that Tolliver was occupying this week. He threw open the door and stormed into the sitting room, followed closely by Simon and Maxwell. A quick glance at the tidy couches and the recently-dusted tables told them that the room was empty. The brothers quickly separated to check the rest of the apartment.

Thomas had barely stepped inside the large, immaculate bathroom when he heard Maxwell calling from the bedroom, in a tone that sent a cold sense of dread running through Thomas' veins.

"Simon! Thomas! You'd better come in here!"

Tolliver's bedroom stood in sharp contrast to the rest of the apartment. The heavy curtains were drawn shut, leaving the room looking as dark and dank as it smelled from the collection of empty wine glasses that lined the surfaces of the tables and dressers, and from the disheveled sheets on the bed, which looked like they hadn't been changed once during Tolliver's stay. Curled up among the tangle of bedclothes was a girl. She was slight and pale, with thick black hair all the way to her waist. Her left eye was a horrible mottled purple and red, nearly swollen shut. She looked younger than Linnea.

Thomas was grateful that Simon seemed composed enough to cautiously approach her. "Who are you?"

"I am … Irene," the girl shrank back as she spoke in a thick, unfamiliar accent. The look in her eyes reminded Thomas of a frightened rabbit.

"Did Tolliver bring you here?"

The girl didn't answer; she only looked down, beginning to tremble as the terror in her eyes grew. Thomas thought he might be sick. He walked slowly to the side of the bed, hoping not to frighten her further. He spoke in a low voice. "There's nothing to be afraid of. We won't harm you."

The girl's head stayed down; her trembling grew stronger. Where are you from?"

The girl looked up, not with trust, but with resignation in her eyes. "I am a servant in his castle."

"Why did he bring you here?"

Irene only shrugged, casting her eyes back down toward the floor. Thomas had to choke back the sudden bile that came into his throat.

"Did he do this to you?"

The girl didn't look up.

"Thomas," Simon's voice was low, "you and Max take her to Nathaniel. I will find Father."

Maxwell disappeared for a moment, and then returned with a heavy robe for the girl to put on over her thin nightgown.

"Irene, will you come with us, please?" Thomas asked softly.

Irene's eyes widened in terror. "Are you taking me prisoner?"

What? "Of course not! Why would you think that?"

"Tolliver said ... if I were discovered here, in your castle, that I would be captured ... that I would never see my family again."

Fierce, white-hot anger coursed through him. It took everything he had to keep his voice steady. "It isn't true, Irene. That isn't the way we treat anyone in Eirentheos. We're only taking you to see a doctor ... a healer. He will look at your injuries; make sure you are all right. You are safe now." After a long moment, Irene allowed Thomas and Maxwell to lead her out of the apartment. Thomas wasn't sure whether she believed that she was safe, or if she was merely resigned to whatever fate was in store. He noticed that she limped as she walked.

Thomas and his father both looked up in stony silence as the office door opened, and Simon and Maxwell entered the room.

"He is not in the castle, Father," Simon's eyes were hard. "Jared in the stables reports that he had his horse readied a while ago and he left. Nobody has seen him since."

"Thank you, Son." King Stephen sighed, then turned a stern look to Thomas, who had stood.

"Sit down, Thomas. You are not going after him. He'll turn up, eventually. And when he does," Stephen added, likely noting the glint in his son's eye, "you'll stay away from him."

"But Father..."

"Thomas, it's not a request. Tolliver is a prince of Philotheum."

"Not rightfully."

"Rightfully, he is not the heir to the throne, no. However, his mother came to be the queen honestly with her marriage to a proper king. All of her sons have the right to the title of prince. As to the issue of the throne, it doesn't matter how we feel about it; it is a separate issue from how we deal with Tolliver now. As long as Hector is Prince Regent of Philotheum and is holding Tolliver up as the heir, we have little choice regarding our treatment of him."

"But he..."

"I am aware of what he has done, Thomas. It is becoming painfully clear what kind of behavior is acceptable in that castle these days. However, our political alliance with Philotheum is on tenuous ground as it is. It is not within our rights to punish another kingdom's prince."

"So you're just going to do nothing? Let him get away with it?"

"Not nothing, Thomas. The girl, Irene, is safe now. Her injuries will be treated. She will not be returned to Tolliver's castle, and we will do what we can to reunite her with her family. They will be offered asylum here in Eirentheos if necessary. She will be offered a position here in our castle, if she would like one."

"And Quinn?"

The sudden flash of fury that appeared in Stephen's eye right then placated Thomas just a little; his father was just as upset as he was. "Quinn will be given the highest level of protection, as will your sisters. None of them are to be alone at any time, until after Tolliver has departed back to Philotheum. Guards will be placed near each hallway and staircase that leads to our family quarters. None of the girls are to be anywhere outside of our private corridors without a male escort. I trust that the three of you are up to the job?"

"Yes Father," the brothers answered simultaneously.

"Quinn is not to be left alone in any circumstance, unless she specifically asks for privacy. I can't imagine how upsetting this must be for her." Thomas didn't understand the look that crossed his father's eyes now. "I will ask Linnea to sleep on a cot in Quinn's room tonight."

"I am sure she won't mind, Father. I'll ask her, if she hasn't already come to that decision on her own."

"Thank you, Thomas."

Stephen sighed. "I am going to go and talk to your mother now. I am sure you can expect quite the visit upstairs once she has heard about all this."

"Yes, Father."

THE NAMING CEREMONY

LONG VINES COVERED WITH tiny white blossoms were strung along the lengths of the pews in the large chapel at the edge of the castle grounds. There were thirteen white candles lit at the end of each pew and white-and-purple linen banners draped down from the upper balcony. The long, wide room was awash in a gentle diffused sunlight, streaming in from tall windows along every wall; all halfway open to let in the warm summer breeze that drifted through the surrounding gardens, leaving the entire chapel smelling of the hundreds of sweet flowers. Soft music could be heard from outside as well, from where the musicians had set up for the party.

Quinn followed Linnea down the long stone aisle, which had been lined with a thick purple runner, bordered with silver ribbon. Thomas and William walked closely behind.

"Are you sure I should be here?" Quinn asked quietly.

"For the hundredth time, Quinn, yes. We want you here. Tolliver still hasn't been seen; his horse is still missing from the stable." Linnea's voice was firm.

"And even if he does show up, he doesn't get to ruin any more of your time here. We'll find a safe spot for you to be able to watch the ceremony," Thomas' eyes were both kind and determined. "And then, you'll be with us again for the party."

"I still think that maybe she should sit with us," William said, shocking her, given that he was the one who wished she'd never come here in the first place.

"That would draw more attention to her, if Tolliver did come," Linnea said. "I know a better place."

Quinn watched silently from her hidden viewing spot above an alcove in the side wall. The guests who had been gathering at the castle for the past several days were formally announced as they entered and filed in along the center rows of pews. The outer rows had already filled with castle servants and other less-distinguished guests of the royal family. She'd watched as Mia had edged her way as close to the front as was possible. The upper balcony had filled quickly with villagers and their guests.

To one side of the center platform was a long line of chairs. Once all of the guests had been seated, the royal children were announced as they proceeded one-by-one down the center aisle. They were presented in order of age, beginning with Simon, except for tiny Sarah who was carried down the aisle by Rebecca.

Then the ceremony officially began. A tall, older man in long white robes walked to the center of the dais, and began addressing the crowd in a droning monotone, pontificating as much on his own importance as on the sacredness of the Naming Ceremony.

Thomas turned in his seat to look up at her, and she stifled a giggle when he rolled his eyes and nodded toward the front.

"It's an even more beautiful view from over here." The disembodied voice came from behind Quinn and she spun quickly to see what or who was there.

"Don't worry, milady, I don't bite – at least not without being asked." Quinn was startled; peeking down from a ledge about halfway up the side of the alcove was the face of a man. His long, flowing white hair signaled age, but his face was free of the lines and wrinkles that usually accompanied the years. His green eyes sparkled with friendliness under his bushy, white eyebrows. He extended his hand toward Quinn, clearly intending that she join him up there. She looked down at the dress she was wearing and then back at the man.

"No one will see you, and don't fuss about me; I'm a complete gentleman." The last words were accompanied by a teasing grin that threatened to split the man's face in two. Quinn hesitated for a moment, but then decided to accept the offer. She let out a soft gasp. From the ledge, she could see over the top of the whole crowd. It was a perfect view of the entire chapel.

"Much better." The old man smiled approvingly.

The two turned their attention back to the ceremony, though the action on the dais now was somewhat less exciting than watching grass grow.

"Curse me! That pompous windbag needs to get over himself," the man said, causing Quinn to chuckle quietly. She and the old man stood there quietly watching together for a few more minutes while the speech ended and the "pompous windbag" stepped to a seat along the side of the dais, waiting until he was needed again.

The music took on a more celebratory tone and a herald stepped forward and called the court to witness. The king was announced and he entered, taking his place by the small altar in the center of the platform. The queen and "the blessed gift of the Maker" were then announced, and the queen came in, carrying her thirteenth child. The girl was placed lovingly into the small cradle on the platform and each of her siblings was called up in turn to bestow on her their gift.

Emma enchanted the crowd when it was her turn, marching confidently up to the cradle with her small silver box in hand, and planting a kiss on the baby's cheek. Little Sarah could not be persuaded to part with her own shiny package, and was quickly returned to Rebecca's lap still holding it, before her impending storm could disrupt the ceremony.

Once all of the siblings had taken their seats again, the room fell completely silent and the "pompous windbag" began collecting himself to rise.

"That's my cue," the man on the ledge said with a grin, and he hopped down to stride into the room, and right up onto the dais, into the middle of the ceremony. Pompous windbag looked beet-faced and horrified, but quickly took his seat in defeat, as the room echoed with whispers of 'Alvin'.

Quinn had no idea what was going on.

"My king." Alvin bowed. "My Queen." He bowed again, but for a bit longer. "My princess." He bent and placed a gentle kiss on the baby's forehead, before taking her into his arms. A hush fell over the crowd as Alvin turned to them, holding the infant.

"We are here today to give this baby a name and a blessing that she may be known by her family and her people and that she may serve the Maker and her kingdom in heath, strength and wisdom."

"The name she will be known by is Hannah Eden Rose. Hannah, you are a special child, and the Maker knows you and loves you. You were lovingly created by your Maker, with a special purpose to serve for him, for your family, and for your people.

You occupy a special position in your family, and I have come here today to bestow upon you a special gift. Your siblings each have their own gifts, those that are required as the keys of the kingdom, From wise leadership to compassionate healing and even understanding how to work with plants and animals, all of these gifts are essential to maintaining a kingdom in service to the Maker, blessed and beloved by the Maker. His greatest blessing, however, to this kingdom, to your family's kingdom, Hannah, is you."

At these words, Alvin reached into the pocket of his long purple robes, and withdrew a tiny silver circle, hanging from a small chain. "Hannah Eden Rose, blessed child of the Maker, I bestow upon you His gift, which you will carry all of your days. Though the name of your gift has no translation in the languages of people, the blessings it carries are both universal and eternal.

May your gift bring true blessings upon this house, upon this kingdom, and upon all of our Maker's people whose lives intersect with yours."

Alvin placed the baby lovingly into her mother's arms before fastening the chain around her neck. He again kissed the baby's forehead, and then kissed Queen Charlotte's forehead as well. The king moved in close beside the queen, placing his hand on his daughter's head.

Alvin turned to face the crowd. "Beloved," he began, "Your kingdom is truly blessed to have the leadership of a family so dedicated to ruling in the Maker's ways. Always support your king and each other, remembering that each of you is truly beloved in the eyes of the Maker."

"Now," he continued, "I hear there's a fantastic party waiting outside." Alvin turned, and walked off the dais, effectively ending the ceremony.

The family remained in their places while the guests filed out.

Quinn couldn't see where Alvin went after he left the platform. She supposed he was leading the crowd outside. So she was surprised when he appeared suddenly back in the entrance of the alcove, standing directly below her, hidden from the view of everyone else.

"Need a hand down, Lady Quinn?" Alvin asked, reaching up toward her.

Quinn frowned; she hadn't told him her name. She did take his hand, and he surprised her again when he picked her up under her arms and placed her easily on the floor.

"Quinn!" Thomas was walking toward her, weaving quickly through the departing crowd. He stopped short when he saw her standing with Alvin. "I … see you've met Alvin."

"Oh yes." Alvin's smile was wide. "Quinn and I are fast becoming dear friends. May I have the honor of escorting you outside, dear lady?"

Quinn glanced uncertainly at Thomas, who smiled and nodded.

Outside, the gardens were overflowing with decorations. Small white tables and chairs had been set up all around a large stone-paved circle that had been cleared for dancing.

Alvin walked with her all the way to the circle, stopping just before they intersected with the small number of couples already twirling in time to the music, and then he turned to her. "May I have the honor of your first dance?"

"I don't know how…"

"You'll be fine; just follow the music." his words were filled with confident reassurance and Quinn fell into step as best she could trying to mimic the other dancers.

"How are you enjoying your visit in Eirentheos?"

Quinn wasn't sure how to answer; she assumed he'd heard the story about her visiting from a neighboring kingdom.

"It's lovely."

"And what is your favorite part?"

Her eyes glanced quickly to where much of the royal family had gathered. A smile spread across her face as she thought of a coy answer.

"I think that the flowers are beautiful."

Alvin's wide smile brightened and his step took on a livelier energy.

"I love flowers," he replied. "They are so different and varied. There are so many different colors, shapes, designs. Each serves its own unique purpose, every variety complementing the others. I think the Maker had an especially fun time creating the flowers."

His eyes twinkled as continued. "Take the rose for example; allowed to grow wild it will quickly become a bramble of thorns. If cultivated properly, however, it becomes strong and enduring. It will survive the harshest weather and you can cut it down as far as you like; it will grow back and blossom."

"Contrast that with say, a dandelion. When cultivated, it grows quite strong; yet it always retains its wild qualities, and when left to grow wild, it unleashes its hearty spirit, vibrant colors and indomitable nature. Its seeds are plentiful and spread far and wide, taking root wherever they land. Left unchecked, though, the dandelion is a weed that chokes out the life of all the plants around it, and then continues to spread its seeds, far past the gardener's original intent."

The music ended and Quinn realized she hadn't even noticed the last part of the song; it had been so easy to follow along as she listened to Alvin.

"Now my dear I do believe that young master Thomas is waiting to share the floor with you next." He kissed her on the cheek, and handed her over to Thomas who had appeared next to her.

"Is Alvin filling your head with his wild stories Quinn?" Thomas asked, as the musicians struck up a new, slower tune.

"His views on the qualities of flowers actually," she replied, her eyebrows furrowed thoughtfully, "but I don't understand any of it. Which I suppose fits in just fine since I haven't understood much of anything going on around me since I arrived."

Thomas laughed. "I can't imagine how strange this must all be for you. You're handling it better than I would, I think."

"So, is Alvin another uncle?"

"No. Alvin..." he said, almost laughing. "Alvin is just... Alvin. He's always been around. Some say he's a prophet of some kind. He's just…there whenever he decides he needs to be. I've seen him at a few royal naming ceremonies and he does exactly what he did today. He just appears, steps in, and names the baby… but not every time. He showed up at the naming of the candle maker's little boy. Sometimes, he jumps in and starts officiating in the middle of a wedding.

"Once, I heard about him showing up at a villager's dinner table – he even brought his own plate. You can't expect him to come, or even find him to invite him. The only thing you can predict with Alvin is that everything he says has some sort of meaning."

Quinn's eyes were wide. "Wow…there really is no end to the surprises, is there?"

"How else would we keep lovely ladies guessing?" Thomas' eyes sparkled as he twirled Quinn around and they both laughed.

Quinn felt Thomas stiffen a second before she heard the voice.

"Now Thomas, didn't anyone ever teach you that it's not polite to be selfish with your toys? I think it's high time you shared such a lovely little plaything."

Her breathing accelerated as she realized that Tolliver was standing directly behind her. A wave of nausea rolled over her when she felt his hand stroking her hair.

Suddenly, Thomas' fist flew past her head, connecting squarely with Tolliver's nose. In the next instant, Quinn felt herself being pulled to the side as Tolliver came up raging.

"Who do you think you are, Thomas?" Tolliver demanded, before returning the punch, slamming Thomas in the mouth. "I am the heir to the throne of Philotheum. I will not be treated this way by a royal brat from this weak excuse for a kingdom! Is one little courtesan really worth this much to you? A war?"

This time, William threw the punch, and Maxwell jumped into the fray right behind him. Even Linnea managed to get in a well-placed kick to Tolliver's groin before they were pulled apart by several castle guards.

"Enough!" Stephen stepped between them. He gave a stern look to Thomas before turning to Tolliver. "I will not allow accusations such as those to be directed at my family."

"What, Stephen, you can't accept that you have raised your son to be a spoiled brat who can't share his toys?"

"I have tolerated you for your mother's sake Tolliver; do not press my courtesy further. To engage in fisticuffs with my sons is poor enough conduct, but to malign the character of a young lady under my safekeeping is unacceptable. I will invite you to return to your rooms, Tolliver. Perhaps you will have time to reflect on the kind of conduct that is befitting of the leader of a kingdom."

Stephen let his steel gaze linger on Tolliver for a long moment before turning away and returning to his guests.

Everything happened quickly after that. Four guards led Tolliver back to the castle, and Simon escorted Quinn and the four siblings who had been involved in the brawl around the castle and over to an outbuilding that Quinn had never seen.

Blood was dripping down Thomas' face as they trooped into the building, which Quinn recognized as some kind of medical clinic. They passed through a reception area and back into a larger room. Five cots and small, metal carts filled with various medical supplies lined one wall.

William led Thomas over to the first bed and made him sit down. Thomas was still shaking visibly, his fists curled into tight balls.

Nobody spoke for several minutes. The only movement in the room came from William, who was working on Thomas' cut.

It was Maxwell who finally broke the silence. "Well, that wasn't good."

Everyone burst out laughing.

A TRIP

QUINN AND LINNEA WERE awakened early the next morning by Mia entering the room.

"Sorry, Miss Quinn and Lady Linnea. I didn't want to wake you, but I was told I had to come in here and start getting Miss Quinn packed and ready."

Quinn sat bolt upright.

"It's alright, Mia," Linnea said, rubbing her eyes and struggling to sit up. "We meant to be up early anyway. What time is it?"

"It's going on half-past six."

Linnea groaned, but Quinn was already halfway to the bathroom, anxiety twisting her insides.

After the incident at the Naming Ceremony the day before, Stephen and Charlotte had decided that it was not safe for Quinn to remain at Rosewood Castle while Tolliver was in Eirentheos. It had become clear that he had made a special target out of Quinn, and Stephen wanted her as far out of Tolliver's reach as he could get her. The public spectacle had also created another issue – people asking pointed questions about exactly who Quinn was.

Apparently, Stephen's announcement that Quinn was "under his safekeeping" carried heavy implications.

"It isn't your fault in any way, Quinn." Stephen had been adamant after she tried to apologize. "You have not done anything wrong. And I don't regret what I said today, nor would I take it back."

"We do regard you as under our care, just as one of our own children," Charlotte had added, with tears in the corners of her eyes and a tender look that Quinn didn't completely understand.

"Please don't feel we are sending you away, dear one, our only worry is for your safety. You are always welcome here in our home, please remember that."

So today, Quinn was to be packed and ready, and sent off with Nathaniel, William, and Thomas as they made the rounds of outlying villages to deliver medical supplies and provide assistance to the small medical clinics they had helped establish.

Linnea was quieter than usual this morning as she helped Quinn get ready, braiding her damp, auburn hair in an intricate pattern that she said would stay in place while Quinn traveled on horseback.

Mia, too, was somber, though her mood had no impact on her efficiency. By the time Quinn had finished taking a quick shower, Mia had already packed a small leather bag for her; it was waiting on the perfectly-made bed, next to an outfit she'd be comfortable riding in. Quinn wasn't even sure what was in the bag; it wasn't like she'd brought anything with her to Eirentheos. She had learned better than to object to accepting gifts here, though, so she didn't ask.

Linnea had just put the final touches on Quinn's hair when Simon arrived to escort Quinn down to the meeting point. Nathaniel, William, and Thomas were already there, having left individually to avoid attracting a lot of extra attention. Linnea wrapped Quinn in a fierce hug.

"Now, make sure you keep Thomas in his place; make sure he remembers he's in the presence of a lady. He'll have me to answer to if he doesn't mind his manners."

Linnea's serious tone made Quinn chuckle. She turned to Mia. "Mia, thank you so much for all of your kindness. You're never around long enough for me to say it, but you've truly treated me in such a way that I've felt like a princess since I've been here."

Mia's rosy cheeks turned a darker shade of pink. "It's been my pleasure, Miss Quinn. You are a princess in my eyes."

"Are you ready, Quinn?" Simon asked, hefting the leather bag onto his shoulder.

"Yes, I suppose I am." She hadn't gotten to know Simon very well; he always seemed to be busy, and it felt a little awkward to be alone with him.

Linnea squeezed her hand tightly and then let go. Quinn felt two pairs of eyes on her back as she followed Simon into the hallway.

The atmosphere at little clearing in the woods was nothing like it had been in Quinn's bedroom. William and Thomas both were buzzing with excitement at being out in the open air, ready to travel. Even Nathaniel was smiling as Simon and Quinn walked into the group.

"Ready, Quinn?" Thomas' grin was contagious.

"Sure ... I think. Where's Chestnut?" Quinn's eyes scanned the clearing for the horse. Not seeing him, she looked back at Thomas just in time to catch the end of the conspiratorial look he had shared with William. "What am I missing?"

Thomas made a soft clicking sound, and a horse stepped out from behind some trees, but it wasn't Chestnut. "I know you were promised a trip to the stables to take your pick, and that never quite happened, but I think you and Dusk will get along rather well."

Dusk was a beautiful mare, though Quinn couldn't identify the breed. She was smooth and silky, a deep gray color that was almost black, but shimmered in the sunlight. Quinn was in awe; she couldn't resist walking straight over to Dusk so that she could touch her glossy coat.

"Here." William tossed her an apple, which she caught easily. Dusk reached over and snatched it out of Quinn's hand before she could turn all the way back around to offer it to her.

Quinn laughed. "Cheeky, isn't she?"

"She does have her own personality," Thomas agreed.

"Do you all have everything you need?" Simon asked, as he and Thomas loaded Quinn's luggage into one of Dusk's nearly-full saddlebags.

"We have as much as we can carry. It will have to be enough for now," Nathaniel answered him. "You'll send word of how things go here?"

"Of course. And you'll let us know if you figure anything out with this illness in the villages?"

"Yes."

"Well, travel safe then. Quinn, it was a pleasure meeting you. I am sorry I didn't get a chance to know you better."

"It was nice meeting you too, Simon." He nodded, and then held out his hand to assist Quinn into Dusk's saddle. The others mounted their horses as well, and Nathaniel led them out of the clearing.

THE CLINIC

THE RIDE TO THEIR first destination, Mistle Village, took about two hours.

It had been many months since Quinn had ridden for that long, and, although they took it at a slow and steady pace, she was feeling it by the time they approached the outskirts of the small village. Dusk didn't seem fazed; she'd barely broken a sweat.

She had a feeling that Nathaniel, William, and Thomas could have made the trip in much less time, but they were taking it easy for her.

Nathaniel led the group up to a long, single-story white house with a wide covered porch that wrapped the entire building. A small wooden sign that read "Mistle Village Medical Clinic" hung from the porch railing. They brought the horses to a stop in a grassy, fenced paddock on the north side of the clinic. Nathaniel and William dismounted.

"Thomas, you should stay here with Quinn and tend to the horses, while we check on things inside," Nathaniel told him. He turned to Quinn, "That was some good riding. You kept up with us the whole way without a break. All those years of riding lessons seem to have paid off."

"Thank you." Quinn felt a little awkward at Nathaniel's praise. She had almost forgotten that he was part of her life in Bristlecone, as well. Maybe she hadn't slowed them down as much as she'd thought.

Nathaniel smiled. "I'm sure you're tired after all of that, though. Why don't you go relax and rest in the shade for a little while?"

Quinn nodded. She was hot and tired.

Thomas was on the ground quickly, offering his hand to help Quinn down. The proud trail-guide side of Quinn thought about protesting all the help, but when she swung her leg over the saddle and felt how stiff it was, her grateful side won out.

"Thanks, Thomas," she told him, after he had to steady her for a second on her wobbly legs.

"Of course."

"I'm going to have to get used to long stretches of riding again. There's not much of a chance to keep up with it in a mountain winter."

Thomas' grin was amused and kind as they walked over to a large shade tree. "I'm sure. I forget how different it can be there. William is so used to it now … and he spends so little time there, comparatively, that I don't know how much he notices about your world, really."

Quinn considered that for a moment. She had only been in Eirentheos for four days, but in some ways, that short span felt like a completely different lifetime. Already, she could not imagine not knowing Thomas or Linnea, or the rest of their family.

With a sudden shock, she realized that she hadn't given much thought to home since she'd been here. Apart from the other night with Tolliver, when she had wanted nothing more than to crawl into bed with her mom, thoughts of her real life in Bristlecone had pretty much been on the back burner ever since Thomas had told her she would only be missing one day there.

Of course, everything here was new and interesting; there had been plenty to keep her mind occupied. Maybe, too, it was because it was so all-encompassing, being somewhere she couldn't go home from. She had no way of contacting her mother, or anyone else. While she was here in Eirentheos, she had to just be here. And when she did leave … the thought caused an odd pang in her stomach.

"I suppose it's a little different for William when he's there," she said. "He always knows he's going to be going back and forth. He's probably worried all the time about what he's missing here. Besides, he has Nathaniel with him, and his medical studies to keep him thinking about home. My world probably doesn't mean much to him."

"True," said Thomas. "After all, how much does our world mean to you?"

Quinn swallowed hard when she realized that she didn't know the answer.

"So what is going on here, exactly anyway?" she asked, changing the subject. "I get the feeling that the three of you are worried about something here in the village, but you haven't really talked about it."

Thomas' expression grew serious, and he stared off for a moment, looking at something in the sky.

"Is it something I'm not supposed to know about?"

"No…It's not that. It's just a strange and scary situation for us, and we hate having to involve you."

"Well, I'm here now. Are you going to keep it from me the whole time?"

"I suppose you're right," Thomas took a deep breath. "Strange cases of illness have been cropping up in many of the Eirenthean villages, including here in Mistle Village."

"Strange how?"

"Strange because we don't know what is causing it, or where it's coming from. It doesn't appear to be contagious, because it is only affecting random people - only children, actually, which is one of the things that are so concerning. But so far, there haven't been any cases of more than one child in a family contracting it."

"Wow."

"Yeah. We don't think it's food either, for the same reason. All the children in a family would probably be eating the same foods. Most of these families have several children."

"Is that common here?" Quinn wondered, thinking of the royal family's thirteen children.

"What? To have many children? Yes. Children are very important in Eirentheos. We consider them to be blessings to our kingdom."

Up on the porch, the wooden screen door opened and closed. Thomas and Quinn both looked up to see a young woman standing there. She wore a long, simple cotton dress, covered by a white apron. Her thick brown hair was pulled back into a long braid down the middle of her back.

Thomas stood as the woman walked toward them, and Quinn followed his lead.

"Welcome, Thomas."

"Hello, Essie. It's good to see you again."

"Always a pleasure to see you as well, Thomas."

"Essie, this is Quinn. She's traveling with us for the next week or so. Quinn, this is Essie White, one of the doctors here in Mistle Village. Also, she's married to my cousin Jacob, who is the other doctor."

"Hello, Quinn. Welcome to our home." Essie's smile was warm and kind, though her eyes looked weary.

"Thank you. It's nice to meet you, Essie."

"Come on into the house, you all must be hungry for lunch after that ride."

Quinn followed Thomas and Essie up on to the porch and all the way around to the back of the house. Essie led them through the back door into a small, cozy kitchen. It was homey; a clean, flowery tablecloth hung over the edges of a circular table in the corner of the room, a glass vase with a bouquet of purple flowers served as a centerpiece. Five wooden chairs surrounded the table. A savory aroma was coming from an enormous pot on the wood-burning stove.

"You live here, in the back of the clinic?" Quinn asked.

"Yes, it makes things easier to be close. This back half is our living quarters." Through the open doorway in the kitchen, Quinn could see a tidy living room, and a hallway beyond it. The whole house felt welcoming and comfortable.

"It's lovely," Quinn said.

"Thank you." Essie smiled. "I like to think so. You must be thirsty. Would either of you like a glass of tea?"

"Yes, please," Quinn and Thomas spoke simultaneously. Essie grinned as she filled two glasses with ice from a small freezer.

The tea itself was different from anything Quinn had ever tasted; it had a slight dark-red tint to it. "This is delicious, Essie, thank you."

Just then, a door in the living room opened, and William stepped through with another man that Quinn didn't recognize, though she assumed it must be Essie's husband, Jacob. This was confirmed when he stepped into the kitchen, and placed a gentle kiss on Essie's forehead, taking her hips into his hands.

"That smells wonderful, sweetheart, thank you."

Essie kissed Jacob on the cheek before turning him to face the guests. "Jacob, this is…"

"Quinn, I've heard. It's a pleasure to meet you Quinn. Welcome. I am Jacob. I see you've already met my beautiful wife?"

"Uh, yes. Thank you. It's nice to meet you, too." She noticed that Essie's cheeks grew slightly pink at her husband's compliment, though she quickly turned and began removing bowls from a cabinet.

"Can I help?" Quinn asked, feeling useless.

"Sure, if you'd like you can slice those loaves of bread there on that counter while I start dishing up bowls of stew." Essie handed her a large bread knife.

As she worked, carefully cutting thick slices of the still-warm bread, Quinn listened to the conversation between the men.

"How is it going?" Thomas wondered.

William sighed, "About the same. Marcus Bracken is more stable now. His fever finally broke, but the rash is blistered and painful all over his hands and face. One of his eyes is swollen shut. He's eating and drinking, though."

"We were able to release little Hally Donner yesterday," Jacob broke in. "There are still some welts on her hands and wrists, but she seems to be recovering fairly well. However, we received a new case late yesterday afternoon, Alyia Hawken. She's eight. Her fever isn't as high as some of the others' have been, thank the Maker, but the rash is all the way up to her elbows and covers her neck and face. She's having trouble keeping down food, though, and we're worried about her becoming dehydrated. Nathaniel's in there with her now, trying to get her to accept some fluids. I'm sure we'll need to take lunch in to him; he won't leave."

Essie nodded. "Sounds like Nathaniel. Right now, we have four patients, and at least one parent for each," she added. "Fortunately, it's still a number we can accommodate here, but if we continue to get new cases..."

"We will get this stopped." William's voice was adamant.

After a lunch of Essie's delicious stew, Quinn asked if she could visit the clinic. Thomas and William both had reservations, but Essie simply said that they could use all the hands they could get, and there was no further discussion of the matter.

Quinn followed Essie into the long, main room of the clinic, her hands full with a tray loaded with bowls of stew and glasses of iced tea.

"Over here, Quinn," Essie led her over to a small cot. The clinic was divided into small, makeshift rooms by low, wooden walls and curtains. The little space Essie led her to was occupied by a young boy, who was propped up on pillows, and his mother who sat in a rocking chair next to him, reading aloud to him from a book. Quinn's heart ached at the sight of the little boy's face; odd patches of small, red sores covered his face, blistered in some areas on his left cheek and forehead. His left eyelid was so red and puffy that she couldn't see that eye. Both of his arms were wrapped lightly in gauze from fingertip to elbow.

"How are you feeling, Marcus?" Essie asked softly.

"A little better," he answered. "But I'm still sooo itchy. And my eye hurts."

"The salve seems to be helping a little," his mother said. "Some of the blisters are starting to heal."

"That's good news." Essie smiled. "Hopefully we'll have you out of here soon - not that we don't enjoy your company. Betta, this is Quinn. She came with William to help. Quinn, this is Betta and Marcus."

"It's nice to meet you. Are you hungry?" Quinn smiled, indicating her heavy tray.

"Yes, thank you."

Essie walked off to another cubicle, leaving Quinn to study the young mother as she set the tray down on a small table. Betta couldn't have been too many years older than Quinn was herself. She looked on as Betta placed a bookmark in the thick book she had been reading to Marcus, and set it on the table before she helped the boy sit all the way up and adjusted a wooden tray table over his lap. Betta's eyes were a twinkling gray framed by thick, dark lashes; she reminded Quinn of Thomas. She smiled at Quinn as she helped her carefully lay the warm, full bowl on the tray table.

"Thank you, Quinn."

"You're welcome. Can I get you two anything else?" She asked as Betta lifted a spoon full of the stew to Marcus' mouth; he tried to reach it himself, but the gauze bandages got in his way.

Once he had finished swallowing, Marcus piped up, "Do you have any candy?"

"Now I know you're feeling better!" Betta laughed, tugging playfully at the back of her son's hair.

Quinn smiled. "I don't think I do," she answered. "But if I find some, you'll be the first to know."

The boy's answering grin was reward in itself.

Across the room, William had taken over for Nathaniel, tending to a little girl who looked very ill. Her rash appeared much worse than Marcus' did; the whole lower part of her face and her neck were covered in blisters and the small, red sores. A few of the blisters were oozing a little. The girl's mother sat next to her, rubbing her leg and looking worried. Quinn had seen the girl's father step out onto the porch, where he was now pacing.

"Maybe a little apple juice, Alyia? Or some more tea?" William coaxed.

The girl shook her head. "Not right now; it hurts my throat when I drink." She closed her eyes and lay back on the pillow.

William sighed, turning and stepping just outside the cubicle as Quinn came to stand beside him. "We need to find a way to keep her hydrated," he spoke in a low voice. "I don't want to place an IV if I don't absolutely have to; those kinds of supplies are scarce here. We would have to send back to the clinic at home for more IV fluids."

"Not to mention how you feel about needles," Nathaniel teased, walking over to join them.

William rolled his eyes. "Come off of it, Nathaniel, you're just as much of a softie as I am with that stuff." He looked at Quinn. "In Bristlecone, he just leaves the room and has a nurse take care of that stuff, and here he's always insisting that it's a vital part of my training."

Quinn shuddered at the thought. "I'm not sure I blame him."

William chuckled as his eyes grew tender. "I don't either. Although it is preferable to watching a little girl lose consciousness from dehydration. I need to see a significant improvement in her symptoms in the next few hours, or I'm not going to have a choice."

"What about trying a popsicle?" Quinn asked.

William frowned. "We don't have them here in Eirentheos. I've only ever had one at school."

"Oh." This surprised Quinn. "We could make some, if we froze some juice in the freezer."

"Why haven't I ever thought of that?" Nathaniel wondered. "We use popsicles all the time at the hospital."

"Probably because freezers aren't all that commonplace in Eirentheos," William said. "That little one in there was enough of a job to get through the gate. But we do have it here, so we can give it a try."

STRANGE

"YOU'RE HANDLING ALL OF this better than I would have expected for someone who just walked into a strange world," William said.

"Really? Because right now I feel about as exhausted as I've ever been."

"I'm sure you are. I've felt that way plenty of times trying to adjust to going into Bristlecone, and it's never this stressful there."

William, Thomas, and Quinn were sitting in rocking chairs on the wide porch of Essie and Jacob's clinic, drinking iced tea and watching as the sun slowly began to set.

"We're all exhausted," Thomas replied. "It has been a very long day."

And it had. They had spent the last several hours caring for the children in the clinic and trying to reassure their parents. The popsicles seemed to be working; all of the children were enjoying the novelty, although Alyia had only been able to finish one.

Things were calm for the moment. They had all helped Essie put together a simple dinner of sandwiches and salad from the garden,

171

and then Nathaniel had taken his horse and headed for the Bracken farm, wanting to let Marcus' father know that he was doing better and to bring back some clothing and supplies for Marcus and Betta. There were apparently three smaller children at the home who Nathaniel wanted to check in on as well.

William, Thomas, and Quinn had retreated to the porch, wanting to give Jacob and Essie a break from feeling they had to take care of their guests. They had told them to take the evening off from their clinic duties; both Jacob and Essie looked completely worn out.

"You still have no idea what is causing this?" Quinn asked.

"No," answered William. "I've never seen anything like it."

"It looks kind of like an allergy, or really bad poison ivy or something … except for the fevers and the vomiting."

"Well, those symptoms could be secondary, from an infection of the sores, or a bad reaction to the toxins, if it were something like that," said William. "We just don't have a lot of plants like that here."

"Only one plant that's at all common ever causes reactions that severe," Thomas added. "Shadeweed. And even little children are taught to avoid it. There wouldn't be this many kids suddenly getting into it all at the same time."

"Not to mention," said William, "you'd have to have repeated exposure to react like these children are. Even with two or three exposures, you'd only have a slight rash, maybe be itchy for a day or two."

"Really?" asked Quinn. "That seems odd."

"It's not particularly odd," William replied. "Even poison ivy doesn't usually bother people the first time they touch it. It's allergizing; your body learns to react to it the next time."

"I didn't know that," said Quinn, "I was always just taught to stay away from it. …And you don't think it's contagious, or from food?"

"It just isn't following a pattern that would indicate that. We would expect to see multiple children, and maybe even adults, from the same household if it were one of those things."

"I suppose you're right. But then ... this is just really weird."

"Yeah, that's kind of the problem."

They sat in silence for a long time, watching the colors slowly fade from the sky, listening to the buzzing and chirping of summer insects. Quinn was comfortable; the quiet rocking and peacefulness of the evening was making her sleepy.

"What about a bug?" she wondered suddenly. "Like a mosquito or something?"

William was quiet, appearing to ponder that idea. "I suppose it's possible; we do have several different parasite insects here..."

"Why wouldn't it affect any adults, then?" Thomas asked, bursting the bubble.

"Maybe they're immune to it?" Quinn asked hopefully.

"But what are the chances that none of these families would have had more than one child affected, then?"

"I don't know."

William sighed. "It's probably better to hope that it's not an insect, anyway. It would be very difficult to stop the spread of this, if that's what it turned out to be."

"It would have been nice to have something to go on, though. It was a good idea, Quinn." Thomas said kindly.

"They must have something in common." Quinn said.

"Yes, but we have no idea what."

The screen door opened then, and a man stepped out. Quinn had met him earlier; his name was Aren Creeve. His son, Braedan, was in the clinic.

"Dr. Rose?"

It was still surprising to Quinn to see William respond to that title; he stood and walked over to the young father - all of these parents were so young. "Yes, Mr. Creeve?"

"Call me Aren, please. Do you really think Braedan is doing better? I know he seems like it, but we're just so worried. My wife is coming back in the morning..."

"I really do think so, Aren," William's voice was patient and reassuring. "The blisters are all gone, and the redness is fading. He is eating and drinking normally now. I think you'll be able to take him home with you tomorrow. We'll send some of the salve we've been using along with you."

The relief in the man's eyes was evident, but worry still tugged at the corners. "You don't think the rash will come back again, do you? He's never had a rash that didn't just go away before. Had one a few weeks ago, but it cleared up by itself in a day or two."

"That's usually what rashes in kids do, Aren. It's normal. But if Braedan does get another rash anytime soon, bring him back here right away to get it checked out, just in case."

"Will do, Doc. Now, Braedan's been asking for another one of those ice things..."

William smiled. "Of course." He looked over at Thomas and Quinn. "We probably should pass some out to everyone again – and put another batch in to freeze. I need to check on Alyia again as well."

Thomas and Quinn stood and stretched; their long day wasn't over yet. They all trooped back into the house.

When Thomas and Quinn returned to the clinic after mixing more ice pops and cleaning up the kitchen, they found William in a corner, speaking quietly to Alyia's parents.

"The juice has helped," he was saying, looking gratefully at Quinn as she walked by, "but I'm afraid it's not enough. Her dehydration symptoms just have not improved enough to make me comfortable, and she's still not able to keep down larger amounts of fluids than one juice pop at a time. I'm going to have to put a needle in her arm so that we can give her fluids directly through a little tube.

"It's really not that big of a deal," he added quickly - when a look of distress appeared in her mother's eyes. "If we were in the castle clinic, where we have more supplies and fluids readily available, I'd have done it already, even before it became necessary."

Quinn was certain she would never go into the medical field - she didn't want to have anything to do with needles. Something about William though, made her want to watch him work; he seemed to have that effect on her quite often. She found herself in the tiny cubicle with William and Thomas as they prepared the IV fluids for the little girl. They had sent her parents out to wait on the porch, hoping to work quickly and keep Alyia from getting anxious. Although she wouldn't have needed the warning, William quietly told Quinn not to mention the needle where Alyia might hear.

It wasn't nearly as awful as Quinn expected it to be; she had never seen anyone be as gentle as William was with Alyia. A strange, warm feeling spread through her chest as she watched him.

First, Thomas sprinkled a small amount of valoris seed powder on the little girl's tongue. Although Thomas wasn't a doctor or even an apprentice himself, it was clear from the interaction between the brothers that this was a well-practiced routine.

Once Alyia seemed a little relaxed – apparently, even children didn't react to valoris seed the way Quinn had – Thomas talked softly to her and stroked her hair back out of her face, working to keep the girl's eyes on his. He'd positioned himself in a way that would block the child's view of what William was doing if she did look up.

William fashioned a splint out of a folded towel, and asked Quinn to help hand him small strips of cloth that he used to tie the girl's arm carefully to the splint, to help secure her arm and keep her from dislodging the IV line once he had placed it.

"Okay, sweetheart, I'm going to put something on your arm now. It's like a big bracelet. It will feel tight, but it won't hurt, and I'll take it off in a minute." William's voice was soft and soothing as he wrapped a rubber tourniquet around Alyia's arm, just below her elbow. Quinn was fascinated at this side of him.

"Now you'll feel something cold and wet," he told her. "It will probably feel good - it's hot in here." He thoroughly cleaned an area just above the inside of the little girl's wrist. Quinn's nose twitched at the scent of the rubbing alcohol.

Thomas smiled at Alyia, "Nice and cool?" he asked.

Alyia nodded.

"Now, my friend Quinn here is going to come and hold your hand." Quinn was startled as she looked at William, and he indicated that she should come and stand right next to him and take the little girl's hand. She did it, but she trained her eyes on Thomas; she couldn't bring herself to watch the next part. Quinn was grateful that Alyia's rash wasn't nearly as bad on her left hand; there were no blisters or painful sores on this side.

"Okay, Miss Alyia," it was Thomas who spoke now, "would you like to play a little game?"

"Okay." Her voice was weak, but it was clear that the little girl liked Thomas and wanted to please him.

"Good. I want you to try to squeeze Quinn's hand as hard as you can. She'll squeeze back, and we'll see who's stronger. I'll bet you can beat her – she's not very strong." Thomas winked at Quinn, who understood his hidden meaning.

"Ready?"

Alyia nodded.

"All right. One...two...three...SQUEEZE!"

The little girl's hand clasped tightly around Quinn's, and Quinn squeezed back, just firmly enough to keep the child's attention. A few seconds later, Alyia let out a small whimper and lost her grip. Tears appeared in the corners of her eyes, but they didn't fall.

"All done, honey," William said quickly, keeping his voice soft and upbeat, "I'm all done. You did a fantastic job." Quinn looked over to see him taping a clear tube into place. "I had to put a little tube in your arm so that we can give you some special water to help you feel better, and you don't have to worry about throwing it up." His voice was incredibly calm and comforting. As he spoke, he connected the tube to an old-fashioned looking glass IV bottle filled with a clear liquid, and hung it from the pole next to her bed. "It won't hurt anymore, but I need you to leave it alone, so it doesn't come out, okay? I don't want to have to put it back in."

"Wow, Alyia, you're sure strong," Quinn interrupted. "You beat me at that squeezing contest. I think we're going to have to find you a prize."

"That was pretty amazing," Quinn told William after they'd walked out of the clinic.

"That's not the word I would use. I hate doing things that hurt, especially to kids," he answered.

"But he is fantastic at it," Thomas said. "He never misses; not even when he was first learning how. That's the real reason Nathaniel always makes you do it, you know."

William rolled his eyes. "Yeah, because I'm so freaked out every time I have to, that I won't even try for a vein I can't see perfectly."

"It didn't seem to bother you much that night with me," Quinn teased.

"Is that how it looked to you?" William wondered, his eyebrows raised.

Quinn felt an unfamiliar heat fill her chest.

"Wow, it is warm out here tonight," Thomas broke in. "I'll go and get us some more ice pops."

"I am sorry that's the first thing I did to you when you got here," William said, when Thomas had gone back into the house. "That had to have been frightening for you, and I wasn't as kind about it as I should have been."

Quinn shrugged. "I'm the one who hurt myself."

"It was an accident. Really, I'm not always that big of a jerk."

She chuckled. "You kind of were."

"I was," he agreed. "Needles are a little worse here in my world than in yours – most of what we bring over is to study and we replicate it with what we have here so we're not so reliant on your world, but we just don't have the technology you have. I could have warned you and been gentler about it."

"You weren't *that* bad," she said. "I was just really freaked out. I mean, I'd just come through a gate into a different world, and I didn't know where I was … and then I saw *that* thing…"

He smiled. "Yeah. I really could have done a better job there. I'm sorry."

"Thank you. I am fine, you know. You don't have to be so hard on yourself about everything."

"Picked up on that, did you?" Thomas asked, coming back through the screen door holding three ice pops. "Maybe you'll be the first one he actually listens to."

Morning came far too early for Quinn, who was still sleeping soundly when Thomas came to wake her up. She had noticed that she hadn't been plagued by the odd dreams since she'd been in Eirentheos.

Quinn had spent the night on a small, comfortable bed in one of Essie and Jacob's two guest rooms - Nathaniel, Thomas, and William had shared the other one. She could see through the little window that the sun was only beginning to rise. She yawned and stretched, trying to ready herself to face the day.

She felt guilty when she reached the kitchen and found Essie alone and hard at work, cracking eggs into a ceramic bowl while something sizzled in a pan on the stove. "What can I do to help?" she asked. Now that she had seen how hard Essie worked all the time, she felt she should give her as much of a break as she could while they were here.

Essie only shook her head, her eyes twinkling kindly at Quinn. "You'll want to go and take a long shower while you're here, Quinn.

We've managed to get clean, running water going in most of the rural clinics now, but electricity for heating it is another story."

"Yeah, we saved the first shower for you," Thomas said, coming back into the house from the clinic.

"You didn't have to do that," Quinn complained. "You all work harder than I do."

"But we're used to it," Thomas answered easily. "Besides, you're our guest."

"How are things going in there?" Quinn asked, tilting her head toward the door to the clinic.

"Okay. We're getting Braedan ready to go home today, and Alyia's color is better. We're going to try breakfast and some regular juice with her in a little while. Marcus and Olivia seem to be about the same as yesterday - not any worse, anyway."

"That's good, I suppose."

"Yes. Nathaniel and Jacob left about an hour ago to go and get some more supplies from the castle clinic. We'll leave most of what we brought here with Essie and Jacob when we head out to Cloud Valley later."

Quinn's eyes widened, "Wow. They never rest, do they?"

"No. Not ever. Now go enjoy a shower, and then you can come back out and help."

Relief flowed through her when she walked into the clinic after breakfast and saw Alyia sitting up, sipping at a glass of juice, a small plate of eggs on her tray table. She didn't look quite so ashen, and she was feeling well enough that she'd allowed her mother to brush the tangle of blond hair back into a ponytail.

"How are you feeling today, Alyia?" she asked, "better?"

"A little," she answered quietly. "My arm hurts, though."

Quinn studied the rash on the little girl's arm. It certainly didn't look any better today. It was raised and red and Quinn thought some of the blisters were new.

"I'm sorry," Quinn told her. "Maybe we could find something for you to do to help keep your mind off of it. Do you want to play a game or listen to a story?"

"We could read your lessons," her mother offered from the chair next to the bed. "You don't want to fall too far behind in your studies."

Quinn was surprised. Studies in the summer? "That might not be a bad idea. It would keep you busy for a little while."

"No writing for now, though," William admonished, walking over to them. "Maybe just read aloud to her for a bit, and talk about it. Alyia needs plenty of rest. She still has a low fever. She can worry about catching up on her schoolwork when she's well."

"Can't I just read it myself?" Alyia asked.

Her mother chuckled "She doesn't like it when I read aloud to her anymore."

"It never sounds the same as it is in my head when you read it," Alyia complained.

William laughed. "I feel the same way sometimes. I like to read to myself, too."

"I like it sometimes when my father reads, and does the voices. But he went home last night. So can I read it myself?"

"All right, Alyia. That would be fine for a little while. As long as you work on finishing that juice, and then take a nap a little later."

"A nap?" Alyia scrunched her face, "I'm too old for a nap!"

"Nobody is too old for a nap when they're sick. Juice, then nap. All right?"

Alyia sighed, but nodded.

"Yes, Dr. Rose. Thank you." Mrs. Hawken took Alyia's juice glass and set it on the table before she pulled a thin, paper-covered book from a bag.

A little while later, when they had brought Olivia and Marcus out to the porch for some fresh air, Quinn managed to catch William alone for a moment.

"There's school in the summer here?" she asked.

"It's different here than in Bristlecone," he answered. "Most of our villages are far too small, and the people too spread out to make having the kind of school you're used to feasible. Also, our education is far more individualized toward particular interests and talents - though of course there are many things taught to everyone.

"Most schooling of younger children in our kingdom is done at home with the help of parents. The kingdom provides many of the books and materials, and there are teachers of different disciplines living in the villages who can provide support and help in designing programs of study. They distribute books and give advice, or proctor examinations for certain courses.

"Children can work on studies year-round. Certainly, Alyia's health takes precedence over a few days of studying."

"What's all the secrecy over here?" Thomas wondered, walking up next to them.

"Quinn was just asking about our education here," William replied.

"Ah. Learning anything interesting?"

"Everything is interesting here," Quinn answered truthfully.

"Well, I hate to break it up, Will, but Alyia is vomiting again. Essie is in there with her now."

William muttered something under his breath that Quinn didn't catch, but it sounded like an expletive, and nearly ran back into the clinic.

Quinn's heart sank as she watched him go. "How can a rash be making kids so sick?" she wondered.

"I don't know," Thomas sighed. "Maybe the rash is just a symptom of something else. But there's a reason nobody's calling me Dr. Rose."

They were busy all morning tending to the needs of the families in the clinic; Quinn had no idea how Jacob and Essie ever managed it all on their own. Braedan and his father had finally been sent off, and Quinn was in the kitchen slicing vegetables with Essie when Nathaniel and Jacob returned. William cut through the kitchen in his hurry to get outside when he heard them approaching; Quinn and Thomas followed, watching from the porch.

They had taken Jacob's wagon with them this morning, and now it was packed full of supplies.

William was digging through the supplies before they had even gotten everything unloaded.

"What's going on?" Nathaniel asked, observing William.

"Alyia is vomiting again."

"Oh, no."

"Yes, it's ridiculous. What is going on here? What *is* this?" William shoved one box of supplies to the side, and started rooting through the next one.

Nathaniel looked at William for a minute before he reached into a different box and retrieved a small package. He handed it to William without saying anything. William grabbed it out of Nathaniel's hand and flew back into the clinic.

Quinn turned to Thomas, eyes wide.

"I don't think he slept last night," Thomas said. "He must have gone back into the clinic to check on things four times before he ever even came to bed. I don't know when he got up, but I was awake before the sun, and he'd been sitting in Jacob and Essie's office reading and making notes for who knows how long."

Nathaniel walked up on the porch and over to Thomas. "He has until after lunch in that clinic. Then you need to take the horses and get him out of here for a while."

Thomas nodded.

"And Quinn..." Nathaniel paused.

"Can come. Might be good." Thomas finished.

Nathaniel looked at Thomas and Quinn for a long time, and then he nodded. "It will be better than hanging around here, certainly. I'll send a message over to Cloud Valley. We won't be making it there until tomorrow."

Quinn turned to Thomas, confused.

"Go help Essie finish making lunch. We're going for a ride after," was all he said before he walked off the porch.

Nathaniel walked into the clinic holding a tray with two bowls of food and glasses of ice water. He stopped for a minute, just inside the door, and watched William across the room. The boy was sitting on the edge of Alyia's bed, adjusting a wet cloth on her forehead. The child was asleep, though fitfully. Nathaniel noted the small, empty syringe of anti-nausea medication William had been so desperate to get into her IV.

It had been William who, after hours of study, had figured out a safe way to create the medicine here in Eirentheos a few years ago when Queen Charlotte had been plagued with excessive nausea during her pregnancy with Alice. William was so compassionate, so determined ... and so young.

Nathaniel carried the tray over to the small cubicle and set it on the table. "Here, Mrs. Hawken," he said, handing one of the bowls to Alyia's mother, who looked exhausted.

"Thank you, Dr. Rose," she said. She took one bite, and then just held the bowl in her lap.

"William," he held out the second bowl to the boy, but William shook his head.

"I'm not hungry."

"I don't care if you think you are hungry or not. It's time to eat."

William looked up at Nathaniel, his gray eyes hard.

Nathaniel wasn't deterred. "Outside. Now. Bring your lunch with you." He headed toward the door. Once on the porch, he leaned

183

against the railing. William was angry right now, but Nathaniel knew he wouldn't defy him.

A moment later the boy appeared on the porch, bowl in hand. He came to lean on the rail beside Nathaniel, eating in stony silence.

Nathaniel waited until William had placed the empty bowl on the rail next to him.

"You're going to get out of here for the day. Thomas is readying the horses."

"I can't leave, not now."

"Essie, Jacob, and I are well-equipped to handle things here for an afternoon, William."

"But..."

"This is hard on everyone. None of us knows what to do; we are all at a loss. You are one person, Will. You are the most talented healer I have ever come across, even when you were small. You are a true fourth-born prince. But you cannot do everything - even if you had reached adulthood, and had completed all of your training - neither of which you have. You cannot do this to yourself."

"What about Cloud Valley? We need to be getting on the road."

"I have sent them a message. We are not traveling to Cloud Valley until tomorrow. You, Thomas, and Quinn are taking the afternoon off."

"Quinn?"

"Would you leave the girl here, to deal with us alone? Besides, her company might just keep you from brooding all day. Quinn is ..." he shook his head. "It will be good. Go and find your brother."

William picked up his bowl and started toward the door, but Nathaniel stopped him.

"Not one foot inside that building," he said, taking the bowl from William's hand. "That way." He pointed down the porch steps.

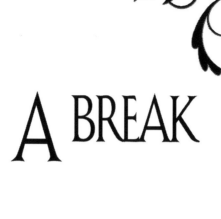

A BREAK

BY THE TIME Quinn had finished helping Essie clean up the kitchen and put together some bundles of food for their ride, Thomas had all three horses saddled and ready to go. Quinn followed him outside after his last trip in for the food.

Thomas was closing up the saddlebags and Quinn was mounting Dusk when William came around the building, stone-faced. Without looking at them, he climbed into Skittles' saddle and rode off.

Quinn looked at Thomas. "Wow. Is he always like that?"

Thomas shrugged. "Give him some time. We'll catch up to him when he's ready."

"How do you know where he's going?"

"I don't."

She frowned, not feeling right about leaving William alone when he was upset like that, but she didn't say anything, realizing that Thomas knew his brother better than she did.

Still, she felt bad for William; she'd seen how he'd poured everything he had into that little girl, and there was an odd pang in her chest as she watched him disappear over the horizon.

Thomas led them away from the clinic and past the outskirts of Mistle Village, down into a wide, wild river valley. The day was warm, but a light breeze blew across the river. After the challenging morning in the clinic, being outside, riding, with no real destination in mind felt wonderful.

Quinn soaked in the sunshine and the breathtaking scenery. Everything here was lush and green, the trees, tall waving grasses, the low bushes along the riverbank. It was so different than home, beautiful in an entirely new way.

When they reached a flat, open area, Thomas turned to her and grinned. "Let's see what they can do."

Quinn smiled back. A moment later, the horses were galloping through the field. They let them run for several miles, racing at times, but never wanting to put too much distance between themselves. It was exhilarating, and Quinn was laughing by the time they finally slowed and walked the horses down to the riverbank.

They sat in the grass and watched Storm and Dusk drink from the edge of the river. Quinn lay back and watched a few puffy clouds drift slowly across the brilliantly blue sky. They didn't speak for a long time, but the silence was comfortable. She felt like she had already known Thomas for a long time.

"Where do you suppose William is?" she finally asked.

"If he doesn't find us soon, we'll find him," Thomas answered.

"How?"

Thomas made a chirping sound, and less than a minute later, he pointed to Sirian, circling in the sky over their heads.

"Oh," Quinn had forgotten about the seekers. "They followed you all the way here?"

"Always."

"That's amazing." Quinn was thoughtful as she watched them, her thoughts drifting again to William, to how hard he'd worked last night, to how upset he'd been when they'd left the clinic.

A soft breeze blew across her forehead, refreshing in the heat, even if her thoughts were turbulent.

"This is really hard on William, isn't it?"

"Yes. He feels so responsible for everything, all the time. It's too much sometimes."

She thought about that. It was a lot of responsibility for a seventeen-year-old boy. It hadn't taken Quinn very long in this world to realize that, even if William and Thomas had lived more days than she had, and even if they'd had more experiences and more time to learn things, they were still teenagers, with the same emotions and difficulties navigating the transition to adulthood as she and her friends faced at home. "Is he okay, do you think?"

"He will be."

Quinn watched as Sirian completed several circles overhead, and then swooped down, coming to a landing a few feet from Thomas. He strutted over to Thomas, pecking gently at his hand.

Thomas chuckled. "All right already! I'll get something for you." He reached into the saddlebag he had laid a few feet away, and pulled out a slice of meat. He pulled off pieces, feeding them to Sirian one at a time. Sirian let out a squawk of approval.

"How are you doing?" Thomas asked Quinn. "Is all of this getting to you yet?"

Quinn considered the question. "I don't know how much I've even thought about it," she answered honestly. "This is all so strange and different, I'm not sure I even believe it's actually happening. It's like a dream – I'm going to wake up at any moment, and none of it will have really happened."

Thomas laughed, but then nodded. "I guess I can understand that. In a way, that's somewhat true for you. You'll go home in a few days, and it will be as if you never left. You'll go back to your life."

She was quiet as she thought about that, not sure what was causing the lump that had appeared in her throat. She stared at Sirian, still accepting small strips of meat from Thomas, and then looked over at

Dusk and Storm, who had moved up the riverbank a little way and were contentedly grazing in the grass.

She did miss home, when she thought about it, but she had worked hard to keep her mind away from Annie and Owen, her mom... And Zander – she couldn't bring herself to think about Zander at all.

It hadn't been quite as hard as she would have expected, though, being away from them for this long. Maybe because she had been so busy – there was always so much going on here. She'd fallen into bed utterly exhausted every night. Maybe even more so because this didn't feel real. It still felt like a dream.

Besides, if what Thomas had told her was true, she wasn't missing anything at home, except spending a Saturday alone in her house. But the whole idea that she could just "go back to her life" as if nothing had happened, nothing had changed – she wasn't sure she could really do that.

What was it going to be like with William at school, now that she knew his secret, now that – she realized – he would be the only one who knew hers. She would never be able to tell anyone at home about this.

She sighed. "Probably better if I don't think about it too much," she finally said.

Just then, Aelwyn joined them, swooping gracefully from the sky and snatching the last scrap of meat from Thomas' hand. Sirian took three steps backward and bowed his head, which made them laugh.

"Who's in charge here?" Thomas chortled, as they watched Aelwyn swallow the treat before strutting back toward Sirian.

A minute later, they heard the sound of hooves on the grass, and they looked up to see William ride up and dismount Skittles. They looked on as he unsaddled her and let her join the others.

Nobody said anything as William walked up to their little spot and sat down beside Thomas.

William looked at both of them; Quinn couldn't read the expression in his eyes. Was he still mad – or a little sheepish?

"Gorgeous day," he finally said, breaking the tense silence. "A little warm, though."

Quinn heard Thomas' quiet sigh of relief. "Yes it is." He answered. "Want to go for a swim?"

"Sure." William was actually smiling.

"What? In the river?" Quinn was surprised.

"Where else?" Thomas asked.

"Is it … safe?"

"Definitely… it's wide here, and the current's not strong at all."

It was William who caught her concern. "Water's safe here, Quinn. No pollution in our world. You could drink right out of it. Warmer than Colorado, too."

She looked down at the brown short-sleeved shirt and woven pants she was wearing. "I don't have a swimming suit."

Thomas shrugged. "Wear your clothes. It's warm enough today, you'll dry. There's some extra stuff packed, anyway."

She still wasn't sure. "I'll think about it," she said.

"Suit yourself." Thomas stood and pulled off his shirt, then waded into the river. William followed him.

Quinn stayed on the shore and enjoyed the sunshine as the brothers walked out almost to the middle of the river, into water up to their waists. Thomas, always the bolder of the two, was the first to disappear under the surface and bob up a second later, shaking his head and splattering William.

William responded by using his hands to send a huge wave of water rolling toward Thomas, who failed to move to the side quickly enough. Within seconds, it degenerated into a full-blown water fight, both boys laughing and splashing water. Quinn found herself laughing as well.

While Thomas was the more muscular of the two, now that he was shirtless, Quinn could see that William was not at all as lanky as she'd thought. It was clear that he, too, put in plenty of physical work during his stays in Eirentheos. She felt herself blush when she realized she was staring.

The afternoon was growing hotter. The clear water in the river looked more and more inviting as the boys' friendly war calmed, and they spent time swimming up and down a short, wide span. Finally, she decided she would at least wade in. She took off her shoes and socks, and rolled up her pants legs as far as she could.

Even with only her toes in the river, the water felt incredible. William was right; it was much warmer than the mountain river at home, but it was still cool enough to be refreshing. The riverbed was smooth sand under her feet. She'd never seen such clear water; she could see every grain of sand below her, every rock a little further out where the water was deeper.

The afternoon sun sparkled off the small waves created by the gentle current. Before she realized what she was doing, she was in water up past her knees, and the bottoms of her pants legs were wet. Suddenly, a giant splash completely soaked the front of her.

"Th..." she started to yell, but stopped after she wiped her eyes, surprised to see William standing right in front of her, laughing. "Hey!" she shouted instead.

William laughed. "You were going to get wet anyway," he teased. "This is too nice to resist."

He was right, she knew. So she responded by aiming a giant splash at his face, which he neatly avoided by ducking under the water and swimming away, leaving her with no choice but to follow.

An hour later, the three of them climbed back on to the riverbank, exhausted and dripping. Quinn's cheeks hurt from smiling. Thomas handed her a blanket to wrap herself in, though he and William just went and lay in the grass.

She followed them, and the boys cleared a space for her between them. She sat for a moment, watching them.

"What are the chains for?" she wondered. Both boys wore identical silver chains around their necks, with some kind of silver pendants hanging from them, very visible now against their bare chests, though she had never noticed them when they were fully dressed. She supposed the chains were long enough that they'd stay hidden underneath their shirts.

Neither boy opened his eyes. "They symbolize our gifts," Thomas answered.

"What?"

"You were there at Hannah's Naming Ceremony. When a child of the royal bloodline is named, he or she also receives a gift. The pendants we wear symbolize our gifts. Most people wear them all the time. Hannah received her pendant that day. We have to change the chains every once in a while, of course." Thomas sat up now, leaning toward Quinn and holding out his pendant so she could see.

The pendant was a small silver circle, engraved on one side with the same design she'd seen on the silver bars the princes had worn across their capes and on their hats that night at the dinner party. On the other side was a different design, a delicate heart with an intricate pattern in the middle.

Quinn frowned. "Your gift is love?"

William laughed, sitting up to join them. "A heart isn't a symbol for love here. Thomas' gift is grace, or as we like to tease, 'charm'."

Thomas grinned widely, clearly affecting his most charming smile. Quinn rolled her eyes. "What's your gift, William?"

"Can't you guess?"

Quinn thought she probably could, but she was afraid to embarrass herself with the wrong answer, so instead she just raised her eyebrows.

"Healing," he finally answered, holding out his pendant which featured some kind of flower she didn't recognize.

"It suits you," she said. "So who gets to choose who gets what gift?"

Thomas smiled at her convoluted question. "Nobody chooses. The traditional gifts are given in the order that you're born. First-born has the gift of leadership, second-born discernment, third, hospitality ... Will is the fourth child, and I'm the fifth."

"Oh... traditional gifts?"

"Yes," William finished. "There are twelve 'traditional' gifts that have been passed down through the generations. Hannah is the thirteenth child in our family, so her gift is unique."

"That's ... wow. So, what happens if there aren't twelve children in the royal family?"

"Nothing happens; the family just doesn't have a child with that gift." Thomas lay back down lazily, closing his eyes against the bright sun. "It's beautiful out here."

Though her mind was swimming with questions, Quinn lay down with them.

They lay there for a long time, staring into the blue sky, the grasses waving lazily around them. Quinn could hear the twittering of birds in the nearby trees, the buzzing of insects in the grass, and Thomas and William breathing on either side of her. She felt worn out ... and wonderful. It felt like they could have stayed there forever, right up until they were interrupted by another sound – Thomas' stomach growling.

Quinn giggled, and the three of them sat up slowly.

"I suppose it is time to put together something to eat," William said.

"For sure," Thomas answered, grinning. "Quinn, do you want me to get you something to change into?"

Quinn stood and nodded; she really didn't want to stay in her wet clothes until they got back to the clinic.

Thomas rummaged through one of the saddlebags and pulled out a shirt and a pair of long shorts. Quinn recognized them from the bag Mia had packed for her. She looked at Thomas quizzically.

He shrugged. "I like to be prepared. You never know when you're going to need extra stuff out here."

"I could have helped you pack, you know."

"You were busy with lunch. This is what I do. It's why they bring me."

Quinn sighed, slightly embarrassed at the idea of Thomas going through her bag. She couldn't fault his intentions, though. "Um, where should I change?" she asked, looking around.

"What about over there?" William broke in, pointing to a stand of trees about fifty feet down the riverbank from them. "That's probably about as good as you're going to get. Want me to walk you down?"

Quinn thought about trying to change in the trees with William standing close by, and a wave of heat washed over her face. "Uh, that's okay. I think I can handle it."

It was shady and cool in the little cluster of trees. Through the leaves, Quinn could see the flowing water of the river several feet away. Getting chilly, she dressed quickly, blushing again when she discovered dry underclothes folded neatly inside the shirt. When she was dry and comfortable, she decided to take a few minutes to explore and enjoy the privacy.

She didn't recognize any of the trees or plants here. They were certainly nothing like the ones in Colorado, most of which she'd known on sight for years. She was used to forest floors that were covered in pine needles, rocks, and pieces of bark, but here there was lush vegetation underneath her feet. Green grasses and leafy plants were everywhere, even in this dark, sheltered area.

There were flowers, too, in brilliant colors popping out of nearly every shrub. Quinn was fascinated by the deep purple and red blooms of one of the bushes, growing right at the base of a tree. The leaf-covered stems of the bush were beautiful as well, a very dark, glossy color that was almost black.

She couldn't resist; the flowers were so amazing, and it had been such a fun day - a couple of blossoms would make a nice souvenir if she took them back and dried them. Maybe one or two would make a nice little secret gift for Annie. Quinn had already put a few rocks in her bag for Owen, who liked to collect unusual stones.

She gently pulled off two red and two purple flowers, careful not to damage the rest of the plant, and carried them out of the grove, blinking as she stepped back into the bright sunlight.

When she got back over near William and Thomas, she discovered that they'd both changed, as well. They'd laid out their clothes in the sun to dry, so she did the same with hers, though she hid her bra and underwear underneath the wet shirt. She set the flowers next to her clothes, and walked over to where the boys were sitting near the river.

"Hungry?" Thomas asked, holding out a sandwich.

"I'm starving, thanks," Quinn accepted the sandwich and bit into it without even looking. She turned to Thomas in surprise. "Peanut butter and jelly?"

William laughed. "Not exactly, but the closest thing we have here. Nathaniel's the one who brought back that idea years and years ago. It's caught on."

"It's perfect for today," Quinn smiled. "It would be even better if we had milk."

"You'll have to make do with fresh water from the river today." Thomas told her.

She was in the middle of her second sandwich when she noticed William staring at her leg.

"What?" she asked him.

"I was just thinking that it's probably about time for those stitches to come out. It's been over a week, and your leg looks like it's healing very well."

Her eyes widened. "They don't just dissolve on their own or something?"

William smiled. "We don't use that kind for a cut on your leg. Those ones need taken out – it won't hurt," he added quickly.

"Are you sure?" she asked suspiciously.

William looked straight at her, a serious, sympathetic expression in his gray eyes that made her heart skip a beat. "Do you think I would tell you that if it wasn't true?"

"Probably not," she admitted quietly, thinking of the gentle way he'd treated little Alyia in the clinic.

And it didn't. Quinn felt a few odd, tugging sensations as William gently pulled out the stitches, but it wasn't painful at all. When he was finished, he applied some kind of oily salve from a tiny jar.

"You'll need to keep putting this on for a few days," he told her. "It will keep you from getting a scar."

"Thanks."

"No problem." The smile he gave her was nothing that she would have ever expected from William Rose. It felt like the more she knew about him, the less she understood.

"Hey, Quinn! Will! Come look at this!" Thomas was several yards up the river, crouched down by the bank.

William and Quinn hurried over, and Thomas indicated that they should kneel down with him. Right in the side of the riverbank there was a little hole, and inside the hole were three tiny, fuzzy animals. They were obviously newly-born; their eyes were still closed. They slept, huddled together in a tiny, quivering ball.

"What are they?" Quinn breathed.

"They're called river boles," William answered quietly. "They're kind of similar to otters."

"Wow." Quinn was fascinated. "Where's the mother?"

"I'm sure she's swimming somewhere nearby, looking for food," Thomas replied. "She probably won't approach while we're standing here. She won't want to call attention to the nest."

They watched the sleeping babies for a few more minutes, before heading back to their picnicking site.

"We should probably be headed back to the village soon," William said.

"Are you really ready?" Thomas asked him.

"Yes. The break was nice, but I need to get back."

Thomas was starting to get the saddlebags back on the horses when Quinn heard him call her name in a strange, strained-sounding voice. William followed her as she walked over.

"Yeah, Thomas?"

"Where did you get these?" He was pointing to the purple and red flowers, lying next to Quinn's drying clothes.

"Um, over in that grove of trees, when I was changing," she answered, not understanding. Was it illegal to pick flowers here?

"Quinn, those are shadeweed flowers," William told her, a serious tone in his voice.

Quinn frowned. The name sounded familiar, but she couldn't place it...

"They're very poisonous," William said. "Let me see your hands."

The tone in his voice set her heart beating faster, she held her hands out to him, suddenly remembering the conversation about shadeweed from yesterday. She sighed; of course she would pick flowers from the one poisonous plant. "I ... didn't know," she stammered.

"I know," William told her, examining both sides of her hands and wrists carefully, though he didn't touch them.

"It's my fault," Thomas' expression was mortified. "I should have shown you..."

"Both of us are at fault, Thomas. I'm sorry, Quinn. But you look okay, no signs of a rash, at least yet. It's usually not dangerous the first few times you're exposed. Just keep an eye on it okay? Let me know right away if your hands get itchy or you see anything that looks like a rash. And don't touch flowers like that again."

Quinn nodded. Although she knew it was just her imagination, an overreaction to William's warning, her hands felt just a little tingly.

Thomas handed her a small glass bottle he had pulled out of one of the saddle bags. "This is soap. Go and wash your hands and arms really well in the river. Wash the soap bottle, too."

She blinked. "It's that dangerous?"

William nodded. "The nectar from the flowers and the sap from the branches both dry into a soft, powdery substance that retains the ability to poison for months, sometimes longer if it's in a closed space. You just want to make sure you don't get it on anything else where it might stay. You should take a shower and change clothes again when we get back."

"He's overreacting a little," Thomas said, "but still, we'd rather be safe."

William followed her down to the river, washing his hands and arms too, worried that he might have gotten some on him while he was removing her stitches.

"Wow," Quinn said, watching him scrub. The whole thing was making her stomach a little wobbly.

"It's not actually that easy to pass from person to person. The oils in your skin dissolve the powder and activate the toxin. Only the powder can be transferred. I just think it's better not to take chances."

Quinn couldn't argue with that.

"You should probably wash your legs, and your face and neck, too," he added. "People usually touch those places with their hands without thinking about it."

By the time they had finally finished, Thomas, ever efficient, had the horses completely loaded and ready to go.

SHADEWEED

THE SUN WAS LOW in the sky as the horses walked into the small paddock next to Mistle Village clinic. Thomas offered to take care of the animals so that William could get inside right away. Although they kept claiming that there was really nothing to worry about, both boys were insistent that Quinn's hands and arms be examined again, as well.

Quinn was glad to see Alyia sitting propped up on pillows, holding a little cup with the stick of an ice pop poking up, but otherwise the little girl didn't look too much better. The rash had now spread all over her left arm, too, and there was a painful-looking blister on her right cheek. Essie was sitting with her, and she waved William away.

Marcus and Olivia were both sitting on Marcus' bed, giggling over ice pops of their own, which was a happy sight to everyone. Nathaniel and Jacob were in the kitchen, cleaning up from dinner.

Once he was reassured that things were calm, William took Quinn back to a little treatment room, where he could look at her hands underneath a lighted magnifying glass. "I'm really just being paranoid," he said. "Shadeweed is not that dangerous with minimal exposure. The main concern is that the effects are cumulative. You'd be more at risk if you touched it again sometime and worse still if it happened again. Still, you need to keep an eye out for any kind of a rash in the next few days."

Yeah, she thought, *he's so unconcerned he's repeating himself.* "How long does it take for the rash to show up?" she wondered.

"It takes anywhere from about five minutes to several days, depending on the person."

"Of course, the last time we used a plant from our world on you, look what happened," Thomas interjected. "If you were going to get shadeweed poisoning, you'd probably already be unconscious."

William chortled, but Quinn shot Thomas a dirty look. "It just causes a rash, right? Like poison ivy?" She had never been inclined to touch poison ivy on purpose, but she'd never been afraid of it, the way she already was of this plant the boys were obsessing over.

"No. The rash is not the biggest issue. The toxins from the plant can make people extremely sick. With several exposures and improper treatment, it causes terrible poisoning. It can even be fatal. Not that a rash is always something to take lightly," he added, nodding his head toward the clinic door.

Quinn nodded. The rashes that some of these children had were serious indeed. "You don't think their rashes are from shadeweed, do you?"

William turned off the lamp and looked back at Quinn. "No, it's impossible that those children could be sick from shadeweed. You saw it today; it's a very recognizable plant. Even toddlers are taught to stay far away from it. And to get as sick as they are would require more than just accidentally getting into it. Besides, potential shadeweed exposure is one of the first things we ask about when someone comes in with a rash."

"Right," Thomas added. "Shadeweed poisoning is really rare. There isn't any way that this many kids could be sick with it at the same time."

She considered that. What they were saying made sense, but still... "What would you do if it *was* shadeweed poisoning?" she asked.

William sighed. "We would treat the rash the same way we're treating the children's rashes now. The poisoning has a separate treatment."

"Have you treated any of the children for possible poisoning?"

"No, we haven't."

"What if you tried that? What would it hurt?" she wondered.

"The medication we use for treating the poisoning has risks of its own," William told her. "For very mild cases, there is an oral medication. It's mostly safe, but it can also make people feel awful for a few days, especially if several doses are needed. There are also greater risks with more doses."

"It tastes completely horrendous, too. It's a thick, brown, disgusting liquid," Thomas told her. "You pretty much have to hold a kid down and force them to take a second or third dose, after that first one."

She looked at him in surprise. "Have you taken it?"

Thomas nodded. "A lot of people have."

"We give the medication the first time someone gets the mildest rash, as a precaution - I'd be giving it to you if I saw any signs of it on your skin." William explained.

"And that experience keeps even the most adventurous kids from trying it again." Thomas shuddered at the memory.

"I take it you were one of those adventurous kids?" Quinn teased.

"Would you expect anything else?" Thomas grinned back. "But even I only did that once. Nathaniel had to use one of those syringe-thingies to shove the second dose in the back of my throat. I was in the clinic throwing up the whole next day."

Quinn felt a sudden urge to hide her hands behind her back, afraid a rash might decide to appear.

"In any case," William continued, "the liquid is only effective in very early and very mild cases, but for a long time it was all we had. It

201

was actually Nathaniel who developed a stronger, and much more effective intravenous form."

"So can't you just use that one?"

"It's fairly painful - it stings," William's eyes were down, and he was pulling apart a piece of scrap paper that had been on the desk, "and the side effects can be pretty terrible. It clears the toxins from the body, but also depletes several important nutrients. People are often hospitalized for a week or more after the poisoning clears. It can only be used for so long, as well. There is a metal compound in the medication that can build up in the body if too much is used, or for too long. It's serious stuff."

"Basically, there's no way we use the medication unless we're absolutely positive that it's shadeweed poisoning," Thomas summarized.

"Does shadeweed poisoning ever go away without the medicine?" Quinn wondered.

"Yes. The acute symptoms can go away on their own if the patients are well-rested and hydrated, although they don't always. The rash will also usually heal with topical treatment. The big problem is that the body doesn't always completely clear the toxin. Small amounts of it can stay and then cause problems later, sometimes within several weeks, sometimes even months or years later. It can attack the central nervous system, causing blindness, deafness, even paralysis." William's eyes were tired.

Quinn was well aware that William knew much more about this than she ever would. She was sure he was right. But she couldn't stop herself. "What is the difference between shadeweed poisoning and what those children have?" she pressed.

William's eyes flashed annoyance, and he walked out of the room. Quinn gulped; she'd gone too far. "I didn't mean..." she started saying to Thomas, but then William came back in. He set a thick, red book on the desk between them. He flipped rapidly through the pages until he found the one he was looking for.

Quinn and Thomas sat in silence for several minutes as William read. Finally, he looked up. "Nothing," he said. "There is no difference between the symptoms that those children have, and the symptoms of shadeweed poisoning - except maybe that none of them are bad enough yet that their eyes have turned yellow." He folded his arms over the book, and laid his head on his hands. "You'd better go get the others, Thomas."

Nathaniel, Jacob, and Essie were all just as shocked and upset at the idea as William was.

"It's not even possible!" Essie said, wringing her hands. "There is no way all of these children could have shadeweed poisoning. All of their parents told us that their children hadn't been playing in the woods before the rashes appeared."

"It's too risky to treat them for shadeweed if that's not what it is," Jacob was adamant.

"Riskier than not treating them if it is?" Nathaniel asked quietly.

Quinn was awake before the sun the next morning. Nathaniel had ordered her, Thomas, and William to bed early the night before. She was surprised when she reached the clinic and found only Thomas in there. He sat in a chair in the middle of the room, reading a book. When he saw Quinn, he held a finger to his lips, and pointed over at Alyia's cubicle.

She tip-toed over. Alyia and her mother were both curled up, asleep in the small bed. The difference in the child was obvious; the awful blister on her cheek had faded to a purple-red blotch, and the raised red sores over her face and arm had blended into the more tolerable-looking rash. The child slept peacefully, her breathing even. She was clearly not feverish.

Quinn looked at Thomas in surprise. He nodded and rose, indicating that she follow him into the kitchen.

"So, it looks like you were right," he said quietly, once the door had closed behind them.

"I wasn't trying to…"

"It isn't something to apologize for, Quinn. It's a wonderful thing to worry about other people's feelings, but not at the expense of doing what you think is right. You were right."

Quinn felt her cheeks turning pink. "Is everyone else still asleep?" she asked, changing the subject.

"Yeah. Will was completely crashed when I came out here. I'm glad; he needed it. He almost never sleeps."

She nodded; she'd noticed that. Every morning for the whole time she had been here, William had already been awake when she'd gotten out of bed. "How long have you been up?"

"I don't know, a couple of hours, maybe? Jacob was in the clinic when I woke up, worrying over Alyia. I sent him to bed. Told him I'd wake him up if he was needed."

She looked out the kitchen window. A thin strip of pink was beginning to appear right at the horizon. "A couple of hours? Do you ever sleep, either?"

"Sure." He shrugged. "I have plenty of time for sleeping in when Will and Nathaniel are gone."

She studied him for a moment.

"You miss them when they're away, don't you?"

Thomas paused, "Do you have any brothers or sisters, Quinn?"

"Yes. I have one of each. Owen and Annie."

"Is one of them your best friend?"

"Not exactly. They're both a lot younger than I am. But I love them both very much … And yes, I miss them." Looking in Thomas' clear gray eyes, it was obvious how much he loved his brother. She swallowed hard, thinking about what it must be like for him when William was gone for long stretches of time. A single school week for William in Bristlecone meant his missing fifty days at home.

What would it be like to be away from Annie and Owen for that long?

He squeezed her shoulder. "Want to help me get breakfast started?"

William must have really been exhausted; everyone had already eaten breakfast when he finally walked into the clinic. He went immediately over to Alyia, who was sitting up and nibbling at some toast. Quinn was just returning with a fresh cup of tea for Mrs. Hawken as Nathaniel followed him over.

"I just gave her the second dose a little while ago," he told William quietly. "I followed it with a dose of your anti-nausea med; that seems to be helping."

William nodded; his eyes were still tired. He stepped out of the Hawkens' earshot to speak with Nathaniel more. Quinn couldn't resist walking close enough to hear.

"Have you started the other children on the oral meds?"

Nathaniel shook his head. "We wanted to get breakfast in them first, and talk to their parents. Jacob is pulling together all the records of children who have been seen for this so far. They're all going to need to be treated to make sure the toxin is cleared."

William nodded, staring over at Alyia. "She's so little. Probably need to start a second line. Need to keep her hydrated and replace the nutrients." It was clear from the tone in his voice that he did not intend to do it himself.

Quinn watched William as he walked away from Nathaniel. His face was hard, unreadable. He disappeared into the small supply closet and re-emerged a few minutes later with a bulging leather bag, which he carried outside. Quinn looked at Nathaniel quizzically.

Nathaniel only shook his head. "Leave him be. We'll finish doing what we can here this morning, and we'll follow William to Cloud Village before lunch."

Quinn frowned. "Follow him?"

"Yes. I'm certain that's where he'll be headed in the next few minutes."

TWO KINGDOMS

THE MORNING HAD PASSED by in a busy blur. There was so much to do in the clinic. By the time she found herself on horseback again, Quinn was starting to wonder what exactly it was she did with all of her time in Bristlecone.

They rode for about an hour before Thomas suggested they stop for lunch. Nathaniel found a shady spot near a stream where they could lay out a blanket and unwrap the neat little packages that Quinn and Essie had put together that morning.

"You doing okay, Quinn?" Nathaniel asked, once they were sitting down.

"Yes." Although she could tell there was more to his question than just the trail ride, she decided to avoid the bigger question for now, and she smiled. "I'm getting used to being on horseback all the time again."

Nathaniel smiled back. "I'm glad that hasn't been an additional hardship on you." He paused for a moment, thoughtful, "You've been a lot of help to us here the past couple of days. Thank you."

She shrugged. "What else is there to do?"

Nathaniel frowned. "That's a fair question, I suppose. This whole situation has to be pretty strange for you."

"It is. It's been interesting, though. I never imagined that something like this was going to happen when I followed William."

"No, I'm sure you didn't. Still, you didn't freak out. You just jumped right in and became part of things."

"You're one of us now." Thomas smiled at her. "Our mystery solver."

"I didn't solve the mystery," she said. "We know what the problem is now, but we still don't have any idea how all these kids are getting shadeweed poisoning." Quinn reached across the blanket for an apple, and as she did so, the short sleeve of her shirt pulled up slightly.

Nathaniel almost choked on his sandwich. "Is that what Tolliver did to you?"

Quinn was confused for a moment, but then she remembered the deep bruise on her arm that was beginning to turn fascinating shades of green.

"Yes," Thomas answered darkly, before she could form the words.

"That s..." Nathaniel looked at Quinn, and didn't finish whatever word he'd been going to utter. "I'd like to kill him with my bare hands."

Thomas looked stunned. "I've never heard you say something like that, Nathaniel."

Nathaniel looked sheepish, but not sorry.

"Not that I blame you – I wouldn't mind serving his tongue for dinner myself."

Quinn burst out giggling. Thomas and Nathaniel both stared at her. "Sorry – I know it's not funny," she choked out between spasms, "it's just..." but before she could finish her sentence, they were all laughing.

"I wonder if he's finally left and gone to crawl back under the rock he came from," Thomas said, once they had all calmed back down.

Nathaniel shook his head. "He was still at the castle yesterday when we went back for supplies. I spoke with your father briefly. The talks about the Philotheum crown are not going well."

"He has to know we'd never allow it. And his own people – he'd have a rebellion on his hands." There was fury underneath Thomas' words.

"Never allow what?" Quinn asked.

"We would never allow someone who is not a first-born of the royal bloodline to wear the crown of Philotheum," Thomas answered.

"Can you stop him?"

"We have to," Thomas said.

She looked over at Nathaniel, but he didn't say anything. His expression was dark, but there was something more underneath it. Quinn couldn't describe what it was, but it made her shiver.

"Time to get the horses ready again," Nathaniel said.

The ride to Cloud Valley was long, and some parts of the trail were challenging.

"How do you get wagons back in here?" Quinn wondered at one particularly rocky pass.

"We don't," Nathaniel answered. "Whatever supplies can be carried in on horseback is all we can get in."

"Wow. Can't you build roads?"

Nathaniel smiled. "We could. You know that there are easy trails to access Mistle Village. However, most of the people of Cloud Valley prefer to live as they do, quiet and secluded."

"Why?"

"Lots of reasons, I suppose. Do you ever wish that I-70 ran right through Bristlecone?"

She wrinkled her nose. "No, not really."

"And why not?" Nathaniel raised an eyebrow pointedly.

"There would be so much more traffic, more people in and out all the time, tourists. Bristlecone would turn into another Vail or Winter Park."

"True. But there would also be more stores, restaurants, things to do."

Quinn thought about that for several minutes as they rode. "Some of those things would be nice in a way, but I like Bristlecone the way it is."

Nathaniel only raised his eyebrows and smiled.

About twenty minutes later, as they reached the end of the narrow, rocky pass between two hills, Quinn got her first glimpse of why the people of Cloud Valley might feel so protective of their seclusion.

It was one of the most beautiful places she had ever seen. Nestled inside a nearly perfect circle of low, rolling hills, sat the tiny village of Cloud Valley. In the center of the valley was a sparkling, clear lake. All around the lake, huddled in groves of tall trees, were the small houses and other buildings that made up the community.

As they rode down the hill, closer to the town, Quinn could see the minute outlines of a number of people, mostly children, jumping and splashing in a shallow end of the pristine lake. As the name implied, puffy white clouds drifted low in the sky over the valley, casting cooling shadows on the ground as they passed.

"Amazing," Quinn breathed.

"It is gorgeous here," Thomas agreed.

The Cloud Valley clinic was built in the same style as Jacob and Essie's place in Mistle Village, only rather than the neat white everything was painted there; this clinic had been left its natural rich red wood.

As they approached, Quinn could see Skittles among the horses grazing in the small, fenced field to the side of the clinic. Thomas, Quinn, and Nathaniel were dismounting their own horses in the yard when a young man stepped out onto the clinic porch, and then walked purposefully toward Nathaniel.

"Nathaniel! So good to see you! Thank you so much for coming." The two men hugged.

"It's wonderful to see you too, Eli."

"Welcome back, Thomas. And this must be the lovely Quinn? William told me you'd be coming."

Quinn blushed and nodded.

"Yes, Eli, this is Quinn. Quinn, this is Eli, the doctor here in Cloud Valley."

"Nice to meet you."

"Lovely to meet you, too. Will you all come inside for some tea?"

"I'll be along in a few minutes," Thomas answered, "after I tend to the horses."

Quinn followed Nathaniel and Eli around the back of the clinic, and up into his living quarters.

"So what is the situation here, Eli?" Nathaniel asked when they were sitting at the table with glasses of sun-brewed tea.

Eli sighed. "We had been pretty calm here for a few days. One little girl, Katie Cook, I've been treating for a few days, but she's been recovering well. Actually had a little while there where my biggest worry was a sprained ankle. Then, night before last, Cammie Winthrop came in with her little boy, David. Do you remember Cammie?"

Nathaniel's face looked stricken as he nodded.

"Her husband was killed in a lightning storm last year - a tree fell on him," Eli explained, for Quinn's benefit. "David is terribly sick - he hid the rash from his mother for several days, didn't want her to worry about him. He has a high fever that we just can't get down. Are you really thinking this is shadeweed?"

"The symptoms all match, and the shadeweed remedy seems to be working on the children in Mistle Village," Nathaniel sounded like he was working to keep his voice steady.

"But how could it be?" Eli's brow was furrowed. "We haven't even had any reports of anyone finding shadeweed plants in the valley lately."

"We don't know," Thomas said, entering quietly through the screen door. "It doesn't make any sense."

"Could it be something else? Something that just acts like shadeweed poisoning?" Eli's voice was desperate.

"Even if it is, so far the treatment appears to be working. I think we need to treat all of the children like its shadeweed."

"You know my concerns about it, Nathaniel."

Nathaniel studied Eli's face for a moment. "Yes, I do. But I don't think we can take the chance of not treating it."

Quinn looked at Thomas, confused, but Thomas only shrugged.

Nathaniel caught their exchange and turned to them. "About five years ago, we had a death from the shadeweed treatment."

Across the table, Eli took a deep breath.

Nathaniel's voice was sympathetic as he spoke. "Wyatt was older, Eli. He had other health problems, and he was already weak from the shadeweed poisoning itself. You didn't have all of the supplies you needed that would have helped him, either."

"I know. It just frightens me. William came in here a couple of hours ago, wanting to start the treatment immediately. He explained everything, and while I can't disagree … I still told him I wanted to wait until I'd talked to you."

Nathaniel's voice was soft. "I feel the same way William does. We've already lost a child to this, Eli. We cannot afford to not try treating it this way."

"What am I supposed to tell that boy's mother?" The pain in Eli's eyes was clear.

"Tell her he'll get better."

Eli closed his eyes and rubbed his temples with his fingertips. After a moment, he nodded and stood.

Nathaniel looked at Thomas and Quinn. "Thomas, I think it might be better if we didn't have so many people in the clinic right now.

Perhaps you and Quinn could brush down the horses, and then maybe think about dinner?"

"Of course," Thomas answered. "Quinn?

She nodded, and followed him outside.

Thomas and Quinn had barely begun brushing out Storm and Dusk when she heard the clinic door open and shut and there were sounds up on the porch. She and Thomas turned at the same time to see the two small children who had appeared near the railing. The little girl looked maybe five or six cycles; the boy was probably less than two. Quinn walked over to them; the height of the porch put the little girl's head level with hers.

"Hello," she said through the railing. "I'm Quinn. What's your name?"

"I'm Tallie," the child answered, pushing strands of long, brown hair out of her face.

"It's nice to meet you, Tallie. And who is this?" Quinn asked, looking at the little boy.

"That's Caleb. He's my little brother. He's just a baby."

"Bay-bee!" Caleb repeated, looking delighted and proud of himself.

Quinn smiled, "And you're a big girl?" she guessed.

"Yes." Tallie grinned widely at her.

"What are you two doing out here?" Thomas asked, climbing on to the first porch step.

"My mom said we needed to go outside. She said stay on the porch and watch Caleb. My big brother is sick in there." Tallie pointed at the door to the clinic.

At that moment, Nathaniel opened the screen door and poked his head out. He gave Thomas a pleading look.

"Don't worry," Thomas told him. "We've got them."

"Thank you," Nathaniel said, and he ducked back inside, closing the solid wooden door as well.

"Hey you two," Thomas said, "want to go see the horses?"

"Yes!" Tallie shouted. "Can we ride them?"

"Horsie?" Caleb asked.

"We'll see," Thomas told her, taking Tallie by the hand, and leading her over to the corral.

Quinn reached for Caleb. At first, he wasn't too certain about allowing her to pick him up, but once she said, "Want to go see Tallie and the horsies?" he allowed her to take him.

Caring for Tallie and Caleb became Thomas and Quinn's full-time task, so that their mother could concentrate on David. Tallie did talk Thomas into taking her on a horseback ride, while Quinn, too nervous to take wiggly little Caleb on a horse, instead enlisted the toddler's help in harvesting some of the ready vegetables from the garden. Caleb ate more of the sweet peas than he managed to get inside the little bucket Quinn gave him, but it kept him busy and entertained.

They didn't see much of Nathaniel or Eli all day, and the only time Quinn saw William was for a few brief moments when she carried in bowls of stew for him and for David's mother.

William sat right next to David's bed closely monitoring the child, who looked very ill. He did look up at Quinn when she handed him the food, mumbling a quiet, "Thank you."

David's mother looked exhausted and concerned. "How are Tallie and Caleb?" she asked Quinn.

"They're fine," Quinn reassured her.

"Thank you so much for looking after them … they're not too much trouble, are they?"

"They're no trouble at all, really Mrs. Winthrop."

"Please call me Cammie. I just … I don't want them to see David like this. I don't know what to do."

Quinn's heart went out to the young woman, who was dealing with this alone. She couldn't imagine how difficult it must be. "Thomas and I don't mind caring for them at all; please don't worry about them right now."

Nathaniel walked across the room and joined them. "Your home is quite close by, isn't it Cammie?"

"Yes, Dr. Rose."

"Perhaps Quinn and Thomas could take Tallie and Caleb back to your house tonight? Let them have some time at home, sleep in their own beds, give you a chance to focus on David?"

Cammie looked over at Quinn, tears in the corners of her eyes. "Would you really be willing to do something like that?"

"Of course," Quinn answered, without hesitating.

"I'll take them over there in a little while, Cammie. Is there anything I can bring back for you, or we can take care of while we're there?"

Cammie looked down at her faded dress, and then at her son who lay sleeping restlessly, tiny beads of sweat on his pale forehead. "Some more clothes, maybe? My neighbors have been looking after the animals."

Nathaniel's smile was kind. "Certainly. I'll come back in a while with some more clothes for you. Maybe you should try to get some rest while David is sleeping. I know William is keeping a close eye on him."

William, who had been silent throughout the exchange, nodded.

An hour later, Quinn and Thomas were standing in the small, tidy main room of the house Cammie Winthrop shared with her three children. Tallie had been excited to give them a tour, showing them the hand-carved dollhouse and dolls that stood in the corner, and introducing them to Rupert, the shaggy black-and-white dog. Caleb wandered around the house for several minutes, looking confused and calling out "Mama?"

Quinn picked him up, "We'll see Mama in the morning, Buddy. Everything's okay."

"Mama inna morning?"

"Yes, we'll go back to Mama in the morning."

"It's getting close to bedtime," Thomas announced, pointing to the darkening sky through the window.

"Will you read to us first?" Tallie asked. "Mama always reads to us before bedtime."

"Of course! First, let's go change into pajamas, okay?" Thomas scooped Caleb out of Quinn's arm, and carried him back into the small bedroom that he shared with David, while Tallie led Quinn into a room at the end of the tiny hallway.

"This is my room," Tallie announced proudly.

Quinn smiled, "It's very nice."

And it was; Quinn looked around at the neat little room. There was a small bed in the corner, covered with a beautiful handmade patchwork quilt in bright colors. A little matching rag rug covered the floor, and handmade curtains decorated the little window. The wood walls and floor looked somehow different from those in the rest of the house. Shinier? Newer?

"My daddy made this room for me, when Caleb was born," Tallie told her, as she pulled pajamas from the drawer of a little, white wooden dresser.

"Wow. That's really special, isn't it?"

Tallie nodded, pulling a soft, blue nightgown over her head. "He died."

"I know. My dad died when I was little, too."

Tallie looked at Quinn with wide, brown eyes. "Do you miss him?"

Quinn nodded, a thick feeling in the back of her throat,. "Of course I do." She picked up a brush from the dresser and began pulling it through Tallie's thick, brown hair.

"I miss my dad, too. Can we go read a story now?"

Quinn smiled at how easily the little girl's mind drifted to a new topic, wondering if she'd been so casual about things when she was Tallie's age. "Let's go brush your teeth first."

Tallie and Quinn met Thomas and Caleb back in the living room. Thomas had settled himself into the small couch, with

Caleb curled up on his lap, boasting a fresh diaper and snuggly pajamas. Quinn was impressed. Even Zander, who was so good with Annie and his own little sisters wouldn't touch diapers when they were little. She swallowed hard; it felt odd to be thinking about Zander right now.

She wondered what they were all doing right now – her family, Zander and his family. It was so strange to not even know what time it was there, or even what day. She'd been in Eirentheos for a long time now, was it Saturday at home already? Was it morning or afternoon? It was all a little too much to process, and she decided not to think about it right now.

Thomas cleared a Tallie-sized space on the couch next to him, and the little girl climbed up, eager and holding a book she'd retrieved from David's bookshelf. It was a thin paperback, and Quinn thought it looked strangely familiar. Thomas smiled when he saw it.

"Has David been studying history?" Thomas asked, taking the book from Tallie.

Tallie shrugged. "This is his book from his teacher."

"I had the same book when I was little," Thomas told her.

"It has good stories."

"Yes, it does."

Quinn settled into a chair near them, watching and listening as Thomas began to read.

Long ago, before anyone alive now was born, our land was one great kingdom, ruled by a king and queen.

"That's the king?" Tallie interrupted, pointing to the pictures.

"One of them," Thomas answered. "There were probably many kings and queens before this story started."

Tallie nodded, a serious look on her face.

Thomas continued.

When a king grew old, he would pass the crown to one of his sons. Usually it was his oldest son, but if that son had died, then the crown would go to his next-oldest son.

One year, a young king and his wife were expecting their first child. They awaited the child's arrival with joyous anticipation. However, when the queen's time came, the baby had a difficult time being born. By the time the baby boy was born, the queen was very sick. The midwives were so busy tending to the queen that they almost didn't notice that a second baby was coming.

In their surprise at the arrival of the second child, and their haste to tend to the queen, the midwives simply set the baby in the cradle next to his brother.

When they were finally reassured that the queen would live, the midwives turned back to the babies, who had curled together and fallen asleep. They were amazed at how alike the babies were; not one of them could find any difference between the queen's two tiny sons. None of them could remember which child had been born first.

"So they didn't know which prince should be king?" Tallie asked.

"Nope," Thomas answered.

"Could they both be the king?"

"I don't know. Should we keep reading?"

Tallie nodded.

The princes were named Aaron and Philip. To tell them apart, Aaron was always dressed in purple and silver, while Philip always wore green and gold. As the princes grew, they were generous and kind, and both loved by their people. The king and queen loved them both very much. When the time finally came that the king was growing too old to rule, he didn't know what to do. Which son should he pass his crown to?

One day, the king was visited by a messenger from the Maker Himself. This messenger told the king that his kingdom was to be split into two equal parts, and would be ruled by two kings. Aaron would rule one kingdom, and pass the crown to his own firstborn child. Philip would rule the other. If ever there was a dispute over one of the crowns again, the crown was to be passed to the closest related firstborn child of the royal bloodline.

"Is that a true story, Thomas?"

"It's in the history book, isn't it?"

"Yes," Tallie was thoughtful. "Can a girl be the king?"

Thomas smiled. "A girl can be the queen."

"Yeah, but I mean if a girl was the firstborn."

"You mean like being the queen without marrying a king? Be in charge?"

"Yes."

"I don't see why a girl couldn't; nothing says that one can't. There just never has been a firstborn girl."

"Why not?"

"I don't know, Tallie. It just hasn't happened. Enough questions for now. Time for bed." Thomas stood and scooped both of the children into his arms, carrying them down the hall.

When both children were tucked in and sound asleep, Quinn and Thomas retreated to the living room.

"That was an interesting story," Quinn said, picking up the history book and studying the picture on the cover, the same symbol she kept seeing. "Is it true?"

"More or less," Thomas answered. "That version is a bit watered down for small children."

"What is this book?"

Thomas reached over and took it from her hands. "It's a history book, given to children by a kingdom teacher when they're learning Eirenthean history."

"That makes sense," Quinn told him, "I think Alyia had the same book in Mistle Village."

Thomas nodded, "Pretty much every child around that age in the kingdom has this book." He flipped to a page in the middle, showing her where blank lines had been filled in with childish writing. He ran his fingers over David's answers; Quinn was impressed at the neat handwriting.

"What's the symbol on the front?"

"That's the Eirenthean seal," he said, closing the book again, and looking at the circular design on the front. "It's the same one that's on our pendants."

She nodded. "And it's all over your formalwear, too."

He shrugged. "I think I have underwear embroidered with it. I am a prince of Eirentheos."

When they finally stopped giggling, Quinn looked over at Thomas. "So the other kingdom in the story – is that the kingdom that Tolliver is trying to take over?"

He nodded. "Yeah, you can see, even from that little story, why it's kind of a big deal to us. We really believe that the Maker intends for the crown only to go to a true firstborn. And Tolliver isn't one."

"Is Tolliver the second born?"

"No. He thinks he has a right because he's his father's firstborn, but his father isn't a true royal. His father isn't even actually from Philotheum."

"So the crown can't go to whoever is the second born?"

"No. It can only go to a firstborn. It could go to the second-born's firstborn, but I don't think there's anyone else close enough in line who's old enough."

"And so Tolliver thinks he can just step in."

"Yeah. And he thinks he can get our kingdom to stand behind him, but he's wrong."

"Why would he think that?"

"Well ... he's been trying for a long time to marry into my family. I guess he thinks that if his wife was a princess of Eirentheos, that my father would support his bid for the throne. He tried to court Rebecca, and now he has his eyes on Linnea."

Bile rose in Quinn's throat. "Isn't he a little old for her?"

"I don't think he cares. I don't think he cares much about anything except for what he wants." Thomas eyed Quinn meaningfully.

She shuddered.

A NEW CASE

THOMAS, AS USUAL, WAS up long before Quinn the next morning, though the horizon was only barely turning pink when Quinn first looked out the window. Thomas was outside, working in the Winthrops' vegetable garden, filling a basket with ripe vegetables, and throwing weeds over the fence into a field. A fire had already been set in the little cook stove in the kitchen.

Caleb and Tallie were still sound asleep, and so Quinn attended to what small tasks she could find around the house. She'd never cooked anything on a wood-burning stove, but figured it would probably work like something in between a regular stove and a campfire, both of which she knew how to operate. She filled a kettle with water from the kitchen pump and set it to boil while she took out a rag to dust the living room furniture.

She had barely finished dusting when she heard Caleb calling out from his room. He was upset when he saw Quinn, instead of his mother, but she was able to distract him with a rolling wooden horse before his cries woke Tallie down the hall.

Once he was happy again, she was faced with a new challenge: a stack of neatly folded cloth diapers on a shelf. Her heart sank. Quinn's mother had used cloth diapers when Annie was small, but they were some kind of fancy, new-fangled ones that fastened with Velcro and worked exactly like the disposable ones Quinn was used to. Annie's had been waterproof on the outside, too, but judging from the spreading wet spot on Caleb's bottom, his were not.

Leaving Caleb to play for a moment, she went out onto the porch and called to Thomas.

"What is it, Quinn?"

"Um... I'm not quite sure how to work diapers in your world."

Thomas looked down where he was standing, a garden hoe in his gloved hands. "I'm kind of busy here, Quinn. Can't you figure it out?" There was an edge to his voice that she'd never heard before, and it startled her. Was he angry? Her cheeks felt hot and a strange wetness hit the corners of her eyes.

"I'm sure I can," she mumbled, heading back into the house.

She did figure it out, copying the way the old one had been fastened. Her job wasn't as neat, but the diaper stayed on. By the time Tallie woke up, Caleb was dressed and playing, and Quinn had finished cooking some of the hot, grain cereal that Essie had taught her to make.

Thomas didn't come inside the house for breakfast, and Quinn didn't try to get him to, still worried that she'd somehow made him mad. She tried to think of what she might have done to upset him, but kept coming up empty.

It was when she was helping Tallie get ready, asking the little girl to hand her a ribbon so she could tie her hair back, that Quinn forgot her concern about his feelings and called out to Thomas in alarm.

The sound in her voice must have scared him, because he came rushing into the house, covered in dirt and still wearing the gloves he'd been using as he gardened.

"What's wrong?"

Wordlessly, she pointed to Tallie's hands, where tiny pink spots were beginning to bloom. Thomas' eyes widened, and he leaned down to take the little girl's hands in his gloved ones, looking at them closely. He nodded, his Adam's apple bobbing up and down, a grim look in his eyes that she could see him trying to erase when he made eye contact with the little girl.

"Hey sweetheart," he said to Tallie in a gentle voice, "want to go back over to the clinic and see your mom?"

"Yeah! Can we go now?" Quinn was relieved to hear the excitement in the little girl's voice – she hadn't scared her.

Back at the clinic, Tallie's rash was big news. It was the first definite case of the poisoning affecting more than one child in a single family. Nathaniel and Eli were floored; both of them questioned Thomas and Quinn intensively about any plants Tallie might have touched, and were disconcerted to realize that the child had only been inside her home between the last time Nathaniel had seen her and the time Quinn had discovered the rash.

"What does that mean? Is it something in the house?" Quinn wondered.

"It could mean that, or it could mean that she was exposed sometime in the last few days and is only now developing the rash."

Cammie Winthrop was hesitant about giving Tallie the medication. David's shadeweed symptoms were improving; his fever was down and the blistering on his skin had calmed, but the medicine was making him very sick. He kept getting the chills, and his facial features were tinged with pale gray. William's anti-nausea medication was helping greatly with keeping the boy from throwing up, but he still looked and felt terrible.

"I know she seems fine now, Cammie," Nathaniel's voice was soft and matter-of-fact. "But if we don't treat her, she could get worse. If we treat her right now, while she just has a little rash, she shouldn't get as sick as David got. We'll be able to give her just one or two doses of a medicine she drinks, and she'll be feeling a lot better by tomorrow afternoon."

"Are you sure she has shadeweed poisoning? What if she just has a rash from something else?"

"I'm not saying that's not possible. But is that a chance you're willing to take?"

"I just don't understand how this happened," Cammie lamented. "Where is this coming from?"

"We'll find out." The stress on Nathaniel's face was evident. "We have to," he sighed. "In the meantime, may we have your permission to treat Tallie?"

Cammie nodded silently, looking devastated.

After lunch, Nathaniel and Eli left to go over to Cammie's house, to see if they could find anything that could possibly be a source of the shadeweed. Thomas, who still seemed to be in a strange, distant mood, kept himself busy outside for most of the day, so Quinn found herself spending the afternoon in the clinic with William and the Winthrop family.

The other little girl who had been there when they'd arrived, Katie Cook, had been sent home with her family that morning, and David and Tallie were the only patients.

It had been an epic battle that morning, trying to get Tallie to swallow the vile shadeweed remedy, but she'd finally taken it, and she seemed to be doing okay. She had been sick for a while, but now was keeping down a glass of juice, and Cammie had taken her and Caleb out on the porch to play. Quinn wished she could have offered popsicles to the children.

It was quiet inside the clinic now, and she caught sight of William, who had been keeping vigil by David's bed the whole day, and he didn't show any signs of moving. She pulled up a chair on the side of David's bed, opposite William.

"How is he doing?" she asked quietly, over the sleeping child.

William looked up at her, studying her face before he spoke. "A little better, I think. He's sleeping well, and his body is responding to the treatment. I'm hopeful that he'll recover completely."

"That's good."

"Yes." William's expression was still so dark and serious. Quinn watched him as he adjusted David's blankets, and swept his fingers gently across the child's forehead. It was so difficult to reconcile this William with the boy she had been following at school. That time seemed so long ago now, as if it had happened in another lifetime.

"How are you doing?" she asked him.

"Me?" William's eyes flickered up to hers; his penetrating gaze made her breath catch in her throat. His forehead wrinkled, and his eyebrows pulled into a V-shape, as if he had to think about his answer. "I'm okay, I guess. I'm just worried about these kids, and I'm mad at myself."

"Mad at yourself? Why?" After the words were out, she remembered his angry behavior the other day, and wondered if she was pushing him too far. It would be just her luck to upset both brothers on the same day.

He sighed, but he didn't look angry. "There have been several things lately that I'm not too happy with myself about, but mostly for being too stupid to realize that these children had shadeweed poisoning."

Quinn frowned. "I don't think there's anything stupid about that. How were you supposed to have known that?"

"You figured it out right away."

"Sure, after almost poisoning myself with the stuff. Not to mention that I was coming at this from a completely different angle than you. Nobody else here figured it out, not even any of the ... other doctors." Her voice caught for a second. It was still difficult to think of someone her age as a doctor. "I wouldn't consider Nathaniel stupid. Or Jacob or Essie, or Eli, for that matter."

"It was so obvious though, especially when we were talking about shadeweed that first day in Mistle Village."

Quinn shook her head. "It's not that obvious. It still doesn't make any sense; it's not like any of these kids were out picking shadeweed flowers like I did."

"No... But even so..."

"Why are you being so hard on yourself? Why does it have to be your fault? You didn't do this to them."

William blinked at her, looking surprised. "I ... I don't know."

A sense of empathy washed over her. Although the situations she'd been through in her own life were very different from his, she realized she understood his feelings too well.

"Nobody is perfect, you know."

He managed half a smile. "I've heard that somewhere."

They heard the back porch door open and close; the door that connected the clinic to Eli's living area had been left open. There was the sound of footsteps on the wooden floor in the kitchen, and then water running in the sink, followed by the screen door opening and closing again.

Frustration mixed with – something else welled up in Quinn. "What is going on with your brother today?"

William shrugged. "You've seen him more than I have."

"I don't know if I did something to make him mad, or what."

She was startled when he smiled. "I seriously doubt it. Thomas isn't the type to keep that stuff bottled up. If you did something that made him mad, he would tell you."

"He would?"

"Yes, that's a skill I envy him sometimes."

She smiled ruefully. "I have a problem with that one myself on occasion."

"That doesn't surprise me." William was pondering her face intently; she couldn't fully grasp the emotion in his expression. She wondered what he meant.

"So if it's not me … then what do you think his problem is?"

"I really don't know, Quinn. Maybe he's just having a bad day. Even Thomas gets grumpy sometimes – hard to believe, I realize. But this isn't easy on him, either."

Quinn sighed, "I'm sure you're right." She paused for a moment, watching him fidget with the edge of the blanket.

She watched David breathing in and out as they were silent for several minutes. Suddenly, she realized that William was watching her, and she looked up at him.

"How are *you* doing with everything?" he asked quietly. "This has to take the prize for the strangest thing that has ever happened to you."

"The grand prize," she agreed. She looked down, picking a tiny piece of lint off her woven pants. "You're not the first person to ask me that, and I really don't know if I know the answer. This is so far outside of anything I could have ever imagined, but here I am … unless it's all a dream." She looked back up at him, seeing herself reflected in his wire-rimmed glasses.

"It's not a dream, Quinn. It's real. This is what I am – my big secret."

"I can see why you keep it a secret. Isn't it hard keeping to yourself so much at school, though?"

His forehead wrinkled thoughtfully. "Sort of. I don't really think about it all that much most of the time. It seems like an awful lot of work to be friends with people I'd have to lie to all the time."

She nodded, considering that. "It's going to be weird for me, going home."

He shrugged. "For a day or so, it will be. And then it will probably be like it never happened. Nobody else will know."

"You'll know."

His eyes met hers, and he nodded. "I'll know."

She hadn't thought about it at all, how things would change when she went home. Or how things wouldn't change at all, really. He was right; she couldn't tell anyone else. They'd never believe her if she did, and even if they believed her – she realized that she didn't want to share it. Nobody would ever understand what it had really been like here, what it had, maybe, started to mean to her.

"Do you realize that this is the longest conversation you and I have ever had?" she asked.

William laughed out loud at this, causing the boy between them to stir in his slumber. "That it is. Maybe we shouldn't wait so long again … and maybe we should move away from David and let him rest. I want to go check on Tallie again, anyway."

LEAVING CLOUD VALLEY

THOMAS WAS STILL ACTING distant the next morning as they packed and got ready to ride back to Mistle Village. He certainly managed to get a lot done, though. Breakfast was ready and waiting before anyone else was even awake, and while they were eating it, Thomas finished packing and readying the horses.

Quinn had decided to take William at his word and assume that Thomas was just in an off mood. Things certainly weren't easy for anyone right at the moment.

Nathaniel and Eli had no luck identifying any kind of plant or anything else in the Winthrop home that could have been the source of Tallie's rash. They had spent the late afternoon and early evening traveling to the homes of children who had been treated for the rashes, trying to convince their parents to bring them into the clinic for a dose of the medication. They were leaving Eli with several children to observe on his own.

"You don't think we should consider staying one more day to help him out?" Quinn had asked William that morning.

"It's not an option, Quinn," he had told her pointedly. "The gate will be open tomorrow evening, and Cloud Valley is too far of a ride to make sure we get there on time."

Quinn felt like the room had suddenly started spinning. "That's tomorrow? It's already been ten days?"

"Nine."

"I...don't...wow," she didn't have a better response.

William smiled, "I'm sure you'll be glad to get home."

"Um, yeah … definitely."

He frowned. "Aren't you dying to get back to real showers?"

"You have real showers here. There's a real shower in Eli's bathroom," she pulled on a lock of her still-damp hair. "It's just cold."

He chuckled. "That doesn't bother you?"

Quinn shrugged, "I live in the mountains in Colorado, you know. We spend plenty of time camping every summer. I can't be much less used to cold showers than you are. You're a prince; you don't go without all the time, either."

"I suppose you're right; I don't."

She smiled. "I didn't think so."

"Not missing your cell phone, either?" he teased.

She rolled her eyes.

The ride back out of the beautiful valley was quiet. They weren't in a hurry; everyone was still bothered by the lack of any idea of where the shadeweed poisoning was coming from. There was still so much to do that the long ride felt like a reprieve from the reality of the situation.

Quinn was still reeling from the idea that she'd be going home soon. It was almost making her time here in Eirentheos feel real for the first time, as if it might actually be happening. The thought that she'd go home tomorrow night, and it would be like she had never left, never come here … everything there would be the same. It would only be Saturday night there. Her mom, Owen, and Annie would still be in Denver. She would still have the whole day Sunday, and then … what? Just go back to school on Monday?

Despite the fact that she'd talked about this a little bit with William yesterday, going back home, back to her friends and school – it just didn't feel right. And yet, she didn't have any other choice. She couldn't exactly stay here.

She'd never thought about the possibility that she might not be going back to the castle at all. She hadn't thought that she might never see Linnea again, or William's other siblings.

Even his parents, the king and queen. She'd liked them so immediately, and they'd been so welcoming to her. How could she just go home and leave this forever?

And her life at home… Did she have homework she needed to do? She couldn't remember. She'd been getting behind on some work before she left. There was definitely a trigonometry assignment – that thought wasn't pleasant. A chapter she was supposed to read for World History, maybe? Suddenly, Quinn gasped as several things clicked into place at once. "Stop!" she yelled.

All three men stopped simultaneously; it was almost funny.

"Quinn, what's wrong?" Nathaniel turned to her in alarm.

Quinn ignored him, leading Dusk right up next to Storm, so she was level with Thomas.

Thomas raised an eyebrow at her. "Is everything okay?"

"Let me see your hands," she demanded.

"What?"

"Show them to me."

Reluctantly, Thomas extended his hands toward her, his palms facing up. She could tell by the expression on his face that she'd been right. His hands were covered in small, raised bumps. A blister had formed in the middle of his right palm, and been rubbed away by Storm's reins. The edges were now a raw, angry red. Quinn cringed at the sight.

"Quinn? Thomas? What is going on?"

"Show him, Thomas."

Nathaniel's eyes grew wider than she'd ever seen them when Thomas held his hands out.

There was a long silence before Nathaniel spoke. "I don't understand."

By then, William had come close enough to see. He sat perfectly still on Skittles, wearing a shocked expression.

"How ... How long have you had the rash, Thomas?" Nathaniel finally managed to ask.

"Probably since yesterday morning," Quinn answered for him.

Nathaniel turned to her, a deep frown creasing his forehead. "How did you know?"

"I didn't know for sure until he just showed me. Actually, I was kind of hoping I was wrong."

Nathaniel shook his head. "I don't understand."

Quinn took a deep breath. "I ... I think it's the books."

Nathaniel raised an eyebrow, clearly waiting for more.

"The History books that the kids have. Alyia was reading hers just before she got worse again, and Thomas was reading David's book to Tallie the night before she got the rash. And he's been acting weird and avoiding everyone ever since he woke up yesterday, around the same time I found the rash on Tallie. I don't know how or why, but I think it's the books."

Nathaniel looked at Thomas. "Is this true?"

Thomas shrugged, "All I know is that I woke up yesterday morning at Cammie's house with this rash, and then we found Tallie with one, too."

The look in Nathaniel's eyes became a glare, "Is there a reason you didn't tell us about this yesterday? You've been walking around with that rash for an entire day?"

Thomas' face and neck turned red. "I didn't want to deal with it in Cloud Valley ... I wanted to be closer to home. I thought it would be okay if I just put ointment on the rash and waited."

Nathaniel sighed heavily. Quinn could see William rolling his eyes.

"I didn't know what to do," Thomas said, strain in his voice. "I knew we didn't have time to get stuck in Cloud Valley, worrying about me."

"What you do, Thomas," Nathaniel answered through gritted teeth, "is you tell us things we need to know. What you do not do is put yourself at this kind of risk."

Thomas dropped his eyes to the ground; to Quinn he suddenly looked smaller.

Without another word, Nathaniel began riding again at the front of the group. As soon as he found a spot where they could find shade and water, he led them in. They dismounted in silence. Quinn gulped at the expression on Nathaniel's face. She would never have been able to imagine that the kind Doctor Rose was capable of that look.

"William? Take care of him please. I need some time to think."

William nodded at his uncle, who stalked off into the trees, and began searching in Skittles' saddlebags for his medical supplies. Quinn rushed over to help. Thomas stared at them for a moment before he walked over and sat down near the edge of the small pond.

"So, Quinn, does all of your camping experience mean you know how to start a fire?" William asked her.

She blinked up at him in surprise. William's tone and expression were still unusually friendly, in sharp contrast to Nathaniel and Thomas' moods. "Uh...yeah," she paused. "I don't know that I could do it without a lighter, though. Why?"

"I'm going to need sterile water for that burst blister on Thomas' hand. It doesn't look good."

Quinn was about to make a comment that she'd thought the water here was unpolluted before she caught herself and realized that the warm water in the little pond wouldn't be nearly as clean as the running water in the river. "Right," she said instead.

William tossed her a lighter, which she caught. She looked at him, perplexed. He smiled, "We take advantage where we can. Small things we can carry back and make our lives easier."

Quinn smiled in return, and started searching the area for twigs.

Nathaniel returned to the clearing just as Quinn and William had managed to get a small fire burning. William rose and walked over to him, but Thomas still sat by the pond, staring into the water. Unsure where she fit in, Quinn remained crouched by the fire, feeding it kindling. She wiped sweat from her forehead with the short sleeve of her shirt as she listened to their conversation; the heat from the fire made the already-warm day uncomfortable.

"I'm going to have to return to Cloud Valley, William. I can't just send Eli a message like this and leave him to deal with it all on his own."

"We're already more than halfway to Mistle Village. Are you sure that's the best decision?"

"I think it's necessary. I think we need to investigate this book that Quinn is talking about as soon as possible. But you need to take Quinn and Thomas on to Mistle Village."

"What if Quinn is wrong? I mean, it doesn't make any sense for shadeweed poisoning to be coming from books."

"If Quinn is wrong," Nathaniel said, glancing over at her, "then we need to know that, too. It doesn't make any sense, but it never made any sense for it to be shadeweed poisoning in the first place, and Quinn was right about that."

"But how..."

"I don't even want to think about that yet, William. A big part of me is desperately hoping that Quinn is wrong, because I cannot – and I do not want to – imagine how poison would get into a child's schoolbook. The other part of me wants her to be right, because then at least we know something and we can maybe start dealing with it. Either way, I need to try to find out."

William sighed and closed his eyes for a long time. When he finally opened them, he nodded.

"All right. Will you be okay here, tending to Thomas and getting the three of you back to Mistle Village?"

"Yes, Nathaniel."

"Quinn?" Nathaniel called, "Would you come here for a moment?"

She stood and walked over to them. "Yes?"

"I know you heard all of that. I'm not quite sure where we'd be right now if you hadn't come here with us."

Pink flooded her cheeks. "I don't think I've really done anything."

"You underestimate yourself, sweetheart. By quite a lot, I think."

She swallowed hard.

"Anyway, I plan to try and make it down to Mistle Village by late morning tomorrow, but if I miss your departure, I wanted to let you know that I am truly glad you found your way here to us."

"Um … me too," she responded, feeling awkward.

Nathaniel smiled; his face had returned to his usual, gentle demeanor. "And I'll see you sometime soon in Bristlecone, I hope." He squeezed Quinn's shoulder softly, and stared at her face for a long moment. She couldn't entirely read the emotion in his eyes, but for a second she was sure he was going to hug her. He didn't, though; instead, he turned away and walked back to the horses.

Quinn joined William back at the campfire, where he had retreated during her conversation with Nathaniel. He had rigged up a small, metal contraption over the fire, from which he had hung a little kettle. Steam was already beginning to rise from the spout.

"All right Thomas," William called. "You've had long enough to sulk and worry. Get over here."

Thomas came, but his attitude was still begrudging. Quinn wasn't used to seeing him this way.

"Enough, Thomas," William snapped. "You're the one who chose not to tell us what was going on. I know it's not your fault that you're sick, but it isn't our fault, either. Did you know that you had Quinn all worried that you were mad at her?"

That got Thomas' attention. "What?" Thomas turned to Quinn. "Why would I be mad at you?"

She shrugged.

Thomas' expression softened; there was concern in his eyes. "I'm sorry. I didn't mean to make you feel that way. That was rude of me."

"Yeah, it was rude. So snap out of it already! What in the name of the Maker were you thinking, anyway?" William scolded.

This time, Thomas shrugged.

William let out an exasperated sigh and grabbed Thomas' hand to examine it. He looked alarmed when he touched it; he dropped the hand and stretched out to touch Thomas' forehead. "Crap," he muttered, "you have a fever."

Quinn was taken aback when Thomas nodded, "I kind of thought I might." Her heart sank at his words; Thomas was already getting sick.

"Well, that explains some of your attitude today," William told him, going back to work on Thomas' hand. "Did you not realize how far past crazy this is?"

"I'll be fine, William. Stop overreacting. Ow! What are you doing?" Thomas pulled his hand away.

William sighed, and took Thomas' hand again. "You're the one who rode over two hours on horseback with this blister. Now it's getting infected – like just letting yourself get sick wasn't bad enough." William's tone carried only irritation, but Quinn could see the worry in his eyes.

Thomas made the rest of the ride to Mistle Valley, but it was clear that he wasn't feeling well at all by the time they arrived. Sweat dripped from his forehead, and his complexion was gray. William had done what he could to patch up the burst blister on Thomas' hand, and then Thomas had worn gloves to protect it for the rest of the ride, but it was obvious from the way he favored the hand that he was in pain.

Jacob and Essie both dashed outside to meet them as soon as they rode into the yard. William had sent Aelwyn with a message about what was going on before they had started traveling again.

"How is he?" Jacob asked, as William tried to help Thomas dismount.

"I can talk, Jacob," Thomas answered, "and walk." He looked pointedly at William, waving away the help. "I'm fine."

Jacob eyed him critically, "I'm not sure you and I have the same definition of fine, Thomas."

Quinn had to agree; she watched as Thomas' gray pallor developed a green undertone. He swayed a little, and then asked to be excused for a moment, and walked over behind several trees. The rest of the group eyed each other warily before William went to retrieve his brother.

When they took Thomas inside the clinic, Quinn was pleased to see Alyia, sitting up on her bed and playing some kind of a game with her mother. A single IV line still trailed from the little girl's left arm up to the bottle hanging beside her bed, which was now filled with a clear yellow liquid, but her color was much better. Her rash had faded significantly.

Alyia turned to watch as William and Jacob led Thomas to the only unoccupied bed in the room, right near Alyia's. There were several children in the clinic that Quinn didn't recognize. Fortunately, none of them appeared to be terribly sick. She figured that they must be children who had already recovered and been brought back for the shadeweed treatment.

"Hello, Alyia," Quinn greeted her.

"Hi Quinn." Alyia's grin, which showed her missing her two front teeth, was like a breath of fresh air to Quinn. "Did Thomas get sick, too?"

"Yeah, he did."

"How?"

Quinn shrugged; she wasn't going to be the one to explain her theory right now.

Jacob and William were quietly discussing whether to start Thomas on the oral medication or the IV treatment.

"I vote for IV, if I get a say," Thomas called out, interrupting them. "I don't think there's any way I could keep that liquid stuff down long enough for it to help. Just put a needle in my arm and be done with it." He did look awfully pale again. She was afraid that Thomas wasn't telling them how sick he really was.

Quinn noticed that Alyia's eyes were as wide as her own were as she overheard the same conversation.

"It really hurts, Thomas," the little girl warned him. "You won't like it." Alyia stood and walked over to his bedside, careful of her own IV tube.

Thomas turned to the Alyia, a soft expression in his eyes, and he smiled at her.

"I know, sweetheart. Do you think I could be brave like you were?"

Alyia nodded solemnly, brushing a strand of Thomas' hair back from his forehead, mirroring the way he had comforted her when she was so sick. Quinn felt tears sting the corners of her eyes. It was the single sweetest scene she had ever watched.

As all of the children were doing well enough to be up and around a bit, Jacob and Essie decided to take everyone outside on the porch for lunch and fresh air, while William tended to Thomas. Quinn stayed inside to help, pulling up a chair next to Thomas while William left the room to prepare some supplies.

"Hey, Quinn," Thomas' voice was soft, and the sparkling kindness she was used to had returned to his eyes. "I really am sorry if I've been hurting your feelings. I can't imagine what you could do to make me mad at you."

Quinn shrugged.

"No. It is a big deal. It was wrong of me. I know it's hard enough on you to be away from home like this without people treating you badly. And you've already had that happen to you here. You can't know how badly I feel that I've hurt you, too. That isn't something I ever want. I'm so sorry."

Quinn smiled. "You really are 'Thomas the Charming,' aren't you?"

Thomas flashed his most charming smile, and Quinn couldn't help but laugh, though she could see the effort it was taking him to be so gregarious. Sweat beaded on his forehead, and his breathing was rough. His eyelids were heavy; and there were dark circles under his eyes.

William returned then, carrying a tray of supplies, and Thomas stiffened a little.

"Are you sure about this, Thomas? We can try the oral medication first." William looked uncomfortable; although of course she never would, she felt a sudden impulse to hug him.

She watched the greenish tinge spread down Thomas' forehead just at William's words. Quinn couldn't blame him; she'd had a chance to smell the liquid medication the day before in Cloud Valley. Besides, as Thomas had already argued, he was sick enough now that if they started with the drink, there was a strong chance he'd end up having to take both. She was undecided about which treatment was worse, but she'd never opt for having a firsthand chance to compare.

He nodded. "I'm sure."

"All right, then." William began wrapping a tourniquet around his brother's arm. She had never seen him look so forlorn.

"Quinn, you don't have to stay for this," Thomas told her.

"You were there for me," she answered. "I'll stay unless you want me to leave."

Thomas studied her eyes; she could tell he was struggling with the choice, and then shook his head. Quinn took his hand in both of hers. "Take a deep breath and try to focus on something else," she told him.

Thomas smiled. "Good advice. Where did you get that one?" He locked his eyes on to hers as William cleaned a spot on the side of his forearm. Even though it wasn't her, her pulse accelerated.

"Okay, Thomas, big pinch now. It'll be quick – this is just the IV needle." William said.

Quinn cringed, but Thomas only inhaled deeply and kept his eyes on hers. The only visible sign that anything happened was a slight tightening of his eyes. Then he relaxed and smiled reassuringly at Quinn. She gripped his hand more firmly.

"First, I'm going to give you some of the anti-nausea stuff. It might feel a little cold, or you might not feel it at all." Again, she was impressed at how William could be both matter-of-fact and comforting in the same breath.

Thomas nodded, and then he just kept breathing and looking at her. William's calm, step-by-step explanation even relaxed Quinn a little. She heard the clink of the small glass syringe against the metal tray a moment later. Her eyes accidentally wandered over to William, and she was relieved when she didn't see any needles – the syringes just attached to the small IV port that he had already put in place.

Thomas caught her gaze again. "I'm okay, Quinn. This is not the worst thing that has ever happened to me, I promise. I've told you, William is awesome at this. It hasn't even hurt."

Quinn's face flushed red. "I should have gone outside," she said. "Now you're taking care of me."

Thomas squeezed her hand, "Which helps me more than anything. Please don't feel badly. I'm glad you're here."

William didn't speak again until he had the last syringe hooked in place. "Okay, Thomas, time for the worst one. Sorry. This stuff has a pretty good bite to it, I'm afraid."

He had already begun pushing in the medicine as he spoke. Thomas' hand gripped Quinn's tightly, almost painfully, and she squeezed back as hard as she could. He kept up with the reassuring half-smile toward her for a moment, but finally he looked away and shut his eyes tightly; his jaw clenched.

"Deep breaths, Thomas, just a little bit more." William's voice was strained. Quinn felt tears in the corners of her eyes again. A couple of drops betrayed her and fell after Thomas released her hand. He didn't open his eyes; she could see him concentrating on taking steady breaths as the medicine traveled up his vein. She knew William could see the moisture on her cheeks, but she wasn't embarrassed, because his expression mirrored her own.

He reached into his pocket and pulled out a small, white square of cloth, and handed it to her. Quinn realized it was his handkerchief, and her tears fell more freely. William walked over to her, and brushed her hair back from her neck before placing his hand on her shoulder. She was a little surprised at how natural the gesture felt. He left his hand there until she was calm.

It wasn't long before Thomas was asleep; William had given him a dose of a painkiller to take the edge off of the stinging effect of the shadeweed remedy that also made him drowsy. Quinn and William were sitting in Jacob's office, discussing her theory about the history books.

"That is impossible," had been Jacob's initial reaction.

"We all know it is," answered William. "But we have to investigate it."

So Jacob had gone to Alyia's mother, and borrowed the History workbook. The three of them sat now at Jacob's desk, with the book and a microscope between them.

William donned a pair of black leather gloves, and opened the book. He flipped through the pages, running his index finger down the center of each. After a moment, he lifted his finger to show Jacob and Quinn. The thin layer of white powder showed up perfectly against the dark glove.

Although it was unnecessary, William wiped his finger on a glass slide, covered it, and slid it under the microscope. Jacob looked through the lens, and then sat back, hard, in his chair.

"How?" The harshness of Jacob's voice startled her.

"I don't know, Jacob. I can't imagine a single way."

The room was silent for several minutes before Quinn summoned up the courage to speak. "Could someone be poisoning them on purpose?"

William and Jacob both stared at her, uncomprehendingly.

"Who would do something like that? And why?"

"I don't know. I don't know anything about it. I just keep saying the stupid things that pop into my head out loud."

William chortled, although the tension in the room was thick. "Well, so far that's been a good thing."

Jacob and Essie both left almost immediately, hoping to travel to as many homes as possible in search of more contaminated History books. William spent the next couple of hours meeting with the parents of the children who had come in for one dose of the treatment. He was able to discharge all of them, sending them off with warnings about the books and instructions to return to the clinic at the first sign of any kind of symptoms in the family. By the time it was fully dark, only Thomas and Alyia remained in the clinic.

They both kept drifting to Thomas' bedside to check on him. He slept off and on, clearly uncomfortable from the fever that kept climbing, and the itchy rash. He refused any more pain medication, which was scarce in Eirentheos – he didn't want to waste any. Quinn lost track of how many times William offered it to him, and more than once she found herself wishing Thomas would accept.

William and Quinn were the only ones awake when Jacob and Essie returned. They stumbled in looking exhausted; Essie's eyes were red and shiny.

"We're going to go to bed," Jacob told William. "I'll take a look at the books tomorrow. Both of you need to get to sleep as well, everything looks like it will be okay for the night."

William made up one of the empty cots with clean sheets and blankets for himself, wanting to sleep where he could be close to Thomas. Quinn stood in the doorway for a long time, watching him.

"You really should go to bed, Quinn," William finally told her. "It's another couple of hours on horseback back to the gate tomorrow afternoon."

"It's the same distance for you," she answered pointedly.

"I will rest."

"Will you?" Quinn looked over to where Thomas had finally been able to fall back into a restless sleep, and then back at William.

He nodded, "I promise."

Quinn didn't understand the emotion that hung thick in her throat, the overwhelming jumble of thoughts in her head. She was unable to move from the doorway for so long that William finally walked over to her.

"Are you okay?"

She shrugged. "I think so."

Thomas would have laughed at her, if he were awake. He might even have hugged her. She would have known how to respond to that. The empathetic expression in William's eyes caught her completely off-guard, and she nearly started crying again. They stood there together in silence, his soft, gray eyes on hers in wordless conversation. Finally, William nodded. "Yeah, I get it."

THE LAST DAY

SHE THOUGHT SHE WOULDN'T be able to sleep at all that night, but suddenly sunlight was streaming through the window in the small bedroom. Quinn dressed quickly and walked out to the clinic. William was sitting by Thomas' bedside when she got there; Thomas was awake, propped up on pillows. His face was still a sickly shade of gray, made even worse by the bright red welts of the rash.

Quinn swallowed hard, trying to force a tone into her voice that was brighter than she felt. "How's the patient today?"

"Better," Thomas answered.

William shot him a look. "A little better. His fever is down, but not gone. He's got a couple new blisters this morning, but the redness of his rash has faded some. Hopefully one more dose of the medication when I get back this evening will be enough."

Thomas blanched at his brother's words. "I'm better already, Will. I'm fine."

"You will be – after another dose." Quinn was certain that the twinkle in William's eye was there for the same reason she was feeling better – they were just glad Thomas was well enough to be arguing.

A while later William caught Quinn watching Alyia as she sat on her bed, eating a plate of eggs and toast. "I told Alyia and her mother that if she eats breakfast and lunch today, and does well with her fluids, that I'll take out the IV later."

Alyia smiled and nodded, putting a big forkful of scrambled egg in her mouth.

Quinn chuckled, "Easy there, Alyia. Don't choke."

"I'll eat some toast and eggs," Thomas offered.

"Sure. After you actually manage to keep down some juice," William responded.

Thomas sighed and lay back against the pillows, staring at the glass on his bedside table that was still three-quarters full. He didn't take a drink.

The morning passed quickly for Quinn. Was it possible that she was really going home today? Eirentheos and the people here had been her entire life for the past ten days. She still couldn't quite wrap her mind around the idea of never seeing them again, and she was beginning to wonder if she ever would.

She would still see William and Nathaniel, of course, but even that wouldn't be the same. She didn't know how she felt about that.

Jacob spent much of the day holed up in his office, examining the History books he and Essie had collected the night before. William went in to check on him from time to time.

"It's still very strange," William told Quinn and Essie when he came into the kitchen to help them prepare lunch, "very few of the books are contaminated -- mostly just those from children who have already been sick. So far, we've only found the poison on two books that belong to children who haven't gotten sick. And those parents told Jacob that the children haven't had the books for long."

"Do you know where they got the books from?" Quinn asked him.

"Not yet."

Shortly after they had finished eating lunch, William came over to Quinn, who was helping Alyia put together a small wooden puzzle.

"It's nearly time to get loaded up and start riding," he told her.

Quinn nodded; she supposed it was impossible to be truly ready for something like this. She helped Alyia finish the puzzle, and then sent the little girl out to the porch with a popsicle.

"So you finally get to go home?" Thomas asked from his bed.

"I guess so," Quinn sat down in the chair next to him.

"I'm sure you're excited."

Quinn shrugged, "I am, I think. I'm not sure about anything right now."

"I can understand that. I, for one, will miss you."

A hot lump rose in her throat. "I'll miss you too, Thomas."

He smiled at her, looking deep into her eyes, in a way that made her feel like he was seeing something she couldn't. "It will all be okay, Quinn."

"I'll be worried about you."

He snorted. "Don't be. I'll be fine. If people wasted their time worrying about me every time I managed to land myself in a clinic, nothing would ever get accomplished."

Quinn smiled in spite of herself.

"Come back and visit; I'll be good as new."

She coughed, "Yeah, I'll get right on that."

"Why not? Now that you know how."

That was a possibility that she hadn't considered. It didn't seem very likely, though. How would she ever sneak off and manage it? And what would his parents think of her coming here on purpose? "We'll see, I guess."

"I guess we will." Thomas stretched out his arms, and Quinn leaned into them, hugging him. She tried to be careful of his rash, but he pulled her in tightly against his chest.

"Get some rest," she told him.

"Yes, Ma'am."

CAN YOU REALLY GO HOME AGAIN?

QUINN AND WILLIAM STOOD on the bridge, looking over the vast forest to the northwest. She felt a slight breeze blowing against her, though there was no evidence of it in the nearby trees. The air smelled faintly of car exhaust.

"I guess it's time," she said, with more excitement than she felt. She smiled at William, and took a deep breath, wondering why it had seemed easier when she had thought she was going to end up knee-deep in frigid water.

"I find it's easier if I close my eyes. It makes the transition ... not quite as weird."

She nodded and took a cautious step toward where she expected the gate to be. "I guess I'll see you on the other side?"

"Yeah, I'll see you Monday in school."

"Right," she nodded, wondering how she had forgotten that he wouldn't be going back at the same time as her. "Monday. What will you do in the meantime?"

"I'll head back to Mistle Village. Nathaniel should be back by now; hopefully we can get some more things figured out."

"Will everything be okay now?"

William's eyebrows furrowed. "Well, thanks to you, we at least know what we're dealing with, and we kind of know where it's coming from. If we can get the rest of those books out of the hands of children, then we can prevent any new cases. There are still a lot of questions that aren't answered yet."

Quinn nodded in understanding; thinking about how much larger William's world was than worrying about whether there would be a pop quiz in math class, or which cheerleader was going out with which football player.

She thought about the rest of the kids their age back in Bristlecone, spending their Saturday playing video games or doing laundry. When she compared it to William's world - caring for sick children, acting as prince of his kingdom... This was William's real life.

"So ... Monday then." She forced a smile.

"Have a good weekend." He said it with a joking tone. It was such a common parting remark and yet, coming from him, as she stood here on a bridge between two different worlds, it took on a completely new meaning.

"You too," she replied. He smiled back at her, understanding the humor in her referring to his "weekend" that would last another ten days.

"Remember, closing your eyes makes it easier to reorient on the other side."

She nodded, grateful for the wisdom.

"And go slow ... try not to fall this time."

She glared at him, and he grinned before she closed her eyes and took the careful steps down the far side of the bridge. One moment she was hearing the roaring river and the cries of Aelwyn flying overhead, and in the next, the roaring had quieted to a rush and the familiar calls had been replaced by a few random twitters from the wild birds that were brave enough to weather a mountain winter in Colorado.

She opened her eyes and, sure enough, the familiar sight of the rocky riverbed was there to greet her. A few scattered snowflakes drifted down, and she shivered, untying the warm jacket from around her waist and putting it on.

The embankment that sloped up to the highway and the tall pines that obscured the bridge from passersby all looked the same as they had nearly two weeks ago. Yesterday, she reminded herself. It was only yesterday.

She climbed the riverbank and sought her car keys and cell phone from under the safety of the rock. They were exactly as she had left them.

She flipped open her phone and read the screen. Two missed calls and three text messages from her mom; no surprise there. She quickly scanned the messages and breathed a sigh of relief; her mom wasn't worried yet, only checking in. Quinn typed back quickly.

Sorry, Mom. Bad cell service today. Been out running around. Everything's okay. Love you.

The reply came before she was even halfway up the path to her car.

Glad to hear it, sweetheart. I was almost ready to start getting worried. Hope you had a good day. I'll call in a bit. Love you too.

Quinn had barely climbed into the Pilot and closed the door when her phone rang. She rolled her eyes at her mom's haste and flipped it open. "That was fast."

There was a pause on the other end of the line. "What was fast?" The voice did not belong to her mom. Quinn's face went white-hot as she realized it was Zander.

"Um, sorry Zander. I thought my mom was calling."

"Oh, that's okay. Where have you been? I've been texting you for the last couple of hours."

"You have?" Quinn realized that she hadn't even read any of the rest of her messages. "Sorry – my service has been iffy today." That was an understatement.

"That's okay. Listen, my mom knows your mom is out of town, and she wants you to come over for dinner."

"Tonight?" Quinn was feeling completely disoriented.

"Yes, tonight. You're not doing something else tonight, are you?"

"Um … no."

"Great. I'll be at your house in an hour to pick you up."

"An..." Quinn started to speak, but the line was already dead. Zander would be at her house in an hour.

The suddenness of the transition was making her head spin, and she wasn't sure how to do this. How was she supposed to just come back, and jump into her life like this? Dinner at Zander's? She wanted to do that – didn't she?

Yet when she looked down at herself, at the Eirenthean clothes she'd worn on a long horseback ride today ... she really wasn't sure what to do with herself. Part of her wanted to run back through the gate, make sure everything was all right in Mistle Village, figure out how those books had gotten poisoned.

At least say a real good-bye to Linnea.

She couldn't, though. The sky was already turning black over her head. There wasn't a choice. She turned the keys in the ignition, and hurried home to shower and change.

Quinn's story continues in the next six books of

The Dusk Gate Chronicles

Available now wherever e-books are sold.
Coming soon in paperback editions.

Book 2: Roots of Insight

Book 3: Thorns of Decision

Book 4: Blooms of Consequence

The first four books tell a complete story, but further adventures with Quinn Robbins, and William, Thomas, and Linnea Rose continue, beginning with:

Book 4 and ½: A Christmas Rose

Book 5: Canes of Divergence

Book 6: Leaves of Revolution

And coming in the Fall of 2015

Book 7: Blades of Accession

Also by Breeana Puttroff

Rumpelstiltskin's Daughter

KEEP READING FOR A PREVIEW FROM ROOTS OF INSIGHT

Dear Readers,

Thank you so much for your time in checking out Seeds of Discovery.

If you would like to find out more, or chat with me and other readers of The Dusk Gate Chronicles, you can do so in a number of ways.

My website is at
www.BreeanaPuttroff.net

I am often on Facebook, and respond to messages and posts at **www.Facebook.com/duskgate** -- give me a like!

You can follow me on Twitter. I'm **@bputtroff** – usually chatting about my writing progress, and other silly stuff.

I also have a newsletter, where I send out stories, news, and sometimes exclusive content. My newsletter subscribers even got to read deleted scenes from the first draft of Blooms of Consequence – in the very earliest draft, William, Quinn, Thomas and Linnea *did* get to go for a visit to Bristlecone. I never, ever, use my newsletter list for spam, but I do occasionally send out prizes, especially Dusk Gate swag, to readers just for being part of the list.

If you'd like to subscribe to the newsletter, you can do so on my website.

Again, thank you so very much for sharing your time with me, Quinn, William, and the rest.

Reviews of any kind are always appreciated, and help other readers know whether they might enjoy the books. Thank you!

Sincerely,

Breeana Puttroff
breeana@breeanaputtroff.net

ZANDER

QUINN ROBBINS SIGHED AS she crossed out the third paragraph in her essay for the second time. Homework was the last thing she wanted to be spending this Sunday afternoon doing, but she had been falling behind on her homework during the last couple of weeks, and now she was attempting to tackle the massive pile. However hard she tried, though, she couldn't concentrate. Her thoughts kept wandering to faraway places. She finally managed to complete the paragraph in a way she could live with just as the doorbell rang.

Ugh. Who could that be? Her mom had gone to Denver for the weekend with Quinn's little brother and sister. She wasn't expecting them to be home for another couple of hours. She put down her pen and ran downstairs. When she looked through the peephole, her breath caught in her throat.

It was Zander.

Zander Cunningham was…well, she wasn't sure exactly what he was right now, aside from being the seventeen-year-old son of her mother's best friend, Maggie. She and Zander had been close friends since they both were in diapers. Lately, though, things had been changing.

She took a deep breath and opened the door. "Hey, Zander."

"Hey," he said, his smile reaching all the way to his light brown eyes. "Can I come in?"

She stepped back into the entryway and pulled the front door wide. The blast of cold air made her shiver. The tiny, mountain town of Bristlecone, Colorado had finally gotten its first big snowstorm of the year during the night. Zander pounded snow from his boots and brushed more from the hood of his blue-and-white ski jacket as he stepped inside. He set a large shopping bag down just past the entryway.

"What are you doing here?" she asked, as she watched him take off his boots and line them up with the collection of others on the side of the tile floor.

He grinned. "I told you I would help you with your trigonometry homework, didn't I? Last night you said you'd been falling behind."

She blushed. The night before, Maggie had insisted on her going over to their house for dinner since her own mom was out of town. Quinn had been so exhausted and distracted, though, that she couldn't remember what she might have said during the meal. She could vaguely remember mentioning something about trig as she tried desperately to maintain a normal conversation. "I didn't know you were actually going to come over here," she stammered.

Worry flashed in Zander's eyes. "It's okay, isn't it?"

"Yeah." She smiled in what she hoped was a reassuring way. "I'm glad you came. I haven't even started on it."

"Want to go grab your stuff?" he asked, as he hung his coat on the rack behind the door. "We can work on it in the dining room. I brought a book that helped me." He held up his backpack.

"Sure," she answered. Her mom would probably appreciate it if they stayed in the main part of the house. Her heart fluttered a little at the idea of her and Zander here alone. She swallowed. "What's in the big bag?"

"My mom sent over some of her beef and vegetable stew and a bunch of rolls so you guys wouldn't have to cook tonight."

"That was nice of her," she said, peeking in the bag. It smelled amazing.

"You know my mom. She likes to feed people."

"True," she agreed. Eating dinner with Zander and his family had been a big part of her childhood, and Maggie was forever sending side dishes and desserts home at the end of the day when Quinn picked up her little sister, Annie, from their house.

"When will your mom and the little kids be home?"

"Probably around five or six." She carried the bag into the kitchen and put the enormous bowl of stew into the refrigerator.

"Sweet. We have time to get you all caught up in trig." He was already piling books onto the dining room table.

She hurried back up the stairs to retrieve her trigonometry book, trying to get her thoughts in order at the same time. Her head was still spinning from the strange experience she had just come home from the night before, and she hadn't really been able to process what had happened. She had appreciated being home alone today. Zander was almost an awkward interruption, though she wasn't going to turn him away.

She checked herself in the mirror, running a brush through her auburn hair. She briefly considered changing into a nicer shirt, but then thought that might be too noticeable. She settled for a quick coat of clear lip-gloss and headed back to the dining room. Zander smiled widely when she sat down in the chair he'd pulled out for her.

As soon as she looked at the first problem, she frowned. She couldn't remember this at *all*. Maybe being gone for ten days had somehow affected her memory.

"Why does this look like it's written in a foreign language?"

Zander chuckled. "Have you been paying attention in class at all?" She shot him a dark look, and he held his hands in front of his face. "Sorry, sorry! I've just never seen you actually have trouble with something."

She sighed and buried her head in her arms as red colored her cheeks.

"Hey, welcome to how I feel around you all the time," he said, tucking a strand of her hair behind her ear. The unexpected touch sent a shiver down her spine. "I can help you with this, no problem. I'm just glad I'm here to be your knight in shining armor."

If his words hadn't been setting a blaze in her chest, she thought she might have needed to bite back hysterical laughter as she imagined what Zander would think if he knew she'd spent the last ten days in an actual castle. She breathed deeply a few times to compose herself, and looked up. "I'm glad you're here, too."

His answering smile melted everything else away.

Even with Zander helping, the assignment took nearly two hours. Math had never been Quinn's strongest subject, but this was bordering on ridiculous. How could she have forgotten so much? He never seemed to lose patience with her, though, and as they got closer to the last problems, she realized that it was the first time she had ever really understood a trigonometry assignment, rather than just struggling through.

His smile grew wider as he watched her complete those last problems; she did the final one without any help.

"You're not bad at this teaching thing," she said.

Unless she was mistaken, his cheeks took on the tiniest hint of pink. He shrugged. "It's easy to teach when there's a cute girl involved."

Now it was her turn to blush. Her heart pounded as Zander, smiling shyly, reached over and ran a single finger down her cheek, all the way to her jawline, where he paused, turning her face up so she was looking into his eyes.

At that moment, a sound from the garage made Quinn jump, and Zander dropped his hand. It was the garage door opening, and a car pulling into the driveway. Both of their faces were suddenly bright red, and they started giggling.

I think my mom's home," she said, between gasps for air.

By the time the door between the kitchen and the garage opened, they were both bent over papers on the table, pretending to write furiously, though uncontrolled snickers kept threatening to break through. Zander had scooted his chair conspicuously far from Quinn's.

"Hello Zander," Quinn's mother called from the kitchen, carrying her purse and suitcase in one arm, a sleeping Annie in the other. Owen appeared behind her, diligently toting his own bag.

"Hi, Megan." He stood and walked over to her, taking the suitcase. "Do you want me to take this upstairs for you?"

"Sure. Can you come set it on my bed? I'll carry Annie up to her room."

Quinn was left sitting alone at the dining room table, surrounded by books and papers.

Owen took the seat that Zander had vacated, his eyes scanning over the work that she had finished. "Number six should be 47.2," he told her quietly.

She stared at him. "How do you even know that?"

"I read your trigonometry book." He shrugged.

She sighed. "I should have been asking you for help with it, instead of Zander."

Owen shook his head. "Zander can explain things better than I can. Anyway, Zander helping you makes your eyes look all shiny, and your cheeks are pink." He studied her face intently for several moments, his eyebrows furrowing. "Where did you go this weekend?"

Her heart skipped a beat. "What do you mean? I stayed here."

"Your face and neck are tan."

Crap. She hadn't even thought about that. "I, uh, tried some kind of new fake tanning stuff I read about in a magazine."

"Oh." He was silent again. "Well, this one works better than the last kind."

Heat flooded her face. She had never tried any kind of fake tanning stuff, and she knew Owen knew that.

"I'm going to go read until dinner," he said, "but I'm always here if you need me." He stood and walked up the stairs, leaving Quinn staring after him in disbelief. Owen's mild autism often meant he had difficulty understanding things about people, but sometimes the things he did understand were shocking.

WILLIAM

QUINN ARRIVED AT SCHOOL early on Monday morning. She hadn't slept well the night before, which she hoped wasn't going to turn into a habit again now that she was home. She had left the house earlier than usual, worried about the slick layer of snow on the road. Fortunately, the roads had been better than she'd expected, but now she was wandering the empty halls at school, feeling strangely out of place.

It was like the feeling she sometimes had coming back to school after being out sick for a few days. Anxious, disconnected, wondering what things had changed in her absence. Except that nothing had. She hadn't actually missed anything. She had been here on Friday; now it was Monday. Everything would be the same.

Everything except her.

A few people had started trickling into the halls when she spotted him. He was wearing the same long overcoat she had so often seen him in, a hint of purple wool showing at the collar. She now recognized his purple sweater for what it was: a reminder of his home. Knitted in purple for the royal color of his kingdom. The tiny, silver-embroidered design that she would be able to see on his chest once he removed his coat was a symbol that he was a prince.

"William!" she called down the hall.

She thought William Rose looked a bit startled when he first glanced up. Of course, it was possible that no one had ever called to him in the hallway at school before. He had always kept to himself at school, and he had never had any friends. The confused expression turned into a smile, though, when he saw her.

"Hello, Quinn." His gray eyes were friendly behind his wire-rimmed glasses, so different from the last time she'd seen him here at school, when his expression had always been distant or annoyed. "It's good to see you."

"It's good to see you, too." She was surprised at how happy she was to see him, the one person who wouldn't think her feelings about today were crazy, who knew the enormous secret she was keeping. She almost felt like hugging him.

"I have something for you."

"What?" She couldn't imagine William giving her something.

"Hang on, it's in my bag. How are you?" He asked, as she followed him to his locker.

"Um, good, I suppose." She looked around to make sure no one in the hallway could hear them. "It feels a little weird to be back."

His eyes were sympathetic as he dialed the combination. "I know the feeling. Did closing your eyes help?"

"Yes…with the gate part. It's everything since then that's a bit overwhelming."

He nodded. "It can be."

"How are you? How is … everything?"

The look in his eyes told her that he knew what she was asking. Although Quinn had come back from Eirentheos, the world that was his true home, on Saturday, William hadn't come back until last night, which had given him another ten days there. "Things are better. We think that all of the contaminated books have been found, and all of the children who were exposed have been treated properly. We've identified the teacher who was responsible for distributing the books."

She wanted more details about that, but there were more pressing concerns on her mind at the moment. "And Thomas?"

"Is fine, just as he promised he would be." He smiled, unzipping his backpack. "In fact, he sent me a letter to give to you."

"He did?"

"Yes. As did Linnea." He withdrew two heavy envelopes from his bag, and handed them to her. "And I brought you these."

She gasped when she saw the three small, colorful stones in his hand. She had found them near the river on one of her first days in Eirentheos, the first time she had gone horseback riding with William and his brother and sister. She had put them in her pocket, intending to bring them home to give to Owen, who collected unusual rocks. But they had been forgotten when she'd packed to leave the castle in a rush.

"Mia found them when she was cleaning your room. I thought you would probably still like to have them."

She nodded, a sudden lump in her throat as she thought about "her" room in the castle, and Mia, the kind servant who had taken such diligent care of her. Taking the stones into her hand, she rubbed her thumb against them. They were smooth, like marble, and the sensation flooded her mind with memories.

"And this is from me," he said, holding out another small object. "I figured you might like to have a little something to give to your sister, as well."

Quinn was stunned. The object was a small horse, expertly carved out of soft, Eirenthean wood. She examined the tiny details carefully. "It's Dusk," she said in surprise. Dusk was the horse that William's mother, Queen Charlotte, had given to her to ride during her time in their world.

"Yes, do you like it?"

"You carved this?"

He nodded. "Nathaniel says carving is good practice for surgery and stitches." His eyes followed hers down to the inside of her right leg, where he had stitched a cut after she had fallen on the night she had followed him through the gate.

She swallowed hard. "It's beautiful, thank you."

"You're welcome." He looked up at something over her shoulder. She turned and followed his gaze.

The hallway had filled with people during her conversation with William. Watching them, from a few feet away, was Zander. Though his eyebrows had been knitted together as he watched them, his eyes lit up when they met hers.

"You'd better go," William said quietly.

She nodded. "Thank you so much."

"You're very welcome." His expression was soft as he closed his locker and headed down the hallway.

"Hey, Quinn." Zander's smile was infectious.

"Hi, Zander."

"Were the roads okay this morning?" He brushed snowflakes out of his damp hair. A big drop of water landed on her left wrist, and he reached to wipe it away.

Heat washed over her at his touch. "Yeah, they were fine. I left early, just in case."

"Good." He smiled. "What's all this?"

Quinn's right arm was curled around the two envelopes and the carved horse and the stones were clasped in her hand.

"Oh, just some stuff for a class…" she trailed off, pulling her backpack off her shoulder so she could tuck them inside the first folder she touched, out of sight. She didn't like lying to Zander, but it wasn't as if she could explain it to him, either, though the idea of how *that* conversation would go did make her grin a little.

"Since when do you talk to William Rose?"

"Um, I ran into him on Saturday, and we talked a little." That wasn't completely untrue – it had technically been Saturday here in Bristlecone when she'd been spending time with William.

"Huh. I've never seen him talking to anybody before. He's kind of strange, isn't he?"

She didn't know why the question irritated her. Up until this weekend, she'd felt exactly the same way about William. And, really, by the standards of Bristlecone High School, he was strange – more so than Zander could possibly guess. It still rankled, now that she considered William her friend. "He's just quiet," she said. "He's actually a nice guy."

"Okay." Zander shrugged. She could see from his expression that he hadn't meant to offend her. "Maybe I'll have to get to know him."

Printed in Great Britain
by Amazon